I0679256

# Loving

# Bernadette

# ALSO BY DANIELLE GRAINGER

## THE DENTON HEIGHTS SERIES

*Under Her Wing (Book 1):*
*The Shasti and Madison Story*

*In Her Cage (Book 2):*
*The Jaleesa and Tina Story*

*Within Her Grasp (Book 3):*
*The Marta and Shanice Story*

*By Her Command (Book 4)*
*The Rowena and Minjung Story*

## THE BERNADETTE SERIES

*Wrecking Bernadette (Book One)*

*(S)mothering Bernadette (Book Two)*

*Becoming Bernadette (Book Three)*

*Desiring Bernadette (Book Four)*

*Loving Bernadette (Book Five)*

# LOVING Bernadette

## BOOK FIVE IN THE BERNADETTE SERIES

# DANIELLE GRAINGER

BIBI BOOKS

Copyright © 2022 by Danielle Grainger

All rights reserved. No part of this publication may be reproduced, transmitted in any form or by any means, electronic or mechanical, including photocopy, recording, or any information storage and retrieval system, without permission in writing from the publisher, except in the cases of brief quotations embodied in critical articles or reviews. The characters, incidents, and dialogue herein are fictional, and any resemblance to actual events or persons, living or dead, is purely coincidental.

Paperback ISBN   978-1-953734-11-2

First Edition 2022

9 8 7 6 5 4 3 2 1

Cover design by Sarah (Forcoverservice)

Published by:
Bibi Books Publishing Company, LLC

# Dedication

This work is dedicated to those who continue to educate the world about what loving BDSM is all about. Keep on doing what you do best.

# Acknowledgments

I began the Bernadette series to entertain and possibly educate readers about the world of BDSM, but the series has taken on a life of its own. The promise of a marriage between our two beloved main characters wasn't enough for the readers of the series. Oh, no. The demand for the actual wedding overwhelmed the storyteller in me, and, voila, the readers got their wish. So big thanks go out to the readers who made their wants known. You pushed me to keep going and put a definitive stamp on the lives of Bernadette and Rikki. I am grateful for your push.

I also want to thank my faithful Beta readers, Jiske, Miss S, and Olivia, who find all kinds of things I overlook in my fervor to get the story out. I am forever grateful. And, as always, I thank the community of like-minded people who help me get the details right and continue to encourage me when I get too introverted for my own good.

# Table of Contents

# Chapter 1
## Bernadette

Bernadette opened the rear door of her hybrid and pulled out her briefcase and a box containing the stack of Calculus 1 problem sets. She sighed at the weight but dutifully trudged up the steps of her front porch. Rikki wasn't home yet, of course. It was too early for her to leave the coffee shop, and Bernadette had chores to do before her fiancée got home anyway.

"Fiancée," Bernadette gushed out loud as she unlocked the front door. A grin split her face. *She collared me in March and asked me to marry her in June.* "I've been officially engaged for two whole days." She didn't have a ring to hold up and examine or anything like that. Not yet. Rikki promised one as soon as her financial stuff was straightened out. Maybe then they'd be able to tell all their friends. So far, their engagement was a closely guarded secret between the two of them.

Once inside her three-story farmhouse, minus the farm, she hung up her keys and took the box and briefcase up the stairs to her second-floor office. Rikki said she didn't want to "trip over" Bernadette's boxes, so she took great care to keep them out of the way.

"Mmm," Bernadette said, "this light is perfect for working in here right now." She put the problem sets on her desk and gazed out the window onto her five acres, imagining their wedding on the back lawn. She sighed. They hadn't talked that part over yet. Maybe Rikki wanted a quick wedding at the county clerk's office. Who knew?

She sighed and looked down at the monstrous pile of work she'd just brought home. But, no, she didn't have time to grade right now. After dinner, maybe, unless maybe Rikki wanted to…no, no, no. She couldn't get her hopes up. By accepting Rikki's collar, Bernadette had explicitly and implicitly given

Rikki permission over her body, and she would use it as she saw fit. It's what Dominants did.

And besides, Rikki had given her a deadline to finish painting the walls in the basement today. No, it wasn't a basement. That space was going to be their new downstairs playroom, so she'd better get moving. She hurried to their bedroom and put on her old painting clothes. She had to finish by five to get Rikki's dinner started. Okay, okay, *their* dinner. Bernadette wasn't too keen on the menu for the evening, but whatever. If Rikki was pleased, then all was well in both their worlds.

She grabbed a water bottle from the fridge and headed down the stairs to the well-lit basement. The washer and dryer had already been moved up to the second floor. Rikki said she wanted them convenient for Bernadette and also said they sucked the mood out of a playroom. That made sense, Bernadette supposed. Laundry was infinitely easier now, so she wasn't complaining.

Three of the walls were already painted. The deep purple Rikki picked out warmed the concrete space more than Bernadette ever thought it could. Rikki had a great eye for design, which was good because the coffee shop was about to get some major renovations. Again, once the financials came through.

Before opening the half-empty five-gallon bucket, Bernadette checked her hair in the picture app on her phone because Rikki sometimes liked to video chat. The layered lob cut that Jaleesa had styled for her came a bit below the chin and was close to needing a trim. Rikki loved the natural wheat color, but Bernadette was ambivalent about it. Jaleesa had said Bernadette's hairstyle softened her already soft butch look. Either way, Rikki didn't seem to care, so neither did Bernadette. Now, Rikki's copper-colored hair? Oh, yes, this did exciting things to Bernadette's libido. But no. There was no time to think like that. There were chores to be done.

She checked to make sure Rikki hadn't texted or called. Like most Dommes, Rikki did not like to be kept waiting. She turned the volume up on her phone just to make sure she didn't miss any notifications. She wanted to put on music to make the drudgery more pleasant, but she couldn't risk missing Rikki's text. She grabbed the roller from where she'd left it drying yesterday. She had one more wall to do, and then she would double-check her work for Rikki's inspection later this evening.

She'd pass. Rikki was fair, if anything. Her punishments, though? They weren't "fun-ishments" like a light spanking or something. No, her punishments were truly meant to teach Bernadette lessons. "To help you grow," Rikki always said to her. Bernadette knew they were necessary but hated them nonetheless.

She dipped the roller into the paint and ran it lightly over the bucket grid hanging inside. Satisfied that she wouldn't drip on the concrete floor, she made a W on the wall and then smoothed it in. The original, white-washed concrete sucked in the paint like crazy. "You need some attention," Bernadette said to her house. "Yes, you do." She patted a dry spot on the wall and then threw herself into her work.

She finished rolling to her satisfaction and filled a one-quart handheld pail with paint before cleaning up. She headed to the first wall she'd painted on Monday and did her own quality control inspection. As she filled in a few thin spots all the way around, she couldn't help remembering Bianca's question that afternoon.

"Dr. Garneau, why aren't you teaching the 8000-level mathematics courses?" she'd asked during Bernadette's office hours. "Why are you stuck with first-year students? Undergraduates?" Before Bernadette could answer, the graduate student blurted, "They're wasting your talent, Professor. And your office, no offense, it's a closet. Dr. Baxter's office has all those picture windows, not that he's ever there for his hours." She sat back in a huff and crossed her arms angrily.

Bernadette wasn't one to throw anyone under a bus, but oh, how she wanted to vent her frustrations to someone, anyone. And Bianca had made a direct hit. Bernadette desperately wanted to teach graduate-level courses full-time. She wanted the recognition she thought she deserved, the recognition she had earned. She would be starting her sixth year at the university in August – two months from now – yet she was still stuck teaching the low-level courses to incoming freshmen. She'd even gone to Dr. Wainwright about it. She'd finally mustered up the courage to ask for the higher-level courses, but nothing happened. He'd told her that she was "successful" where she was. His motto was probably *if it ain't broke, don't fix it.* But it *was* broken. *She* was broken. Even Bianca saw it.

"Hey, you never know," Bernadette had said, "maybe after they see the success of this 7000-level Foundations course I developed, they'll move me up." She said the words but wasn't hopeful. Baxter had been teaching the courses she wanted since forever. There was no way she was ever going to get them.

"That would be so deserved," Bianca said. "I mean, c'mon, Professor, you shouldn't be teaching undergraduates." She gestured to the stack of Calculus 1 problem sets on the corner of Bernadette's desk. "In the least, you should be teaching Multivariable Calculus, right?"

Bernadette shrugged but nodded her agreement. There was no sense rocking the boat and having Bianca think she was ungrateful for her job or that she thought her department chair, Dr. Wainwright, was an ass. Which she kind of did. Privately. She sighed quietly and then got her student back on track by going over inductive proofs, an admittedly difficult concept for most.

Bernadette sighed as she stood in the basement, paintbrush in hand. A sheen of anger and frustration had settled over her at the recalled conversation. She closed her eyes and took a deep breath to calm herself. That is until her eyes flew open. "Shit, shit, shit. What time is it?" She ran over to the phone. Crap, it was already 5:30 pm. She liked to have dinner on the table for Rikki by 6:00.

Bernadette hastily but thoroughly cleaned her painting supplies in the utility sink and left them to dry. She did one last look around and was satisfied that Rikki wouldn't find fault with her work. She bolted up the stairs and into the kitchen to pull out the broccoli she loathed, but Rikki loved. And the salmon—not a fan.

"Shit, shit, shit," Bernadette muttered again. "Forgot to defrost the fish." *What is wrong with me?* A glance at the clock told her she might not make the self-imposed deadline. And she still had to change. Rikki liked her in provocative clothing, not in paint-splattered, loose-fitting grunge wear.

Despite her pounding adrenaline, she took a moment to breathe and think what Tina had told her about frozen fish. Oh, yes, right. She put the fish, still in its plastic packaging, and ran warm water over it in the sink. While the fish was thawing, she chopped the broccoli into the size Rikki liked and put them in water on low. Satisfied that all would be well in the kitchen, she bolted up the stairs to wash up and change into a low-cut sleeveless blouse – it was June, after all – and a tight-fitting pair of short shorts. Rikki liked to run her hand over Bernadette's ass as if reminding Bernadette who was in charge. Not that Bernadette needed reminding. She'd signed up for this Dominant/submissive relationship with eyes wide open.

Back down in the kitchen, she threw a maple syrup glaze over the salmon, silently thanking Tina for sending the link to the recipe a few weeks ago, and threw the pan in the oven. She turned up the broccoli and set the table. Candles tonight? It was Friday, after all. Maybe set the mood for some playtime? Maybe plant the seed that Rikki's sub needed some physical activity after dinner?

"Mmm," Bernadette moaned out loud as a surge of lust ran through her. She gripped the edge of the countertop with both hands. Would Rikki throw her up against the wall, press her body against hers, and sear her with a kiss? Maybe rip her shirt open to get to her body? Pinch her nipples until she squirmed? Would Rikki run her hands down Bernadette's torso, causing her stomach to tighten and her pelvis to arch?

Bernadette glanced at the kitchen clock. No, she didn't have time to shave again. Rikki would be here any minute. She'd gotten punished a few times for not being careful with shaving and grooming. Shit, would Rikki want wine with dinner? No, it was best to ask her when she came in and smelled the food. Bernadette didn't want to assume anything. She had gotten reprimanded in the past for assuming she knew what Rikki wanted and getting it wrong. Best to wait and be told.

The oven timer buzzed, causing Bernadette to jump. A quick look out the kitchen window told her Rikki wasn't home yet, so she turned the oven off but kept the salmon inside so it wouldn't get cold. The broccoli was pretty much done, too, so she put a lid on the pot and pulled it off the hot burner.

"Shit, is she going to want dessert tonight?" Bernadette murmured. She pulled out a box of Tapioca instant pudding that Rikki liked, checking to make sure she had the right ingredients. She could throw it together quickly if necessary. Rikki had them on a low-carb, low-sugar thing but broke her own rules every so often, so Bernadette had to be ready.

She glanced at the clock again. It was 6:15 pm. Rikki was usually more punctual. She checked her phone. Nope. No missed texts or calls. She'd probably gotten caught up with something at the shop. The air-conditioning unit was acting up again, so maybe she stayed to deal with that. Or it could be a thousand other things. Being a business owner wasn't easy, Bernadette had come to realize.

She jumped when the phone rang in her hand.

"Hi, love," Bernadette said into her phone. "Almost here? Dinner's–"

"No, I have to stay here," Rikki said. "The contractor and city inspector will be here at 6:30 to go over plans for the parking lot. We're finally getting that done."

"Oh, that's fantastic, Rikki," Bernadette said. She put Rikki on speakerphone and lay the phone on the kitchen counter as she took the salmon out of the oven. She set it on the stove. Once it and the broccoli cooled enough, she'd put them in the refrigerator.

"It's exciting," Rikki said. "Oh, they're here. I have to go."

"Okay, what time will you be home?"

There was a momentary silence on the other end, and then Rikki said, "I'm not sure. I'll send a text. I'll eat something here. You go ahead and eat without me."

"Okay," Bernadette said, trying not to let disappointment creep into her voice. "Thanks for letting me know."

"Victoria," Rikki said, sounding muffled, "you must let your woman wear clothes occasionally."

The last thing Bernadette heard were two female voices bursting out loud, laughing. Then the line went dead.

Bernadette stared at her phone. Calmly, way too calmy, she closed the phone app and turned the phone face down on the countertop. She gripped the edge of the countertop so hard that her fingertips turned pale white. "Which one of them is the inspector, Rikki?"

Anger and hurt fueled her breathing as she struggled not to pick up her phone and throw it. Instead, she lifted her head and remembered something Madison had told her once. Something about not relying on other people for your own happiness. She'd said it was up to you to find your own happiness. Madison was a *little*, but she was wise.

"Fine," Bernadette said to the kitchen as she pushed off the countertop. "I'll find my own happiness tonight." Dazed, she ascended the stairs to the master bedroom she shared with Rikki. "Fuck this outfit." She ripped the revealing clothes off her body. "I feel like a piece of meat in this." She changed into comfortable sweats and a loose t-shirt, grabbed her wallet off her dresser, and her keys hanging by the front door downstairs.

She was in her car, backing out before she knew where she was going. She was just about to pull out onto the road when she hit her brakes hard enough to make her body jerk forward. "No, no, no," she scolded herself. "You will not go down there. You will not make a fool of yourself." Instead of turning right out of the driveway toward the coffee shop, she made a left toward Hungry Hamlet's and their triple cheeseburger combo meal with french fries and a large Coke. And after that, she'd hit up Kroger for a chocolate cupcake or two for dessert. Maybe she'd eat it in her office upstairs while she graded those blasted Calculus papers. Yep, right there in the home she shared with her absent fiancée.

# Chapter 2
## Rikki

Rikki said her goodbyes to the employees and headed out the side door of her office. Lydia was a competent assistant manager and could close on her own. She'd been with Rikki since the shop opened a little over five years ago. And it was Bernadette who helped Rikki see that it was okay to loosen the reins a little bit and trust her people.

"Ha," Rikki said out loud as she got in her old worn-out Subaru. "I trusted Eileen, and that got me broke and almost on the street." Whatever. Eileen had made restitution and, by some miracle, had given most of the money back after stealing Rikki's identity. After the lawyer's meeting in Cincinnati on Wednesday, Rikki and Bernadette had gone to Rikki's bank in Denton Heights and deposited the inheritance check Eileen left her in the will. The funds would be on hold for at least two weeks, the bank manager had told them, but that was fine. She'd never thought she'd see that money, anyway. As soon as it was released, the shop was getting new HVAC equipment, and Bernadette was getting a diamond engagement ring. At least a carat. No, at least two.

Rikki pulled onto Market Street and let the car pick its way toward Bernadette. Ahh, Bernadette, her fiancée. Rikki's cheeks got warm. She'd finally found somebody that was real. Somebody who filled her heart with an overflowing amount of love and adoration. She couldn't believe that someone as smart and so masculinely feminine was her partner. She was one of a kind. And Bernadette craved Dominance – loving Dominance, which was just the kind of thing Rikki offered.

"Mmm," Rikki mused out loud, "that's right. We have the basement inspection this evening, don't we?" *It will be perfect because my little bee is a perfectionist. She never wants to disappoint me.* "One day, I'll convince you, my little bee, that you can relax." Rikki sighed. Of course, there was the other side of that coin. Bernadette was relatively new to D/s relationships and expected so much from Rikki. It was kind of hard being the perfect Domme for her. But she was up for the challenge and felt she had helped Bernadette in many ways so far. Expressing herself sexually, for one.

"Mmm, yes," Rikki murmured again. "Basement inspection. I'll show you where the St. Andrew's cross will go, my little bee. And then I'll whisper in your ear how I'm going to strap you to it and let you feel the business end of my favorite crop." A wave of arousal spiked her core. "And then I'll tell you how I'll redden your back and ass and legs with it. Flogging will be next, but over that already reddened skin, you'll not think it so pleasant, will you, dear Bernadette. And the spanking bench – oh, yes, how you'll be draped over it and spanked until you call yellow." *I have yet to get you to call red, now, haven't I? See? Loving dominance. Not giving you more than you can handle.* "Well, except that one time when you met the end of my whip, and I called red for you."

Rikki pulled up the long driveway and parked next to Bernadette's hybrid. She took a moment to look up at the house, sorely in need of care and attention, and her heart felt full. This was where she intended to make a home with Bernadette. No, not just a home. A life.

She bounded up the porch stairs, suddenly full of energy. Once inside, she called for her little bee. Getting no answer, she hung up her keys and then called down the basement stairs. Nothing. She must be doing her least favorite thing in the world – grading papers in her office. Rikki made her way up the stairs, and true to form, light streamed out from under the closed office door. She twisted the knob, but it was locked.

"Sweetie, I'm home," Rikki called. "Why is this locked?"

"Oh, hang on," came the reply from inside. It took Bernadette an overlong minute to unlock the door, but when she did, Rikki swept her up in her arms and kissed her silly.

"Miss me?" Bernadette said with a laugh, her cheeks tinging bright red.

"I did." Rikki took in the papers and the red gel pen on the desk and prided herself on knowing her little bee inside and out. "Nose to the grindstone?"

Bernadette stepped out of their embrace and looked toward her desk. "Yeah, it never ends. At least I'll get two weeks off in August before the fall semester starts." She walked back to her desk, sat down, and picked up the pen.

Ahh, Rikki read the signs and understood that her little bee wanted to finish the paper she was grading before going downstairs for the inspection. "I've been thinking about those two weeks. How would you like to visit your friend in Tennessee?"

"Lisa?" The pen dropped from Bernadette's hand.

"Yeah," Rikki said. "It's about time you met your bestie in person."

Bernadette leaped from her chair and smothered Rikki with kisses all over her face. The kisses started heating up until Rikki put a stop to it. She stepped back and said, "I'm going to, uh, get changed out of my work clothes."

"Okay," Bernadette said and sat back down at her desk. Something on the floor near her feet glinted in the desk lamplight. Was that what she thought it was? Oh, hell no. "Stand," Rikki barked.

Bernadette flew to her feet, her eyes wide.

"What is that?" Rikki pointed to the object on the floor near the trashcan under Bernadette's desk.

Bernadette lowered her gaze but said nothing.

"Pick it up," Rikki said sternly.

With a visible sigh, Bernadette picked up the wrapper and placed it in Rikki's outstretched hand.

"Mm hmm. I see," Rikki said. "This is what you do when I'm not here? Eat cupcakes? Blatantly disobeying me?"

"I…"

"You have nothing to say then?" Rikki tried to keep the fury out of her voice when she said, "You know that the foundation of any healthy D/s relationship is trust and honesty. You seem to have violated both this evening."

Bernadette's eyes flashed as if she was also angry. But it was fleeting, and Rikki wasn't sure she had actually seen it.

"Downstairs, now." Rikki pointed to the open door. "In your corner."

With a huff, Bernadette stormed past her and down the stairs.

Rikki inhaled deeply and let it out slowly. Aunt Tilda said there would be times when subs would act out and test boundaries. This must be one of those times. Rikki headed to the bedroom and changed into something more comfortable. Originally, she thought she might put on a corset and a mini skirt for the basement inspection to send the message that there would be intimate time ahead as a reward for passing the basement inspection so perfectly. But not now. Yoga pants and a loose T-shirt, it would be.

After changing, Rikki headed down the stairs and barely glanced at Bernadette, who stood stock still facing the corner in the living room. Rikki didn't want the punishment to happen in Bernadette's office. No, that was her sanctuary, and Rikki didn't want to associate bad things there if she could help it.

Rikki walked past her fiancée and into the kitchen. She found the jar she was searching for in the back of the refrigerator and pulled it out. She spooned out more than enough onto the cutting board and used Bernadette's favorite paring knife to cut tiny pieces. She put the jar back in the fridge and brought the cutting board into the living room. Bernadette was still facing the wall, so she didn't see what was in store for her.

"Pick out twenty quarters from your punishment jar."

Bernadette's head sagged, but she leaned over and did as she was told.

"Two under each finger. I'll help with your right hand."

She nodded. Rikki didn't expect her to say anything. In high protocol D/s moments like this, Bernadette didn't speak unless asked a direct question.

She did as Rikki required, and then Rikki placed two quarters under each of the five fingertips on her right hand. Bernadette pressed each stack tightly against the wall. The quarters sometimes slid against each other, threatening to break free, but Bernadette held them tight. Ahh, yes, she was ready for Rikki's questions now.

"Why are you being punished?" Rikki asked and then demanded that Bernadette look her in the eye.

"I ate two cupcakes."

"And why was that something worthy of punishment?"

Bernadette sighed and said, "Because you don't like me eating sugary things."

"It's more than just the sugar, Bernadette. You violated my trust."

She hung her head.

"I trusted you to do as I asked. It's for your own good. You even said how much better you felt after cutting out all that junk food and sweets. Am I right?"

"Yes, Ma'am."

Ahh, there it was. The word *Ma'am* told Rikki that her Bernadette was in submissive mode.

"So, the message I want you to go away with this evening is this. You must trust that I have your best interests in mind when I ask you to do things. Violating that is cause for tearing the fabric of our trust with each other. Do you understand?"

"Yes, Ma'am," she said again with a sigh. She sounded genuinely chagrined about her mistake.

Rikki picked up the cutting board. "And to further hit this message home, I have a treat for you." Bernadette's brow furrowed. Rikki picked up two pieces from the board. "Open," she directed. "Stick out your tongue." Bernadette opened her mouth, and Rikki placed the jalapeno pieces on her tongue. "Hold it just like that." Rikki placed a few more. "I'll let you know when you can start chewing and swallowing."

The burning sensation must have kicked in because Bernadette groaned in surprise. Rikki left Bernadette to her misery and went into the kitchen for a couple of bottled waters. She sat back down on the couch and listened to her fiancée whimper. "Another minute," Rikki declared, only to be answered with a groan.

When the minute was up, Rikki said, "Slowly bring your tongue in and chew. I want this sensation to be associated with those damned chocolate cupcakes. This is what befalls you when you disobey me like this."

Bernadette coughed and gagged as she chewed the hot peppers. At one point, she coughed and used her hands to catch the jalapeno pieces flying out of her mouth. Unfortunately, the twenty quarters fell to the ground. Rikki leaped up and commanded Bernadette to spit out the peppers into the napkin she held. She wiped off Bernadette's tongue, gave her an opened bottle of water, and commanded her to drink. Slowly.

"Come here," Rikki said, pointing to Bernadette's low stool. "Face me." Rikki sat on the couch in front of her.

Bernadette sat but continued to drink and occasionally blow out a sigh to relieve the heat.

"How many times have you done this?"

Bernadette shook her head.

"Words."

"Just this time," she said and looked down, clearly embarrassed.

"Are you upset that you did it, or are you upset that you got caught?"

Bernadette looked surprised by the question. "Ma'am? I'm sorry I violated your trust. I think I'm about to get my period and…"

"And what?"

"And I think maybe I wanted chocolate. It's comforting to me."

"You could have asked," Rikki said, hearing the disappointment in her own voice.

"You were busy," Bernadette countered.

Rikki sighed. There was something more going on there. Rikki had a feeling there was something hidden inside Bernadette that Rikki couldn't reach. Or something that Bernadette wouldn't release.

"Is there something on your mind?" Rikki prompted.

Bernadette shook her head.

"Come on," Rikki patted the seat next to her on the couch. Bernadette stood up and sat next to her fiancée. "Occasional sweets are okay, baby. But we need to be transparent with each other. If you lie about this seemingly small thing, how long before the lies and deceit get bigger?"

Bernadette picked at her fingernails but didn't respond.

"Look, I'm not saying that I think you're a liar or deceitful. Far from it, but I need to make sure my little bee is okay." Rikki tipped Bernadette's chin up so she would look her in the eye. "If there's something you need or want, you have to tell me. This little outburst tells me that my little bee needs something – besides chocolate." Rikki smiled when Bernadette chuckled.

"So, tell me, what's on my little bee's mind today?" Rikki pulled Bernadette's head onto her shoulder and held her tight so she would feel safe.

Bernadette just shrugged.

"Words, please," Rikki said, using a stern yet gentle voice.

"I don't know, Rikki. I just have a lot of schoolwork, and we have our first softball game tomorrow. We only practiced that one time, you know."

"Are you nervous about playing on Jaleesa's team?"

"No, not really." Bernadette snuggled into Rikki and brought her hand across Rikki's stomach. "I mean, a little bit, but I'll be okay. It's just a rec league."

"Mm hmm," Rikki said and kissed the top of her head. "Okay, so can I get you to promise me something?"

"Okay."

"Will you please ask me the next time you want to have candy or cakes or whatever? Keep in mind that I may still say, 'no.'"

"Okay." Bernadette cleared her throat and said, "Yes, Ma'am."

"That's my good girl," Rikki said and kissed the top of Bernadette's head again. "So, I want to put this situation behind us. Would that be okay with you? Never to be brought up again?"

"Yes, yes. That would be good." Bernadette's sigh told Rikki that Bernadette knew she'd messed up and was suitably contrite. Rikki just hoped it was for all the right reasons.

"One more sip of water, my dear, and I believe there is a downstairs playroom I need to inspect," Rikki said, sitting up taller. There would be no playtime that evening as Rikki had previously planned. No, playtime required deep trust, and she needed to sleep on what had happened with Bernadette this evening. Seriously, it wasn't the chocolate that had Rikki concerned. It was what lay underneath.

# Chapter 3
## Bernadette

Bernadette woke to soft kisses on her cheek. They trailed down her chin, her throat, her chest. This was one of the best ways to be woken up on a Saturday morning. Any morning, truth be told. The lips kissing her body latched onto one nipple and then the other but didn't linger long enough for Bernadette's liking.

"Oh, Rikki," Bernadette said and petted her lover's hair. She lifted her pelvis as a surge of arousal hit her.

Her lover didn't speak. She simply…continued. Kisses landed on her stomach, her hip bones, her lower abdomen.

"Mmm," Bernadette moaned. Early in their relationship, she protested that it was her job to "service" Rikki, not the other way around. At one point, she remembered struggling to get up and do just that, but Rikki wasn't having it. Rikki wanted what Rikki wanted, and Bernadette quickly learned not to go against the flow.

A quiet voice broke the morning darkness. "I'm going to fuck you now." Bernadette's legs were yanked apart. Bernadette still hadn't quite gotten over the slight embarrassment about bearing her most private parts like this, but that was her head speaking. Her body loved it. The head of the dildo strapped to her lover's body rubbed over her slit and clit.

"Yes. Yes," Bernadette said.

"Yes, what?"

"Make love to my body."

"How?" Rikki said, her voice thick with lust.

"Fuck me, Rikki. Please."

"Begging already?"

"Yes, yes, yes."

With no further words, the tip of the lubed phallus pushed against Bernadette's wet opening. Agonizingly slowly, Rikki pushed inside. Bernadette moaned at the welcomed intrusion and arched her pelvis to pull Rikki in. Rikki pushed in with one fluid motion. She pulled all the way out and laughed when Bernadette groaned. Entering her lover again, Rikki steadily increased the pace. Bernadette's moans grew with each thrust. And then Rikki undid her by stroking her clit. Bernadette detonated with a string of profanities. Her body flushed with release as she let herself soar in the endorphins flooding her body.

Rikki slowed down momentarily to lift Bernadette's legs up and over her shoulders. Every time Rikki thrust, Bernadette felt her quad muscles stretch. Rikki moved up and over Bernadette's body in such a way that Bernadette's center pointed right at the ceiling. Rikki basically looked like she was doing pushups as she pile-drived her lover. Each thrust smashed against her cervix, causing Bernadette to moan with each one. Her breasts kept rhythm with Rikki's thrusts, too. Yes, they would also be sore.

"Fuck, Rikki." Bernadette fisted the pillow in a death grip as another orgasm built up deep inside.

Rikki's answer was a low moan. Bernadette knew the signs. Rikki was about to cum. Bernadette tried to time it, but her body betrayed her and blew a good minute before Rikki's did. It didn't matter. Nothing mattered.

Rikki slowed her thrusts and then let Bernadette's legs fall to the mattress. Staying inside Bernadette, she let her body fall on top of her lover. She was breathing hard. Rikki kissed whatever skin she could reach with her lips and then lay still.

Bernadette thought Rikki had gone to sleep, but then she moaned and blew out one last sigh.

"I hate fucking you," Rikki said as she pulled out, causing Bernadette to groan. She was a bit sensitive at the moment.

"Didn't seem like it," Bernadette said with a laugh.

"When I fuck you, I don't get to taste you." Rikki removed the strap-on and tossed it in the basket they kept near the bed. They both knew Bernadette would be cleaning and sanitizing it later. "I don't get to feel your pussy seize up and possess my tongue, my lips, or my fingers." She crawled up the bed and spooned Bernadette. "But later, I'm going to make you scream when I go down on you."

Bernadette inhaled air through her teeth. "I wish we didn't have this game to go to." She pulled her lover's arms close for a quick squeeze and then wiggled out of her grasp and sat up.

"Where are you going?" Rikki asked.

"To make coffee and get ready," Bernadette said.

"Sweetie, it's only two in the morning."

Bernadette burst out laughing and got back in bed. "Sleep or round two?"

"Sleep and then round two," Rikki said, resuming her life's work as the big spoon.

"Yes, Ma'am." She didn't need to be told twice.

~~~

As they drove to the softball field that morning, Bernadette let Rikki think her quiet demeanor was due to nerves about the game. Although that was partly true, she was more upset that Rikki had found out about the cupcakes. What Rikki didn't know was that there had been eight cupcakes, not two. Bernadette had eaten the entire box.

Rikki also didn't know about the Hungry Hamlet's binge, either. She probably thought Bernadette's upset stomach after they'd gone to bed was from the nerves of getting punished. Nope. Not entirely. The lovemaking in the middle of the night wasn't deserved, either. Not at all.

Truth be told, Bernadette was more than a little miffed that Rikki was hanging out with Victoria again, the woman who had taken advantage of Bernadette. Was Rikki's long-time friendship with Victoria more important than the relationship she had with her? And then there was Alyssa—always wearing the least amount of clothing she could get away with. They were both there at the coffee shop last night. Was a contractor really there, Rikki? Or an inspector? You talk a lot about trust and honesty, but—

"This is the turn," Rikki said.

Bernadette jumped at the sudden break in silence. "Okay." She swallowed hard and had to knock back her rabbit-hole thoughts to focus on the game ahead. This was supposed to be a fun morning with her new friends. Like she always did, she pushed everything down and plastered what she hoped looked like a genuine smile on her face.

Bernadette shouldered her softball bag and let Rikki hold her hand as they walked to the field for the start of the eight-week women's summer league.

"Professor!" Madison called and ran out of the dugout. She was one of the resident *littles* in their community and was the one who had accidentally-on-purpose brought Bernadette and Rikki together. "I mean, hi, Miss Rikki." Madison amended, her cheeks turning a brilliant pink as she quickly fixed her mistake. "Sorry, Miss Rikki," she murmured when Bernadette and Rikki got closer.

"You are forgiven, little one," Rikki said. "Just remember for next time, okay?"

"Yes, Ma'am," Madison said, looking properly chastised. "Hi, Professor," she said again.

"Hey, kiddo," Bernadette greeted her with a hug. She whispered loud enough for Rikki to hear, "Always greet the Dommes first. You know that."

"I know. I forgot." Madison reached for Bernadette's hand and said, "We're in this dugout. Miss Jaleesa says you're the shortstop, and I'm the catcher today."

"Whoa, that's a big responsibility," Rikki said to Madison. "Jaleesa assigned me to sit in those comfy bleachers next to your Mistress."

Madison's expression melted as she looked over at Miss Shasti, her Mommy Domme, sitting on the bleachers. Bernadette and Rikki waved their hellos. Madison said, "She's worried I'll get hurt."

"You won't," came Miss Jaleesa's booming voice from the field. "And if you do, young Madison, I will personally sew your arm back on myself. I'll make the stitches nice and even so they won't leave a big scar."

Madison squealed in terror at Miss Jaleesa's teasing. Miss Jaleesa was a tall Dominant Black woman who had a house full of subs that she called family. Her heart was as big as her voice, and everyone adored her. Today, her shoulder-length dark hair was straightened and pulled back in a functional ponytail. Her dark sunglasses made her look badass.

Bernadette said to Madison, "You'll be fine. Come on. We'd better get in there."

Rikki leaned in for a kiss and told Bernadette to have fun.

"Enough of that kissy kissy," Miss Jaleesa barked. "Both of you players, get in that dugout and get ready for the game."

"Yes, Ma'am," Bernadette and Madison called out in unison and then laughed.

Getting her old college softball cleats and glove out of storage felt good. Last weekend's practice told her how out of softball shape she was and how sore she would be after today's game. Maybe Rikki would rub her shoulders out, which would lead to something else. A girl could hope.

As both teams got ready, Bernadette looked around and felt surrounded by love and friendship. Shanice took up residence in the far corner of the dugout in her wheelchair, the scorebook in hand. Miss Jaleesa had made Miss Marta's *little* the team's official scorekeeper. Miss Marta was out in right field, looking one part lost and one part excited. That morning, Miss Lydia was working at the coffee shop so Rikki could go to the game, but her *little* Pammy was covering the hot corner at third base. Three of Miss Jaleesa's subs were playing that morning as well. Tina at second base, tall Kari at first, and petite Dana in left field. One of Miss Jaleesa's oldest friends was going to be their resident pitcher. She wasn't in *the life*, but she knew about Miss Jaleesa's unconventional family and was cool with it. Another friend of Miss Jaleesa's, someone who had driven up from Cincinnati, was playing center field. And Miss Jaleesa was apparently going to be the designated hitter for Miss Marta.

As the game wore on, Bernadette noticed that the infielders handled hard-hit grounders and line drives fairly well. Bernadette had been throwing the ball to her teammates tentatively until she realized she could unleash, and they could handle it, especially Kari at first base, who was showing a mature confidence that Bernadette had never seen before.

Playing the game she loved and getting a hit every time she got up to bat had Bernadette beaming. She must remember to thank Miss Jaleesa and Tina for inviting her to play with them. They were such an interesting couple. Tina was Miss Jaleesa's alpha sub and was short, five feet tops, mid-thirties, and pale white. On the flip side, Miss Jaleesa was six-foot-tall, just turned forty, and medium-toned brown. Her physical stature and the way she carried herself were intimidating to most, but it was obvious that Miss Jaleesa was putty in Tina's hands. Tina's asymmetrical platinum-blonde short hair almost looked gray and suited her well. A Miss Jaleesa creation, for sure. And Miss Jaleesa constantly changed her hairstyle from full-out afro to short and relaxed to pulled back in a hair tie. Yes, they were sort of polar opposites, but their affection and love for each other was clear and almost tangible.

Bernadette sighed. An involuntary groan escaped without her permission. Yikes, she was getting tired. Thank the stars they only needed one more out, and the victory was theirs. The opposing team's batter dug in and waited for the arc pitch to fall toward the plate. She swung hard and fast and sent a sizzling ground ball to Bernadette's non-glove side. Four years of college ball were still in her muscles, and instinct took over. She dove to her right and backhanded the ball on the first hop. It smacked resoundingly in her glove. Ignoring the pain in her ribs, she leaped to her feet and threw off-balance to Kari at first base. Kari stretched, and the umpire called the baserunner out.

Bernadette pumped a fist in the air and then lost the ground beneath her feet as someone picked her up. Her probably bruised ribs protested, but she had no choice as her teammates mobbed Miss Jaleesa, who was carrying Bernadette around the infield in celebration.

"Way to go, Professor," Miss Jaleesa said when she finally put her down. "That made me wet."

Bernadette burst out laughing along with her teammates.

After the season-opening win, Miss Jaleesa announced a team party back at her house. Tina balked at the obviously unplanned event, saying they had nothing at the house to feed the team, and she wasn't even sure if the bathrooms were cleaned. Miss Jaleesa pulled Tina into her arms in front of the whole team and said, "Rikki and I will pick up supplies, oh love of my life. You take Bernadette, Dana, and Kari home to get ready, okay?"

"Okay, babe," Tina said, sounding satisfied with the plan. "We can do that. Thank you for helping."

"I have to be reminded to help on occasion," Miss Jaleesa said to the group, causing their teammates to chuckle. "Everyone else, come on by anytime. You all know where we live."

Rikki walked Bernadette to Tina's family van and made sure Bernadette felt comfortable with the arrangements, which she did, and kissed her one more time. Bernadette handed over her keys and watched as her fiancée and Miss Jaleesa walked back to the Prius.

Tina was a careful driver and got them to her home in no time. Bernadette had never been to Miss Jaleesa and Tina's house before. She wasn't sure what to expect. Human cages lining the living room? Deshawn or Harriet or Bailey, none of whom had been at the game, chained up on crosses? Not only did she not see any of that when she entered the two-story house with a large yard, but what she did see warmed her heart. This was clearly a place of love and affection. Family pictures graced every wall and flat surface. There were a couple of couches and more than a few pillows on the floor. *Ahh*, Bernadette thought, *that's where the subs sit.* But the one big thing she saw in the living room tugged at her heart. A grand piano stood regally in one corner. Bernadette knew she should ask Tina if she could help get ready for the party, but she was drawn to the piano.

"Do you play, Bernadette?" Tina asked as she placed her softball bag in a hall closet.

"I used to," Bernadette said sheepishly, her cheeks growing warm. "A long time ago."

"Oh, honey, please go for it." Tina gestured toward the piano.

"You don't mind?"

"Not at all. No one plays it," Tina said. "Jaleesa got it about a year ago. She sees something new and shiny and just has to have it."

*Like me*, Bernadette thought. *Oh, God, Tina must hate me.* Bernadette hoped her face remained neutral while she died a thousand deaths in front of the woman whose girlfriend she had sex with sometimes.

Tina acted like nothing was untoward and said, "She's toying with the idea of getting lessons for Kari, though."

"That could go either way," Bernadette said low so only Tina could hear. Kari was the newest sub in Miss Jaleesa's household and was putting up a bit of a brat shield.

"Don't I know it," Tina said and rolled her eyes, but then her entire face lit up. She was as fond of Kari as Miss Jaleesa was. It was plain to see. "Listen, truth be told. This house is always ready for company. Jaleesa has a big heart, and I learned early on that she loves to invite people over. I'm surprised it has taken this long for you to be invited here."

Bernadette shrugged, even though she had a sneaking suspicion why she'd not been invited yet. But maybe that was mere speculation in her mind. She couldn't read Tina.

Tina patted her arm and encouraged her to play while she and the other subs got ready for the team party. She reassured Bernadette that she, Dana, and Kari were more than capable of preparing for the team's arrival and that Bernadette should make herself comfortable as her guest. Bernadette couldn't help thinking that maybe Tina had a hidden Mommy Domme inside her. Being the alpha sub in a household with how many other subs? Five? Yes, there had to be a Mommy Domme in there.

Bernadette thanked her and then ran her hand lovingly along the instrument's painted side. "You need some attention, don't you, girl?" She lifted the cover to the keys reverently. She'd had eight years or so of piano lessons growing up. It had been hard balancing academics, sports, and music, but her music teachers thought she was good enough to major in music in college. Bernadette had stronger passions, though. Mathematics and music were closely related, weren't they? You know? Numerical patterns and everything?

She tapped the middle C key to get a feel for the weight of the keys. It felt good under her fingers. She ran a C-major scale with her right hand and then let her left hand join in. She played some of her old practice scales but quietly. She didn't want to disturb Tina or the other occupants of the house. It was funny how easily her fingers remembered where to go. She played a soft Braham's lullaby to warm up gently and then segued right into Debussy's *Claire De Lune*, one of her mother's frequent requests. The music was still in her, flowing from her heart straight to her fingers. Gone were the hours and hours of practice, replaced by this moment when she made actual music. She now understood what her teachers and her mom had been telling her.

She missed this.

Her mother liked Beethoven as well, so Bernadette switched to *Fur Elise*. She had played the piece at one of her long string of recitals to good marks.

*Mom loved Moonlight Sonata*, Bernadette thought, getting a little choked up. She missed her mother. Bernadette rocked gently with eyes closed as she picked out the notes of the C-sharp minor piece. Her left hand hit a dead key in the low notes, but she played on. She held out the last note, and then a burst of applause rocketed her to her feet, her heart pounding.

The room was filled with her teammates cheering and clapping. *Shit, I'm not alone.* How had she not heard them?

"Rikki Carmichael," Miss Jaleesa bellowed, "if you don't put a ring on that, then I will."

Everyone laughed, but Bernadette was mortified. Everyone had seen her in an unguarded moment. And not only that, but everyone also knew she and Miss Jaleesa fucked sometimes. Oh, God, what were they all thinking? She looked for her rock, her anchor, her foundation, and was shocked to see tears welling up in Rikki's eyes. Rikki opened her arms wide, and Bernadette bolted into them, hiding her face in Rikki's shoulder.

"That was so good, little bee," Rikki whispered, wiping her eyes. She soothed Bernadette, who was now crying softly. "Why are you crying, baby? You were so good."

Bernadette was relieved when she heard Miss Jaleesa and Tina usher everyone out of the family room.

"I didn't know anyone was watching," Bernadette said. "It wasn't good. It wasn't…"

"Wasn't what, sweetie?" Rikki pulled Bernadette away from her and gave her the Domme look, which said she wanted the truth.

Bernadette swallowed hard against her emotions. "It wasn't perfect."

Rikki pulled Bernadette into her lap in one of the oversized chairs. "You need to change your definition of perfect, sweetie. Because that *was* perfect."

*No, it wasn't.* Bernadette nuzzled into Rikki's neck. *If I'd known people were watching, I would have … stopped.*

"Don't be afraid to be who you are, my little bee," Rikki said. "I'm embarrassed to say that I didn't know you could play."

Bernadette shrugged.

"And, just so we are uber clear, I want you to know that I *am* going to 'put a ring on it' as soon as that inheritance comes in."

"And then we can tell people?" Bernadette asked sheepishly. She was shocked at herself for asking so boldly. That made her sound needy or judgmental of Rikki. "I mean, I don't want to pressure you or anything."

"No pressure, my love. I'm the one that asked *you* to marry *me*." Rikki kissed the top of Bernadette's head. She leaned lower and whispered in Bernadette's ear, "In fact, the moment I get you home, I'm going to put all kinds of pressure on *you* in all the right places."

"Can we go now?" Bernadette sat up and then leaped off her fiancée's lap.

When Rikki shook her head, Bernadette pouted. But then she couldn't help the grin creeping up her face. She leaned in for a kiss that heated up so quickly that a wave of lust ran through her. She wanted to pull Rikki out of the chair and head home instantly.

Big arms wrapped Bernadette in a hug from behind. "Getting her ready for me, Rikki?" Miss Jaleesa's voice was thick with intent.

"Keep it in your pants, big woman," Rikki chided. "Next weekend."

"It's next weekend?" Bernadette gushed. She hated that they never told her when these liaisons were going to happen.

"You didn't tell her?" Miss Jaleesa said with a laugh. "You old dog," she said to Rikki. "Keeping her in the dark." She released Bernadette from the bear hug and said, "Speaking of dark – I think I'd like her served up to me blindfolded. Like last time."

Another wave of lust hit Bernadette at the memory of being blindfolded and chained to the wall when they'd had their first threesome, and she knew her countenance betrayed that fact.

"Well, uh," Miss Jaleesa said, clearing her throat, "Tina sent me in to tell you that the burgers and dogs are ready out back." She ran a light knuckle over Bernadette's cheek, turned, and walked out of the room.

"I bet this will now be the longest week ever for my little bee," Rikki said and stood up. She wrapped a possessive arm around Bernadette's waist and guided her toward the back door.

Bernadette felt a pang of guilt for being attracted to Miss Jaleesa. Rikki should be all she needed.

# Chapter 4
## Rikki

Rikki sat at the desk in the coffee shop's office Monday evening, letter opener in one hand, an unopened collections bill in the other. Neither of her hands was moving, though. No. Her mind was the only thing moving at that moment. It was working on how to make Bernadette's thirty-third birthday special. She still had a couple of weeks, but somehow, she had to find out what Bernadette wanted. More often than not, Bernadette would say, "Whatever you think is best" or "I don't know. You decide."

Rikki put the bill and letter opener down. The bills could wait. However, what couldn't wait was finding a way to get Bernadette to open up more and tell Rikki what *she* wanted. They'd been together almost four and half months, and Rikki still hadn't quite gotten into the pure essence that was Bernadette. She was sure she'd gotten further than others – loving BDSM relationships tended to facilitate that – but there was something not yet complete in their relationship. Rikki knew that all relationships were dynamic and ever-changing. Still, it felt like the hold she had on Bernadette was slippery, and Bernadette might slide out of her grasp at any moment.

Rikki leaned back in her chair. The soundproofing in the office ensured that she didn't hear the goings-on in the shop on the other side. Good. She didn't want that distraction. No, she wanted to relive last night's glorious Sunday evening.

She'd given both Mark and Lydia the entire Sunday off and managed the shop on her own. It was a brave move since Sundays could be busy with churchgoers and shoppers alike. But she pitched in when she needed to, and her well-trained staff took care of the rest. And that included Kari, who seemed to have settled in reasonably well. Almost too well. Almost like she was trying to butter Rikki up for something. What was that? The stars only knew.

Rikki had texted Bernadette throughout the day, getting good reports on the stack of papers she was grading, her yoga workout, and her work outside in the front flower gardens. Rikki was surprised that Bernadette even found time to research the type of interlocking mats that would be best for their home dungeon, although Bernadette wanted to call it a playroom. Fine. Rikki could give her that.

Since her girl had worked so diligently and communicated so well, she had been rewarded when Rikki got home the night before. Rikki sighed at the memory.

"Strip off your outer layer," she'd said to Bernadette before the front door had even closed.

Bernadette kept eye contact as she took off her sleeveless tank. The revealed black lace bra underneath cupped her breasts perfectly. Rikki licked her lips as she hung up her keys. Rikki slipped off her flats and watched as tight shorts shimmied down Bernadette's legs and landed on the floor. The matching black thong – which her little bee was still getting used to wearing – was an attractive contrast to her pale skin. Maybe a trip to the lake was in order. Soak up some sun.

"Don't move," Rikki said and walked to within inches of her fiancée. She didn't touch her, though. Not yet. Bernadette's small movements betrayed the fact that she wanted, maybe even needed, Rikki to touch her. "Undress me," Rikki commanded.

Bernadette made quick work of Rikki's shirt and bra and then slowed as she unzipped Rikki's skirt. Rikki tossed a pillow at her feet and pointed. Bernadette knew what to do. She kneeled and looked up, waiting for instructions. "Finish the job." Bernadette reached up with both hands toward Rikki's panties. "With your teeth."

Bernadette squeaked in anticipation and did as she was told.

"Make me cum," Rikki simply ordered and spread her legs.

Bernadette moaned in surprise at how wet Rikki was. Well, why not? Rikki had been dreaming of this moment all day, especially when she knew there would be no protest at the command. Bernadette was her collared submissive and bound to do as Rikki wished. Within reason, of course. There were safewords and all of that. And Rikki wasn't a monster, just slightly sadistic with a huge libido. The woman licking her pussy also had a huge libido and would get her own rewards that evening. Somehow, she needed to keep her girl hungry for the release Jaleesa would give her the following weekend.

"Good fucking work, baby," Rikki said, undulating her hips against Bernadette's working tongue. "Go in deep with your tongue." Rikki gasped when Bernadette jammed her face in Rikki's pussy, her tongue digging in as far as it would go. It was hard to breathe that way, Rikki knew firsthand, but she was so close. Bernadette could breathe later. She clawed both hands into Bernadette's scalp, holding the head firm as she rocked against her. She gasped as the orgasm roared its way out of her body. Bernadette continued to suck and lick and fuck Rikki with her tongue until Rikki pushed her away and fell back into her chair, spent. Bernadette rocked back on her heels and licked her lips as if Rikki's spendings were the best thing she'd ever tasted. Good. That's the way it should be.

Rikki took about two minutes to recover before leaping to her feet and shoving Bernadette against the wall face first. She slid Bernadette's thong down to the floor and commanded Bernadette to step out of them. Rikki tossed them aside. She unclasped Bernadette's lacy bra, slowly pulled it down her arms, and then tossed it toward the basket near the wall. Rikki rubbed the bra strap marks on Bernadette's shoulders. She leaned down and kissed the indented skin. It helped that she was 5'10" because Bernadette was also tall at 5'8". Rikki had always been taller than her subs.

Rikki cuffed her fiancée to the brackets they'd had installed in the living room. A St. Andrew's cross in the living room might have been a little too blatant, even for Rikki, so they made do with the metal brackets that Bernadette could either hold on to or cuffs could be clipped to. Today, it was cuffs. A spreader bar connecting Bernadette's ankles and another above her knees kept her thighs well apart, making Bernadette exceptionally vulnerable to the whims of her Domme.

"Kiss it," she said to Bernadette and placed the business end of a riding crop at her lips. Bernadette did as she was told. She *always* did as she was told. Well, almost always. What was that cupcake thing all about, anyway?

At the first strike, Bernadette's cry of pain powered through Rikki's core. She hit the fleshy part of Bernadette's ass again and toyed with making her count the hits. Counting always let Rikki know how her sub was doing. A shaky count meant to slow down. Subs typically didn't like to displease their Dominants, so they often ignored their own discomfort. Bernadette was no exception. But, no, Rikki wouldn't make her count this time. She would know when Bernadette had had enough.

The backs of Bernadette's legs, her ass, and her back reddened up nicely. Bernadette's squirming body and high-pitched yelps empowered Rikki. Yes. She was the one giving her lover this pain. Five more rapid strikes hit Bernadette's ass, and Rikki threw the crop into the basket to be cleaned later. Early on in their relationship, Rikki had toyed with the idea of easing Bernadette into face-slapping, but she quickly abandoned the notion. Her girl was too sensitive emotionally for that. Instead, Rikki grabbed her faux rabbit fur and smoothed out her girl's heated skin.

"Oh, yes," Rikki cooed near Bernadette's ear. "I bet that feels good."

"Mm hmm," Bernadette moaned. She tended to go quiet during impact play as if she needed to focus her entire being on the pain. But holy cow, it was a different story when the woman came. It was as if all the pent-up pain was released at the moment of climax.

Rikki reached for the clit vibrator. She hadn't told her girl she was introducing vibrators into their playtime; it was better this way. A former abusive Domme once strapped Bernadette down to a hotel bed and forced orgasms from her using a magic wand vibrator. Bernadette had been dead set against vibrators after that. But Rikki was starting small.

She turned the vibrator on and watched her girl tighten up instinctively. She pulled against the cuffs.

"Only for your pleasure, my love," Rikki said and showed Bernadette the four-inch vibrating device. "I promise." She waited for a response. An ever so slight nod on Bernadette's pensive face gave her the green light.

Rikki embraced her girl from behind, loving the skin-on-skin contact. She reached around and splayed her left hand on Bernadette's smooth stomach, holding her tight. With the other hand, she placed the round head on one of Bernadette's nipples to get her used to the level of vibration.

The sharp intake of breath told her all she needed to know. It felt good. Rikki moved to the other nipple, lest it feel left out. Bernadette relaxed against Rikki's body, yet another sign that it was okay to move on. Rikki trailed the small vibrator down Bernadette's body and let it come to rest on her mound, near her clit, but not close enough for anything fun.

Avoiding Bernadette's clit, she slid the vibrator lower, running it over Bernadette's nether lips. She used a light touch. She just wanted Bernadette to get used to the sensations. Rikki tucked the head of the vibrator inside Bernadette's pussy, thoroughly coating it. Her girl was wet, as Rikki knew she would be.

She slowly moved the vibrator up and let it linger just below the clit. She felt Bernadette tense in her arms.

"Color, sweetie?"

Bernadette exhaled but didn't respond.

"Color?" Rikki asked again gently. This was a critical moment, and she didn't want to overpower her girl. She needed it to come naturally.

"Yellow, Ma'am," Bernadette said. The *Ma'am* let Rikki know that Bernadette was in submissive mode and would do whatever Rikki wanted. But that wasn't the point. Rikki wanted Bernadette to also want it.

"Why yellow, baby?" Rikki held the toy where it was. The vibrations surely must be reaching her most sensitive spot, even if tangentially.

Bernadette simply shrugged.

"I need more than that," Rikki prompted. "Are you anxious because the vibrations hurt, or are you anxious because of what happened in the past?"

Bernadette shrugged again.

"Tell me," Rikki said. "Is your color yellow, or is it red?"

"Yellow," Bernadette said quickly.

Rikki chose to believe it was the truth and not a way to placate her Domme.

Rikki moved the vibrator making wide circles around Bernadette's clit. "Relax, sweetie. I want this to feel good for you."

One quick nod of Bernadette's head was all she got.

Rikki nudged the vibrator closer to the sensitive nub that was her ultimate goal. She felt Bernadette tense up again.

Rikki pulled the vibrator away and turned it off. She stepped back. Bernadette groaned, obviously thinking playtime was over and that Rikki was upset with her. Rikki reached up and undid the wrist cuffs from the wall brackets. She removed the cuffs from Bernadette's wrists and rubbed the spots. She then took a moment to undo both spreader bars and placed them out of the way. She wanted her girl to be comfortable.

"Deep breath," Rikki commanded and took one herself. "Let it out. Yes, good."

Satisfied that Bernadette was more comfortable, Rikki wrapped herself around her lover's body from behind. She flicked the vibrator on. "Guide me, baby." She tucked her hand into Bernadette's.

"Okay," Bernadette said with a shaky voice. Ahh, good. There was no *Ma'am* attached to her response.

Rikki leaned the vibrator against Bernadette's clit, this time with Bernadette's help.

Bernadette blew out a shaky sigh and seemed to relax. It wasn't long before she moved Rikki's hand to place the vibrator directly over her clit. She made small circles with the device. Her hips undulated, forcing the head of the vibrator to slide over her nub. Bernadette's breathing labored and increased in pace. She was feeling it.

"Let yourself go, baby," Rikki said gently. "I have you."

Bernadette moaned softly as the good feels took over. Her entire body quaked as she pressed the vibrator harder to her clit using Rikki's hand. She turned slightly in Rikki's arms, her lips seeking Rikki's as she climaxed. Once her shaking slowed, she pulled the vibrator away and continued to kiss Rikki.

"Thank you," Bernadette said breathlessly. "I love you."

"I love you, too, sweetie." Rikki pulled her lover to their favorite chair and sat down with Bernadette on her lap. She switched off the vibrator and tossed it toward the basket, completely missing but not caring one iota.

A familiar soft knock on the office door snapped Rikki out of her reminiscence. She opened the door only to find her very own special little bee on the other side. Wordlessly, she pulled Bernadette inside and pressed her against the closed door. She kissed her passionately and said, "That ought to hold you." Bernadette's dimpled smile melted Rikki to her core. Yes, she had gotten so lucky with her little bee.

Bernadette chuckled and quipped, "Hold me for how long?"

"Until we get home and fire up that vibrator again."

Bernadette's eyes grew wide. "Again? I figured you wouldn't let me, you know, until Sunday."

"I was going to, but I think we're on the brink of getting you past some old traumas." Rikki grabbed her girl's chin and kissed her again.

When she released her, Bernadette said, "I'm not complaining."

"Oh? Color?"

"Green with a touch of yellow."

"Got it," Rikki said and smiled. Her girl was admitting that she was still a bit tentative about the whole vibrator thing. Good to know. Rikki reached to the coat rack and grabbed Bernadette's apron. "Do you mind?"

"Helping out?" Bernadette said, her face brightening. "Of course. Of course. Do you want me to bus or help Marta in the back?"

"I gave Marta the night off to spend time with her girl."

"Aww. So, who's back there?"

"Kari."

"Whoa, you've given her a lot of responsibility," Bernadette said. "I guess I'll be going back there then."

"Thank you," Rikki said, gave her girl a quick peck, and then smacked her playfully on the ass.

Bernadette turned back through the open door. "Is it okay if I take a break when Madison and Miss Shasti get here? I feel like I haven't visited with them in forever."

"Of course, sweetie," Rikki said. "Thank you for helping."

Bernadette flashed a genuine grin and closed the door behind her.

"Oh, yes," Rikki said. "I am one lucky son of a gun." She picked up the picture of her mother that she kept on the desk and asked, "What do you think, Mom? I did good, right?" Not waiting for an answer, she said, "Yeah, I think so, too." She turned to tackle the bills piled high on her desk. "Soon," she said to the bills. "Soon, I will be rid of you. All of you." She followed it with an evil laugh.

# Chapter 5
## Bernadette

Bernadette never minded working at Rikki's shop. It wasn't work, not really. She was disappointed that Miss Marta wasn't there because she adored the slightly older woman. Early on, Bernadette's punishments were to help Miss Marta in the kitchen after hours. In the nude. It had been Rikki's way of sending the message home that whatever Bernadette had done wrong must be remembered and not repeated. Usually, the offense had been that Bernadette was too focused on something and didn't hear Rikki speaking to her. Bernadette quickly learned to have a sixth sense radar when it came to Rikki and her needs.

Kari was in the kitchen that evening, so Bernadette worked with her for a good twenty minutes. Kari could be moody, but that evening, she was exceptionally chatty and gushed over Bernadette's softball skills. Bernadette paid her a few compliments as well, but other than that, the conversation stuck to the needs of the kitchen. Thank goodness Kari didn't bring up the piano-playing thing. That was just embarrassing. Finding that Kari was more than capable at her new duties, Bernadette excused herself and left her to it.

After getting a coffee, Bernadette went to sit on her usual couch in the far corner of the shop. Just as she sat down, two things happened simultaneously. Madison and Miss Shasti walked in, and she got a text from her buddy Lisa. Lisa was her first friend and confidante on the kinky website, *Kinks*, which had led Bernadette through many trails and rabbit holes as she discovered the BDSM world she never knew existed before then.

Madison looked around the entire shop, probably checking for Dommes or Doms to greet first, and then called, "Hi, Professor." She weaved through the tables and plopped down on the couch across from Bernadette.

"Hey, kiddo," Bernadette said. Madison liked to have her back to the rest of the shop for some reason. Fewer things to distract her ADHD, maybe? Bernadette shivered at the thought of not knowing what or who was behind her.

Bernadette waved at Miss Shasti, who was ordering coffees at the counter. It had taken a while to get used to calling her *Miss* after meeting her as Shasti. Once Bernadette had become Rikki's collared sub, though, every Domme was to be referred to as *Miss*.

"Let me just answer my friend Lisa's text, and then we'll have a nice visit," Bernadette said.

"She's your *Kinks* friend, right?" Madison asked. "She leaves funny messages on your page."

Bernadette nodded but remained quiet, hoping Madison would get the hint.

> LISA: What's up, my Ohio friend? Rachel is taking me to the dungeon tonight. Pics on Kinks later. Maybe. If anything fun happens. What are you up to this fine Saturday afternoon?

Bernadette could almost hear her friend's Tennessee accent. They had spoken on the phone many times and texted often, but they had yet to meet.

> BERNADETTE: At the shop. Getting ready to hang with M & Miss S. Guess what?

Bernadette was always careful with the identities of her friends. They didn't know Lisa. Bernadette barely even knew her.

> LISA: Excellent. What?

> BERNADETTE: Rikki said that maybe we can visit you in Tennessee. I have this two-week break at the end of the summer semester.

LISA: WHAT?!?!?!?!?!? Yasssssssss!

LISA: Rachel just said it was okay. She'd like to meet you and your Domme.

BERNADETTE: Can't wait. I'll send details once I know. I'll send the potential dates later (I don't have my school calendar with me).

LISA: Can't wait. Oops. Rachel's giving me that 'we gotta go' look. Love ya, B! Can't wait to see you.

BERNADETTE: Have fun tonight. Pics on *Kinks*, please.

She and Lisa had established a no-pics-over-text rule with each other. Bernadette couldn't chance a student or anyone *not* in the life seeing anything damaging or awkward. She wished she'd had that rule with Victoria. A good Domme would have protected her from that. No, no, no, Bernadette chastised herself. That particular regret had long sailed out to sea. It was hard to forget that kind of thing, though.

There was no response from Lisa, but that was often the case when Lisa's Domme was tapping her foot for Lisa to get a move on. Bernadette tucked her phone and said to the uncharacteristically patient Madison, "How was school today?"

"Good. Really good." Madison bounced on the couch now that Bernadette was paying attention to her. Madison's coffee intake had recently been changed to decaffeinated by her Mistress. Madison had protested this new rule, but honestly, Bernadette couldn't tell the difference. Madison was as bouncy as ever.

"What's with the glasses, kiddo?" Bernadette asked.

Madison pushed them up her nose. She didn't answer for a moment and then said, "Mistress is making me wear them instead of my contacts."

"Because?"

Madison sighed the most soulful sigh Bernadette had ever heard. "She says I have to wear my glasses instead of contacts because I sometimes take out my contacts when they bother me, and then I don't see well and can't judge distances adequately, which is not safe when driving."

It sounded like Madison was quoting Miss Shasti. "Your Mistress is wise."

"I know. Hey, Miss Bernadette, did you hear the good news?" The question was clearly a tactic to change the subject.

"No, what's happening in your world?" Bernadette took a sip of her hot vanilla latte. It was June. Maybe she should switch to cold lattes for a while.

"Not *my* world, Professor," Madison said and pushed her glasses back up the bridge of her nose. "Yours." She sat back smug like she knew a secret.

"Hmm," Bernadette said with narrowed eyes. "Soldier, do I have to beat this confidential information out of you?"

Madison sat bolt upright and saluted. "Madison. *Little*. Student," she said, giving Bernadette her name, rank, and occupation. She stared straight ahead.

"Ahh, is that right, private?" Bernadette loved going along with Madison's silliness. "Must I waterboard you?" She narrowed her eyes and held her chin in her hand while tapping a finger along her cheek as if deep in thought. "No, no. That's not it. I will tickle you!" She lurched forward, wiggling her fingers menacingly.

"No!" Madison screeched and recoiled out of reach. Her giggles caused customers to look over at the fun. "Hard limit." Madison leaned in closer. "Mistress tickles me sometimes until I have to call red. She is kind of sadistic."

Bernadette laughed and put a hand over her mouth. Miss Shasti was standing right behind Madison.

"Who's sadistic?" Miss Shasti asked innocently. She wasn't fooling Bernadette. She'd heard the whole statement from her *little's* mouth.

"No one," Madison said innocently, but her grin betrayed the fact that she knew her Mistress had heard everything.

"Here's your decaf." Miss Shasti handed Madison a coffee with whipped cream. "How are you, Professor?"

"I'm doing all right. I'm a little sore from softball on Saturday," she admitted.

"Drink plenty of water," Miss Shasti said. "Light stretching, light activity, and Epsom salt baths if you can."

"I'm sore, too," Madison blurted and then whispered, "but Mistress gave me a thorough rub down on Saturday night when we got home. *Very* thorough."

Miss Shasti chuckled as she rolled her eyes. "Absolutely no filter on that girl."

Bernadette laughed. It was true. Madison had no filter.

"Guess what?" Madison blurted again.

"What?" Bernadette said, giving Madison her full attention.

"Shoot. I forgot." She scrunched up her face and looked to the ceiling as if the thing she wanted to say was written there. "Oh yeah. Mistress let me drive here."

"Wait," Bernadette said. "You already know how to drive. You're a good driver."

"I know, but Mistress says I need to get better, so she's letting me practice. And, besides, she *always* drives us, but today she let me. I mean, she had to do the parallel parking part, but once Miss Rikki gets that parking lot fixed up, I won't have to worry about that anymore."

"Or you can learn how to parallel park, Peanut," Shasti said.

"I guess," Madison said, clearly not wanting to entertain the thought of that. "Once I get more practice, I can be Mistress's full-time chauffeur."

Miss Shasti nodded and said, "Did you see the construction markers out there, Bernadette? The parking lot is really happening."

"In the lot next door? No, I didn't see it."

"Someone from the city came Friday evening."

"And the contractor, too, Mistress," Madison added. "He had a clipboard and a big belly. It was funny."

"Madison," Miss Shasti said in such a way that Madison understood she'd crossed a line.

"Sorry."

*So, a contractor truly was here on Friday night.* Bernadette was embarrassed at her own jealousy. She cleared her throat and said, "Miss Marta told me that Shanice test drove a wheelchair-accessible van last week. And once those handicap spots go in, it'll be so much easier for them."

"It was love at first sight for the two of them," Miss Shasti said. "For Marta anyway."

"How did they meet?"

"At the hospital after Shanice's accident," Miss Shasti said.

"They didn't know each other before?" Bernadette asked.

"No. Apparently, Marta was visiting someone else in the same wing of the hospital. I don't remember who or why, and she heard a patient crying hysterically in a nearby room. She went to investigate and found the nurses unable to get the young woman under control. They were about to sedate Shanice when Marta asked if she could try. Apparently, they let her. And Marta, you know how gentle she is; she was able to get Shanice to calm down and tell her what the issue was."

"The amputations?" Bernadette offered.

"That had already happened," Miss Shasti said. "I think Shanice was upset about what her future was going to bring her."

"A valid concern, for sure."

"Marta visited her every day. She told me she spent more time with Shanice than with the person she was supposed to be visiting. No one visited Shanice."

"No family?"

"She has none," Miss Shasti said. "As I understand it, her mother passed a long time ago. I'm not sure what the story is there."

"Wow. How long ago—wait," Bernadette interrupted herself. "How did *you two* meet? How long have you been together?"

"A little over three years, Professor," Madison said. Mistress scooped me up when I was twenty-two and floundering about what I wanted to be when I grew up. I had just moved to Denton Heights, and so had she."

"Before you ask," Miss Shasti said, "there's a ten-year age gap between us. I found myself all alone after moving here to join a family practice. After a few careful Internet searches and cryptic questions, I found the community I hoped was here. Rikki's Aunt Matilda was part of that community."

"That's the *kinky* community, Professor," Madison clarified for Bernadette, who didn't need clarification.

"She introduced us," Miss Shasti said. The look she gave her *little* was one of pure love and affection.

"Aww, you two are so well matched," Bernadette gushed.

"And we're both Asian," Madison declared. "Did you know that?"

"I did," Bernadette said. Madison was the cutest.

"But did you know that Mistress was born in India?"

"No, I didn't."

"I don't remember it," Miss Shasti said. "My parents moved to D.C. when I was a baby. It's where I went to medical school, but I knew I needed to relocate if I wanted to live this lifestyle. Something they would never understand."

"I was born in Columbus, Ohio," Madison announced proudly. "My great-grandparents moved to Ohio from Korea way long before I was born. My parents had me first and then had my brother ten months later because you have to have a boy, you know? And since girls aren't supposed to like girls, they made me leave home, so I took the bus to Cincinnati on my own. Well, to Denton Heights, where I lived with Mrs. Park for a while."

Bernadette sensed Miss Shasti tense up at the mention of this Mrs. Park.

"Oh," Madison continued, still on a roll, "and did you know that Mistress and I had a trial period? She didn't collar me right away, even though I knew she would eventually."

It was a lot to unpack, but Bernadette simply said, "I think Miss Rikki and I had a trial period, too, although I didn't really know it."

"Madison," Miss Shasti said, "you kind of buried the lead. Tell Miss Bernadette your news."

"I got a job, Professor."

"Whoa, that's fantastic, kiddo." Bernadette reached over and swatted Madison on the knee. It was her version of an atta-girl. "Doing what?"

"I am the new veterinary receptionist and tech trainee for Dr. Addison." Madison sat up a little taller.

"That's fantastic! Congrats."

"Yeah, yeah. Dr. Addison said that I can be a full-time tech there as soon as I get my degree. Of course, I still have to pass *Pharmacology* this summer. The names are so long, and it's so hard."

"You're a smart young lady," Bernadette said. "You passed my Calculus course with an A, didn't you?"

"Yes, Ma'am." She wiggled in her seat.

"Professor," Miss Shasti said, "I don't think I've thanked you enough for helping out my little peanut. She was on the verge of quitting school, but I convinced her to go for one more semester. That was the semester she took your class. You showed her that she *was* capable and that, with hard work, she could be successful. She probably wouldn't have gotten this job if it wasn't for your guidance and patience."

"That is so sweet," Bernadette gushed. "I appreciate you sharing that with me. I think she just needed a bit of a kick in the pants."

"Don't I know it," Miss Shasti said and rolled her eyes.

"Hey!" Madison protested. "Never mind. It's true."

Bernadette chuckled along with Madison's Mistress and then asked Madison, "When do you start?"

"On Saturday after our doubleheader in the morning, and I'll also have some hours in the evenings, and Mistress is growing her practice, so she can't drive me everywhere, so I need to get used to doing it."

"Take a breath, Madison," Bernadette said with a grin. She caught motion at the front entrance and groaned. Victoria and Alyssa had just entered.

The trio of friends grew quiet. Although Bernadette had told everyone she was over the abuse and had forgiven Victoria – or Daddy Vic as she was more popularly known – she wasn't so sure she truly was. First of all, Bernadette knew she should have asked what was in the *supplements* Victoria was giving her, but she stupidly didn't and blindly took them. She was lucky they hadn't done damage.

Victoria leaned down and whispered something in Alyssa's ear. Alyssa nodded and headed to the restroom. Victoria ordered a single drink at the counter and then sat down with it near the restroom. Apparently, she hadn't noticed them in the far corner, or maybe she had. Who knew?

Usually, by now, Madison would have leaped up and greeted Daddy Vic with an enthusiastic hello, but not this time. Madison had had her own troubles with Alyssa recently. Alyssa had taken advantage of an incredibly naïve Madison. And even though Madison told everyone she had gotten over Alyssa giving her edible gummy bears without her knowledge, it was uber obvious that she wasn't.

"You can't step into the same river twice," Madison muttered as she stared in the direction of the restroom.

"Preach it, philosopher," Bernadette muttered right back.

"Heraclitus said that," Madison said and turned around. "Did you know that he was a Greek philosopher who lived in, like, 600 BCE? Did you know BCE means 'Before the Common Era'?"

"I did not know that," Bernadette said.

Madison rambled on happily about the philosopher she'd learned about in one of her college courses, but after a while Bernadette stopped participating and watched as Victoria checked her watch and then headed to the restroom. Bernadette swallowed the bile forming in her throat. Victoria had done the same thing to her. She'd made Bernadette go into that same restroom to ready herself. She'd had to bare her breasts and make her nipples large and ready for Victoria to torture. And then she got smashed against the wall and dry humped from behind until Victoria orgasmed against her. And then she left her there alone to put herself back together. And, no, not all of it had been consensual.

"Baby, are you okay?" Rikki said, shaking Bernadette's shoulder.

"Hmm?" Bernadette realized where she was and took a deep breath to clear her head. "Yeah, sure. I'm okay." She watched Rikki and Miss Shasti exchange a concerned glance but ignored it. Instead, she said icily, "I'm pretty sure the women's room is out of order again."

"Are you kidding me?" Rikki's anger was clear and immediate. "She'd better not be." She stomped over to the restroom and banged on the door. Alyssa emerged first, buttoning up her shirt. Daddy Vic simply stared Rikki down as she walked by. Rikki pointed toward the front door. There were no words exchanged, just hard glares. Rikki followed behind and waited to make sure they didn't come back in.

From all the way across the shop, Bernadette watched Rikki take a deep breath and let it out slowly. She moved her head from one side to the other, clearly trying to release tension. She turned around slowly and looked toward Bernadette. She did not smile. She just shook her head and mouthed, "I'm sorry."

Bernadette nodded and then motioned for Rikki to come back over.

Rikki sat on the arm of the couch Bernadette was sitting on and started to apologize again. Bernadette put up a hand to stop her. She wanted no further reminders of her brief relationship with Victoria. Instead, she cleared her throat and said, "Hey, kiddo, what was that classified intel I was trying to waterboard out of you earlier?"

"Oh, yeah," Madison said. "I forgot to tell you. Dr. Baxter is retiring after the summer session."

Bernadette's jaw dropped open.

"Baby," Rikki said, "isn't that the professor who teaches the courses you want? Those 8000-level courses or something?"

Bernadette looked up at her fiancée in disbelief.

"What? I listen," Rikki said.

Miss Shasti and Madison broke out laughing.

Bernadette smiled. She'd have to verify Madison's intel, but if it was true, then that changed everything. Absolutely everything. It meant that Baxter's top-floor office would be up for grabs. She was still too low on the totem pole to be awarded that, but maybe Dr. Yang would move up there, and then Bernadette could have his office. It was the exact same as Baxter's, only on the third floor. It had the same amazing views of the Myammia Creek, a tributary to the great Ohio River.

Dr. Yang wouldn't want those Group Theory and Abstract Algebra courses, would he? Would any of her colleagues? She sincerely doubted it. They were all stuck in their ways and comfortable with their yellow-sheet courses—lecture notes so old that the paper they were written on had yellowed. No. She was the only one who had expressed interest and who was qualified.

Finally, she was going to get the recognition she deserved. After all, everyone wanted to be noticed, needed, and appreciated, right? And loved, of course. She sat back in her chair and smiled at Rikki, who was decidedly not smiling. Oh, shit. She'd lost herself in thought again.

"Did you hear what I said?" Rikki asked. Her arms were folded. Her eyes were in full Domme mode.

Bernadette gulped down her fear and said meekly, "No, Ma'am. I'm sorry." Crap. She was about to get punished again.

Rikki's sigh was enough to make Bernadette fall to her knees in front of her, but she checked herself. They were in a public place.

"I'm sorry," Bernadette said again. "What did you say?" She reached up and fingered the stretchy day collar around her neck.

There was a long pause as Rikki took a deep breath and looked over at Miss Shasti. Bernadette wasn't sure what their silent communication was about, but Rikki simply nodded and then put an arm around Bernadette. "We'll talk about it later." She squeezed Bernadette close and said low, "Are you okay?"

"Yes," Bernadette said succinctly. "I'm good." *No, I'm more than good. I'm great!* Hopefully, they would announce the new course assignments soon. They didn't have a department meeting until the end of the summer term, but maybe they'd announce it early. Of course, Wainwright might call her into his office before that and give her the good news. He probably knew all about Baxter's impending retirement and wanted to surprise her. Obviously, he understood that five years in her closet of an office with no windows was demeaning and needed to be rectified.

Bernadette looked up at Rikki's concerned face and smiled. "I'm okay, Rikki. Things are looking up."

Bernadette just smiled at Rikki's confused expression, but oh, how proud Rikki would be when Bernadette told her about the promotion.

# Chapter 6
## Rikki

Rikki smoothed the mat on the living room floor, satisfied they were ready for Jaleesa's arrival. She had all the supplies they might need and then some in a plastic bin on the coffee table.

"Little bee?" Rikki called to her fiancée, who was in the kitchen spiffing up for the millionth time.

"Yes, honey?" Bernadette zipped around the corner.

"Oh, you look so cute," Rikki gushed. Bernadette wore the shortest daisy dukes and a plaid shirt, the ends tied underneath her breasts. The shirt was tight enough to press her breasts together and make the most intriguing cleavage. Rikki had half a mind to call Jaleesa and cancel so she could have Bernadette to herself. "Do you have a minute for me?"

Bernadette's eyes grew big with confusion. Rikki usually demanded her presence in front of her, but this time she was asking as if Bernadette had a choice. Which she did. Which she always did.

"Um, of course, I have time," Bernadette stammered and hurried to sit on her low stool at Rikki's feet. The stool was the equivalent of kneeling in their house in deference to Bernadette's weak and injured knees.

Rikki asked if she was excited about their afternoon playtime, and Bernadette nodded, but the response felt a little too automatic. It made Rikki think that maybe Bernadette wasn't up to an intense play session with Jaleesa today. "You'll tell me if you want to stop anything we're doing, won't you, baby?"

"Yes, Ma'am," Bernadette said and looked up. "She knows my hard limits, I think."

"Yep. No piss, scat, public humiliation or public sex, forced orgasms, breath play, CNC, needles, maiming, killing, dirty shoes in the house—"

"Stop." Bernadette playfully smacked Rikki's arm.

Mm hmm. There she was—Rikki's playful girl. Rikki reached over and took off Bernadette's stretchy day collar. Wordlessly, she wrapped the sturdy leather collar around her submissive's neck. The D-rings made attaching a leash or chains easy.

"So, what should be the first thing we do once the inheritance becomes available?" Rikki asked.

"Your shop, Rikki. The furnace and air conditioning."

Mm hmm. That was so like her little bee to think about Rikki first. "What do you want to do here in this house? That's kind of what I meant."

"Oh, uh, we have the new floor to buy and install for the playroom downstairs."

"Mm, hmm," Rikki said with a nod. "And then what?"

"Some equipment? You wanted a cross and a spanking bench?" Bernadette shrugged again, and it was clear to Rikki that her girl had become uneasy when asked what she wanted for herself.

"C'mere." Rikki pulled Bernadette up and into her lap. Once she settled in with her head on Rikki's shoulder, Rikki said, "Someone has a birthday coming up."

Bernadette's eyes brightened. "Who does?" The grin spreading on her face was positively adorable.

"I was going to surprise you, but sometimes the anticipation is just as fun."

"What do you mean?"

"The Reds are in town on your birthday."

Bernadette sat bolt upright. Her full weight on Rikki's lap was uncomfortable, but she didn't let on. "Are we going? Did you get tickets?"

"Yes, yes, yes, little bee." Rikki readjusted her girl so that her legs weren't crushed. "It's an afternoon game. Shasti, Madison, Marta, and Shanice are all coming. Jaleesa has to work, and Lydia will cover the coffee shop."

"Thank you, Rikki." Bernadette hugged her again. "I can't wait. When I first moved here, I went to a couple of games, but then, you know…"

"What?"

"Oh, Jen didn't like baseball, so I didn't go again."

"Well, we'll go as often as my little bee wants to," Rikki said, leaning down and rubbing noses with her girl. "That makes you a happy little bee, doesn't it?"

"Yes, Ma'am. Thank you so much," Bernadette said and then got a far-off look on her face.

"Tell me," Rikki commanded.

"Umm, do you think maybe…" Bernadette looked away and didn't finish her thought.

"Tell me," Rikki said again, careful not to use her full-on Domme voice. It was clear that Bernadette had a request but had second thoughts about voicing it. "I might say, 'yes.'"

"No, no," Bernadette said. "It's okay. Never mind."

"Absolutely not." Rikki couldn't help the irritated edge in her voice. She nudged Bernadette into a sitting position and directed her back on the stool. It was clear that Bernadette needed to remember her place. "Ask me."

Bernadette remained quiet for a moment, her eyes down. She sighed and then said, "Umm, do you think maybe I can wear something comfortable to the game? Something not so revealing?" She gestured to her current garb.

Rikki didn't give her a direct answer right away. Instead, she asked, "Do these clothes make you uncomfortable?"

"It's okay. Never mind. Forget I asked."

Rikki let out a disgusted sigh and immediately wished she could take it back as she watched Bernadette fold in on herself. *She needs guidance,* Rikki thought. *I need to make her comfortable enough to tell me what she's feeling. Is there such a thing as being* too *submissive?*

In a vulnerable move, Rikki asked, "As your Domme, I sometimes arrogantly think I know everything that you need. It's my job, no, it's my *passion* to know what you need. But clearly, there's no way I can know everything, and if I don't know, then I can't help you. So, you have to help me, little bee. Communication is one of our agreed-upon ideals, right?"

"Yes, Ma'am," Bernadette said without looking up.

"You are an amazing communicator when it comes to teaching your students. Madison loved going to that Calculus class of yours. And we all witnessed your communication skills at the masquerade ball last month.

Thanks to you, all the Dominants in Denton Heights and beyond are getting the best foot massages known to humankind."

A small smile crept up Bernadette's face. Good. She was listening.

"That event was hard for you," Rikki continued and stroked Bernadette's cheek. "But you did it. You spoke in front of that room of people and taught them." Rikki lifted Bernadette's chin with two fingers. "Sweetie, I know that some things are difficult for you. But I'm in your corner. I need you to trust me, okay?"

"Okay," Bernadette said with a nod. Rikki released her chin.

"So, we'll back up for you to answer my question. Do these clothes I have you in today make you uncomfortable?"

"Yes," Bernadette said succinctly.

"Because you feel exposed?"

"Yes, Ma'am. I feel like a piece of meat."

Rikki smiled. "My intent was to celebrate your gorgeous body. And not just for our guest. For me, too. Gotta tell you, I'm a little bit aroused at what you're wearing right now."

"I like wearing stuff like this for *you*," Bernadette offered. "Privately."

Three loud knocks interrupted Rikki's next question. Oh, well. She would definitely pick up the thread of this conversation later.

Bernadette stood up to get the door.

"Sweetie?" Rikki said. "Two things before you open that door."

"Yes?"

"One – yes, you can wear whatever you like to the baseball game. And two – we won't do anything today that you don't want to do. Okay?"

"Okay," Bernadette said, giving a nervous smile. "Thank you."

Rikki gestured for her to answer the door.

"Greetings, lovely ladies of the five-acre non-farm," Jaleesa bellowed. "Look, Bernadette, I'm wiping my feet."

Bernadette chuckled genuinely and opened the screen door to let Jaleesa inside. Rikki rejoiced as her girl seemed to relax in the presence of their friend. Jaleesa wore her hair relaxed, pulled back into a chic tight ponytail with a hair wrap around the base. Rikki had seen her wear this style before when in dominant mode. Her black vest, tight t-shirt, and jeans completed the look. Yes, Jaleesa was all style. All the time, even when she wasn't trying.

"Hey, Jaleesa," Rikki said. "Bernadette has been in an amazing mood all week. I wonder why."

"Have you?" Jaleesa asked Bernadette.

"I guess so, Ma'am," Bernadette said.

"Go on," Rikki encouraged. Her girl could become so reticent when her submissive nature took over.

"Oh, uh, I was looking forward to today, of course. And my students were good this week for some reason. They asked questions and did their work. It made me feel like I was reaching them."

"That's so good, sweetie," Rikki said. "I know how much teaching means to you."

"I like working with young people," she admitted. "Keeps me young, I guess."

"You're still young," Jaleesa said with a chuckle.

"Thank you, Miss Jaleesa," Bernadette said and lowered her eyes.

"And I thank you, Miss Daisy Dukes," Jaleesa murmured and sucked air through her teeth. She turned toward Rikki and said, "That's some pretty packaging you got on that fine piece of ass."

"Don't I know it." Rikki smiled as she watched Bernadette's cheeks turn pink.

"Oh, Rikki," Jaleesa said, "before I forget. You asked about joining my family on a bird-watching hike. Our next official date is the weekend after the fourth of July. That's about three weeks from now. I'll text you the actual date later once I confirm with Tina – the keeper of my schedule."

"Excellent," Rikki said. "You'd like that, little bee, wouldn't you?"

"Yes, Ma'am," Bernadette said as she closed and locked the front door. "Um, Ma'ams, may I offer you some refreshments? We have cheese and crackers and a small fruit tray. Water or unsweet iced tea?"

"Water's fine," Jaleesa said. "And thank you for the snacks."

Bernadette's shy grin was so endearing that Rikki wanted to hug her. Instead, she said, "That would be great, Bernadette."

"Let me give you a hand," Jaleesa said and followed my girl into the kitchen. Rikki lost sight of Bernadette as she went to the refrigerator. She reemerged in Rikki's sightline when she put the tray on the countertop. That's when Jaleesa made her move. Bernadette turned to get something, the waters maybe, but Jaleesa blocked her way. She put an arm up and leaned against the top cabinet, trapping Bernadette between her and the countertop. She leaned down, her face inches away from my girl's.

Bernadette's mouth dropped open slightly as she bit her lower lip. They stayed in that pose, never touching, for almost a full thirty seconds. Bernadette swallowed hard, and maybe that was the cue Jaleesa took to push off the cabinet and release her.

"I'll get the waters," Jaleesa said and turned her back to Bernadette.

Rikki smirked at their guest when she returned with three waters and then made herself comfortable on the couch. Yes, the attraction these two had for each other was very mutual. The knot of jealousy Rikki knew she would have that afternoon hadn't manifested yet. But it would at some point. Guaranteed.

Once the snacks were brought out, Bernadette sat on her low stool and fed Jaleesa grapes one at a time at Jaleesa's request. Jaleesa teased by snapping her teeth, which made Bernadette giggle like Madison. It was a truly wonderful sight to behold. The roles switched, and Jaleesa fed Bernadette. Fairly quickly, the snacks were forgotten, and Jaleesa's fingers pumped in and out of Bernadette's mouth.

"Domme Rikki," Jaleesa said, her gaze never leaving Bernadette's, "this pet belongs to you and will remain yours. I will respect any and all ground rules and limits you set for her."

"Domme Jaleesa," Rikki responded. "I accept your words. You may direct and use my submissive as you please within her hard limits."

"Thank you," Jaleesa said to Rikki. "Stand," she commanded Bernadette. "Back against the wall." Bernadette did as she was told. "As much as I like those clothes on you, they need to come off." Bernadette reached up to undo the top button, but Jaleesa stopped her. "Allow me," she said, and one by one, undid the buttons before sliding the blouse off.

Jaleesa reached down to the plastic bin filled with toys and play objects and picked out the jewelry she had given Bernadette at her housewarming party last month. She lifted one of Bernadette's breasts to her mouth and sucked the nipple hard. Less-than-gently, she attached the first nipple clip. Bernadette gasped at the pain, her eyes rolling slightly as she absorbed it. The low moan a moment later told Rikki that the pain had aroused her.

The second clip was attached in the same fashion and with the same effect. Jaleesa held up the dangling third clip as if asking Bernadette if she knew where this last one was going. Jaleesa surprised both Rikki and Bernadette by pulling down Bernadette's lower jaw and commanding her to stick out her tongue. This time, the clip was attached gently. Bernadette's high-pitched groan of pain had Rikki on high alert.

Rikki threw her girl a thumbs-up with a questioning expression on her face. Bernadette raised an upwardly facing thumb, so Rikki relaxed a bit.

"We both have safe words," Jaleesa whispered into Bernadette's ear. "You can snap your fingers if your mouth is otherwise occupied like it is now. Do you understand?"

Bernadette nodded.

"I'm going to take off your adorable shorts now." Jaleesa unfastened the metal button. The slowness at which she lowered the zipper made Bernadette squirm. Jaleesa's smirk betrayed the fact that she liked teasing her subs, even temporary ones.

"No panties," Jaleesa said. "I like that."

Once the shorts were off, Jaleesa leaned down and kissed Bernadette's mound. Bernadette squirmed. A sharp slap to the ass made Bernadette center herself and remain still.

Jaleesa got down on her knees on the mat. She nudged Bernadette's legs apart and then licked her from back to front and back again. Bernadette's surprised moan was almost comical. Neither of us had expected Jaleesa to go down on her today. Or ever.

Jaleesa used the fingers on one hand to open up Bernadette's lower lips and then drove her tongue deep inside. Bernadette's hands came crashing down on Jaleesa's head to pull her closer to her need. Jaleesa didn't protest this bold move but continued to suck, lick, and thrust with her tongue and lips. It was obvious that Bernadette was having trouble staying still, but Rikki was proud of her, nonetheless.

Jaleesa stopped her ministrations and looked up at Bernadette from her subservient position below. It was sexy as hell, arousing Rikki in her chair. Two fingers parted the skin over Bernadette's clit, freeing it. Jaleesa moaned at the sight and leaned in, pulling the clit into her mouth. Bernadette's hips arched and undulated slightly. It was up to Jaleesa to stop her, but she did not.

Bernadette's moans were reaching a fever pitch, and Rikki knew her girl was close to orgasm. Jaleesa must have known it as well because she stopped all movement. She reached up and released the clip on Bernadette's tongue and brought it down. We all knew where it was going, and Bernadette groaned in fear. The clip seized her clit between its teeth.

"Fuck!" came the one-word retort to Jaleesa's betrayal.

"Ride it out, pet," Jaleesa said softly. She was still on her knees, eyes on the clip. "Ride it out."

Sharp measured intakes of breath told Rikki that Bernadette was handling the pain as best she could. Her eyes were closed, and her head lolled from side to side. Oh, yes, her baby was approaching a delicious sub-space. And the afternoon had only just begun. It was too bad that a ball of jealousy had manifested in Rikki's gut like she knew it would eventually. Or maybe it was hurt pride. Rikki was the giver of Bernadette's pleasure, not… She let the thought drop. She was the one who had arranged this whole thing to please Bernadette, after all.

# Chapter 7
## Bernadette

Bernadette steadied herself against the wall and breathed through the pulsing pain of the clit clip. She lifted her head and searched for Rikki. There she was, still in her chair. Good. She couldn't do this without Rikki there.

Miss Jaleesa stood up, but Rikki said, "Not yet."

Bernadette took a deep breath in and blew it out slowly. She closed her eyes briefly. Yes, the pain was still pulsing, but it was manageable now. Never in a million years did she think Miss Jaleesa would torture her this way.

"She's good now," Rikki said.

Miss Jaleesa nodded again and moved closer. She reached for one of the nipple clips and gave it a flick. Bernadette sucked air through her teeth but managed the surging sensations. Her legs separated slightly on their own. She still didn't understand the pain-to-arousal connection, but at this moment, Miss Jaleesa could throw her down and do whatever, and Bernadette would welcome the relief.

"You'll need to undress me now, pet," Miss Jaleesa said, her face in serious Domme mode.

"Yes, Ma'am," Bernadette said and giggled. She untucked the white t-shirt with writing across the front that read, *Yes, Ma'am is the only answer* in black letters. "Undressing you is a privilege, Ma'am," Bernadette said bashfully. Miss Jaleesa made a noise of surprise but said nothing. Bernadette worked quietly, removing the vest and t-shirt. She undid Miss Jaleesa's bra and then unbuckled the belt. Was that belt going to be used on her ass later? Maybe? Hopefully? The jeans and panties came down next, and then Miss Jaleesa was as nude as Bernadette.

Miss Jaleesa pulled Bernadette into a hug. The clips on Bernadette's nipples pressed against Miss Jaleesa's body, continuing the confusing pain-to-pleasure sensations. "I bet you're sore from our double-header yesterday."

"Oh, yes, Ma'am," Bernadette said, feeling her sore shoulders and back and core muscles all over again. "Rikki made me take an Epsom salt bath last night."

"She is a good Domme," Miss Jaleesa said, still hugging Bernadette tight.

"I love her, Ma'am."

"Aww," Miss Jaleesa gushed.

Bernadette turned her head and found Rikki smiling at the sight. Bernadette mouthed the words, "I love you." And Rikki mouthed the same words back.

"Do you have cuffs, Rikki?"

"How many?" Rikki was already up and heading to the plastic bin of supplies.

"Just two for now."

It wasn't long before Bernadette was sitting on her low stool with her hands cuffed together behind her back. She was one part anxious about losing control, but she was also one part grateful. In the right setting, giving up control was comforting. To give herself over to someone, two someones in this case, who made all the decisions was incredibly and contradictorily freeing. In analyzing this dichotomy, she came to realize that her Dommes were sending her the message that she would be taken care of, that she didn't need to decide or handle anything. With decisions taken away, she could turn off the part of her brain that did all the worrying. She simply needed to follow instructions, something she was quite good at. She would let herself be led wherever they wanted to take her.

It was no wonder that trust was such a big talking point in BDSM. Bernadette's problem, though? She trusted too quickly, too easily. Rikki and Miss Jaleesa were cut from a different mold, though. They practiced loving and focused BDSM, and Bernadette trusted them implicitly. So, when Miss Jaleesa guided her to her knees on the mat, she didn't hesitate.

"I'm going to blindfold you later, pet," Miss Jaleesa said. "For now, I need you to see what you're doing." She reached down and pulled off the nipple clips one at a time. Bernadette gasped as the blood rushed back in. She knew what was next and spread her legs wide.

Miss Jaleesa laughed. "Anxious, are we?" Carefully, she set Bernadette's clit free and chuckled again as Bernadette slammed her legs closed with a groan.

Miss Jaleesa snapped the leash onto Bernadette's leather play collar – not the purple collar. No, that one was reserved for playing with Rikki only. This collar might be considered the collar for guests. Is that what Miss Jaleesa was? Just a guest? Bernadette didn't have time to ponder that interesting question as the leash tugged her toward Miss Jaleesa's wide-open legs. Miss Jaleesa scooched to the edge of the chair, giving Bernadette free and full access.

Bernadette moaned in anticipatory reverence. She hadn't meant to. It just popped out. She shimmied forward for a better vantage point. Before diving in, she turned her head and looked at Rikki for permission. Rikki nodded, and only then did Bernadette lean forward and take in Miss Jaleesa's musky scent. She kissed the shaved mound in front of her and then rubbed her cheek along the skin. "So smooth, Ma'am."

"I'll be sure to tell Tina. She shaved me right before I left. She said she didn't want me to embarrass myself."

So, Tina knows and supports Miss Jaleesa's visits? Interesting. Bernadette had so many questions, but a gentle nudge on the back of her head reminded her of the business at hand. It was hard to balance with her hands clasped behind her, but she managed with Miss Jaleesa's help.

Bernadette sucked on the skin of Miss Jaleesa's inner thighs, making sure to leave marks. It would be hard to see on Miss Jaleesa's dark skin, but for some reason, Bernadette wanted to possess her at that moment. Was it the mention of Tina, Miss Jaleesa's long-term partner? Did Bernadette want two Dommes? Again, these were questions for another time.

Since she had no use of her hands, she had to exaggerate her head movements as she licked the pussy in front of her. *Just warming you up, Ma'am,* Bernadette thought as she licked from bottom to top and back again. She momentarily stopped at the clit and sucked it between her lips gently. *Just a tease, Ma'am.* She moved on to suck in the fleshy outer lips and then the inner. She swirled her tongue around the opening and then darted inside.

Miss Jaleesa stroked Bernadette's head gently, signaling that she was doing well.

Bernadette moved back to the clit and circled it with her tongue. This caused a great moan from Miss Jaleesa, who suddenly pushed Bernadette's head away. "Get up. Sit centered on your stool."

Oh, no! What did she do wrong?

"Pleasure pose," Miss Jaleesa said. Bernadette tilted her head back and stuck out her tongue in the pose that Rikki had taught her early in their relationship. "Flat." Miss Jaleesa stood up and maneuvered over the flattened tongue. She rocked her hips and then said, "Hard." Miss Jaleesa exposed her clit and placed a bullseye on the tip of Bernadette's hardened tongue. "Side to side." The single hand petting Bernadette's head told her she was pleasing the Domme guiding her. "Oh, yes, fucking yes, pet. Good fucking girl." The petting continued until Miss Jaleesa said, "Light switch." Jaleesa grabbed a handful of hair and pulled Bernadette tighter to her center. "Swirl," came the next command. "Suck it now, baby. Suck me off. C'mon, little pet."

Then Miss Jaleesa went quiet. Her pussy tightened and spasmed against Bernadette's lips and tongue as she came. Oh, God. This was the part Bernadette loved the best. Feeling a dominant surrender to Bernadette's power, albeit temporary. It was energizing. No, it was more than that. It was revitalizing and life-affirming.

Yes, making a woman orgasm did that to Bernadette.

"Oh, my little pet, look at you between my legs like you belong here." She ran a finger down Bernadette's cheek. "Good girl," she whispered and cradled Bernadette's chin. "I am pleased with you. Very pleased. This bodes well for your future."

Bernadette beamed with pride.

Miss Jaleesa stretched and then grabbed Bernadette's water, offering her a couple of sips. She turned to Rikki and said, "She deserves a reward for being such a good pussy licker, doesn't she?"

"Always," Rikki said and stood up. "Strap-ons?"

"Indeed," Miss Jaleesa said. "And then a flogging afterward. This girl needs to fly. Is she stretched?"

"No, but that can be done while you both rest." Rikki reached into the bin, and Bernadette's eyes grew wide when Rikki pulled out the largest anal plug. Bernadette must have squeaked because Rikki reassured her that it would be all right.

"I just need a minute," Miss Jaleesa said, taking a few sips from her own water bottle. "Rikki, can you undo her hands? Let the circulation back in my shortstop's arms. We need those arms to be fully functional next Saturday."

Rikki did so and whispered, "You make me proud, little bee."

"Thank you, Ma'am." Bernadette felt her face flush. She rubbed at her wrists and swirled her shoulders to get the blood flowing again. "Ma'am?" she said to Rikki.

"Yes, sweetie?"

"Can you kiss me now?"

"Aww," Miss Jaleesa gushed. She put on the red kimono robe that Bernadette had laid out for her.

Rikki pulled Bernadette up to her feet and pulled her into a passionate kiss. Bernadette was breathless when Rikki pulled back. "Mmm, my little bee is hungry, isn't she?"

"Oh, yes, Ma'am," Bernadette said with a sigh.

"C'mon, face down on my lap. You know the drill." Rikki moved to the center of the couch. "Ass up. Arch up. Yes, that's it. Reach back now, spread your ass cheeks for me."

Bernadette complied and was only slightly embarrassed to be so vulnerable in front of Miss Jaleesa. Cold lube hit her tiny hole, and then Rikki's fingers massaged the slippery gel around the hole and inside. More lube was applied, and Bernadette allowed her body to relax. The tip of the plug entered, causing Bernadette to moan.

"She likes anal, doesn't she?" Miss Jaleesa asked.

"Mm hmm," Rikki said. "I didn't need to train her."

"Victoria?"

"No, no," Rikki said. "Her first Domme, the one in Columbus, introduced her to it. Probably the only good thing that woman did."

"Humph," Miss Jaleesa muttered. "Incompetent Dommes need to be caned."

"Agreed," Rikki muttered back.

Listening to the conversation, Bernadette lost track of Rikki's maneuvers and was surprised to discover that the plug was all the way in. Rikki gave it a twist for good measure.

"Are you purring, little bee?" Rikki asked with a laugh.

"Maybe," came the answer.

"Your arousal is dripping all over my leg."

"Sorry, not sorry?" came Bernadette's sheepish response.

Rikki leaned down and kissed Bernadette's shoulder – the only thing she could reach.

"All right," Miss Jaleesa bellowed. "Enough of that lovey-dovey stuff. Face down over that stool, pet."

Rikki laughed, but Bernadette did as she was commanded. Miss Jaleesa blindfolded Bernadette and said, "Lift that ass in the air." Miss Jaleesa's large rough hands stroked Bernadette's ass. "Yes, yes. Spread your legs like you're asking me to pound you good." Miss Jaleesa grunted her satisfaction. "So," she said nonchalantly to Rikki, "show me how far you've gotten on the dungeon downstairs."

Bernadette groaned at the treachery, and the two Dommes laughed.

"Keep that ass up, pet," Miss Jaleesa said. "If the package delivery chick stops by, I want her to see that plug in your gorgeous ass ready to receive." Jaleesa's laugh was playfully evil when Bernadette groaned with worry. "Oh, yes, she'll toss her clipboard down, throw on that strap-on, and do you right there."

Bernadette groaned again as her two Dommes headed down to the basement. She knew Miss Jaleesa was just teasing her. The front door was locked, and all the blinds and blackout curtains were closed, right? Yes, yes, she'd seen to that herself. She wished she could turn and look, but the blindfold prevented that.

"She keeps a lot inside, doesn't she?" Miss Jaleesa asked in a low tone. Bernadette knew she shouldn't be listening, but there really wasn't anything she could do about it.

"She does," Rikki said. "Too much. Being submissive doesn't necessarily mean that you're shy, but Bernadette definitely is. I'm working with her on a few things. She's had a lifetime of being submissive without a positive or accepting outlet for it. I'm trying to bring her out of her shell if you will."

Miss Jaleesa burst out laughing. "Perfect analogy. She's a turtle inside that shell of hers."

"I was hoping you could help me with something," Rikki said.

Their voices got fainter as they moved away from the stairwell. Good, Bernadette didn't want to hear anymore. Her muscles were getting tired from holding the ass-up position and, not for the first time, wondered why, oh, why do Dommes love to torture subs like this? She thought about relaxing her core but heard them climbing the stairs.

"Guess what, pet?" Miss Jaleesa said. "I'm going to make you moan. I'm going to make you scream." She laughed that evil laugh and then helped Bernadette get up off her stool, shake out her muscles, and drink the water Miss Jaleesa put to her lips.

Rikki guided Bernadette down on the mat and then sat behind her with her back against the couch. She instructed Bernadette to scoot back and sit in the well between her legs, both of them facing Miss Jaleesa. Bernadette must have seemed anxious because Rikki said, "You'll be okay, little bee. I've got you." She wrapped her arms around her lover gently and squeezed. Bernadette burrowed back into her fiancée's arms and sighed contentedly.

Bernadette felt something soft fall between her legs. "Ass up on this pillow, pet," Miss Jaleesa said. "I need room to work. Excellent. Lean back, you two. Let those legs fall open for me. Ahh, yes, look at that plug inside you. We'll keep it there while I take your other hole."

Bernadette's breathing was steady and deep. She knew what was coming and soon enough felt the tip of a dildo, a strap-on most likely, at her entrance. She moaned in anticipation. She tilted her pelvis, giving Miss Jaleesa that invitation she wanted.

"Do you want this, pet?"

Bernadette nodded and got a slap on the breasts from Miss Jaleesa in response. "Words."

"Yes, Ma'am," Bernadette said sheepishly. "Sorry. Yes, I want this, Ma'am. Very much, please."

"Good girl," Rikki whispered in her ear.

Miss Jaleesa penetrated Bernadette's body slowly at first but then picked up speed. The moving dildo alongside the anal plug made Bernadette feel oh-so-full. She lifted her pelvis and undulated her hips. Miss Jaleesa's strokes were different than Rikki's. Not harder, per se, but just more intense or something. Maybe because Miss Jaleesa was still a bit of an unknown. Or maybe because Bernadette was blindfolded.

Bernadette felt so loved and protected between her Dommes that her orgasm sparked quickly. Her moans deepened, and Rikki held her tighter. Bernadette wailed when, un-fucking-believably, Miss Jaleesa pulled out.

This time, Miss Jaleesa didn't laugh her evil laugh. She didn't laugh at all. Instead, she reached up and pulled off the blindfold. Bernadette blinked at the sudden influx of light. Wordlessly, Miss Jaleesa took off her strap-on. Bernadette silently cursed sadistic Dommes. They built you up and then left you hanging. She must have groaned because Rikki reassured her gently.

"Trust us," Miss Jaleesa said and showed Bernadette an object that made her recoil.

"I've got you," Rikki said. "You are so safe with us, little bee. It will only be pleasurable. Okay?"

Bernadette couldn't think. She had to process the information coming at her.

"Let's give her a minute," Rikki said. She motioned for Bernadette's water and let her lover drink. To Bernadette, she said, "Trust us, little bee. You will be in control. Just like we've been doing all week, okay?"

Bernadette looked from Rikki to Miss Jaleesa to the object still in Jaleesa's hand and said, "Okay." It was said so meekly that Rikki awed in sympathy.

"You are in charge, pet," Miss Jaleesa said gently and handed the magic wand vibrator to Bernadette.

Bernadette took it and couldn't help flashing back to the time Mama_Luvs tortured her with forced orgasms with one of those things.

"Take back your power, Bernadette," Rikki whispered.

Miss Jaleesa showed her how to turn it on and put it on the lowest setting. "Now, let me hold it since your Domme tells me that your orgasms are never allowed to come from your own hand."

"No, Ma'am. She is the giver of pleasure. I guess maybe you are, too." That was a little confusing to Bernadette's endorphin-filled brain. She'd think about it later.

"Okay, so I'll hold it, but you guide me."

Bernadette nodded and wrapped her hand around Miss Jaleesa's. Together, they moved the head of the powerful vibrator to Bernadette's inner thigh. She wanted to feel the power of the setting before getting anywhere close to sensitive parts. Bernadette let out a long, slow sigh, resigned to her fate. Okay, she was ready now. She guided Miss Jaleesa's hand and the wand toward her center. So far, so good. The vibrations actually felt nice. She made wide circles around the whole area. She moved it closer to her clit, but not directly on it like Mama_Luvs had done over and over and over.

"You're doing great, pet," Miss Jaleesa said. She sat on the mat and contorted her body in such a way that her own center was now near the wand's head. "Let's both enjoy this, shall we?"

"Okay," Bernadette said. She felt Miss Jaleesa press her pussy against the vibrator, which pushed the head against Bernadette's. The sight before Bernadette was pure heaven. Miss Jaleesa moved her pelvis so her exposed clit rubbed on the vibrator. Bernadette did the same. The sight of both clits rubbing on the wand sent a flicker of pre-orgasmic lust through Bernadette, and her whole body shook.

"Yes, pet," Miss Jaleesa said. "Go with it."

The spark of orgasm was back, so she swirled her hips slightly, allowing her entire clit to feel the sensations. A long, low moan started way back in her throat.

"Fucking sexiest sound in the whole damn world," Miss Jaleesa said and sucked air through her teeth. She was close, too. Her hips moved as much as Bernadette's.

"Rikki," Bernadette screeched, pushing back on the woman holding her.

"I'm here. I'm here," Rikki said urgently. "Cum for us, baby. Cum now."

Bernadette exploded a moment before Miss Jaleesa did. Bernadette continued to rub her clit on the wand milking out the sensations. She slowed down and nudged the wand away. Once she came back down to earth, she turned her head and kissed Rikki so passionately that Rikki moaned in Bernadette's mouth. Bernadette pulled away to lunge at Miss Jaleesa for a kiss.

When they broke apart, everyone chuckled. The moment had been intense for all. "Let's rest, pet," Miss Jaleesa said and took a seat on the couch. She patted her lap. Once Bernadette was nestled in Miss Jaleesa's strong arms, Miss Jaleesa said, "We're going to rest, maybe have some more of your snacks, and then go for some impact. Your Domme tells me you're more of a thuddy than a stingy girl."

"Yes, Ma'am. I think so."

"Well then, I can't wait to tan your hide with those paddles. You'll be nice and stretched after our break, too. A little double penetration, maybe? And then end with a good old-fashioned flogging?"

"Oh, yes, Ma'am," Bernadette said, her voice bright. "Yes, please. All of that. Thank you."

"You have a voracious appetite, little turtle. And you are the politest sub I have ever fucked," Miss Jaleesa said with a laugh. "But for now, we rest."

# Chapter 8
## Rikki

The gorgeous Sunday afternoon in June was perfect for their outing at the Cincinnati Reds ballfield for Bernadette's birthday. White puffy clouds floated lazily against a deep blue backdrop. The green grass of the ball field below was bright and vibrant. Even the Ohio River and the hills of Kentucky gleamed just over the center field section.

Rikki had been to a couple of games before but hadn't been enamored by the experience. Until today. She rarely sat out in the sun like this for too long. Her Irish complexion meant instant sunburn, but she had taken precautions: liberal sunscreen, a floppy hat, and a long-sleeved shirt. Bernadette had given her an odd look about the shirt since it was summer, after all, but Rikki explained that she had once gotten sunburned *through* a shirt. And it hadn't been fun. Bernadette completely understood and double checked that she had enough sunscreen for everyone. So compassionate, Rikki thought.

They sat in one of the many designated wheelchair sections. This one was on the lower level above the regular seats behind the Reds dugout. Bernadette gushed when she saw the seats. She said they were "amazing." Currently, Bernadette sat in between Madison and Shanice and seemed to be having a good time. There were so many endearing things about her lover that Rikki was sometimes humbled and overwhelmed. Like now.

"Earth to Boss," a voice said next to her.

"Hmm?" Rikki lifted her sunglasses to wipe a tear from her eye. "Sorry, Marta. What's up?"

Marta was a Domme that Rikki had hired for her coffee shop not too long ago. Marta needed a job with a relatively flexible schedule to take care of Shanice, her new *little*. Rikki took a chance, and it had paid off in large dividends. Marta not only became a model employee but also became a friend. Marta was in her late thirties, about ten years older than Shanice. The car accident that led to the double below-the-knee amputation of Shanice's legs hadn't quieted Shanice's bright spirit, and Rikki knew that had a lot to do with the love, nurturing, and support that Marta gave her.

"You hit this one out of the park," Marta said, gesturing to Bernadette, who was leaning forward, elbows on her thighs, intent on the baseball game below. Her loose Cincinnati Reds jersey, an early birthday gift from Madison and Shasti, fit her perfectly. The Reds baseball cap was a birthday gift from Marta and Shanice that they purchased at the park just before the game. Rikki was proud of her little bee for speaking up about wanting to pick out her own clothes to wear to the game. Maybe Rikki needed to give Bernadette a little more freedom. Maybe that's what the cupcake thing was about. Supposedly, the event and subsequent punishment were over and done with, but they kind of weren't. Rikki still hadn't gotten to the bottom of it and wasn't sure how.

"I just want to make her happy," Rikki said after a moment.

Marta pushed a lock of her wavy blonde hair behind her ear as they stood up for the seventh-inning stretch. Marta wasn't tall by any means, but she was stocky and strong. Especially her hands. Marta was a woman used to physical work. Good thing because lifting Shanice in and out of the wheelchair required strength. "Sounds like a long-term kind of statement," Marta said suggestively.

Rikki smiled but didn't elaborate. The proverbial cat would be out of the bag soon enough.

Bernadette stretched her arms high in the air and then turned toward Shanice, who nodded. Shanice wrapped her arms around Bernadette's neck, and Bernadette lifted the tiny young woman into her arms.

"Oh, my God," Marta gushed. "It's no wonder Shanice has a crush on your girl."

Shasti leaned over, "So does mine." She pointed to Madison, who had wrapped a hand around Bernadette's forearm.

The three submissives swayed and sang the words to "Take Me Out to the Ballgame." When that was over, the lesser-known "Cincinnati, Ohio" song came on. Rikki and her friends laughed as they tried to match the words dancing on the big screen to the melody playing over the loudspeakers.

Madison messed up so badly at the end of the song that everyone in their group howled with laughter.

When the laughter died down, Madison said to Shasti, "Mistress, can I have Cracker Jacks?"

A small shake of Shasti's head had Madison pouting and looking away. It was obvious that Madison asked for sweets often and was rebutted almost as often.

"Hey, kiddo," Rikki said to Madison. "I know what will cheer you up."

"What, Miss Rikki?" Madison's forced frown was almost comical.

"Reading the scoreboard messages."

Madison furrowed her brow, as did Bernadette, but as Rikki predicted, everyone turned their attention to the messages now projecting on the big screen. There were birthday and anniversary announcements, and there was even a gender reveal. It looked like the Millers were having a girl.

The next message scrolled on the screen. Madison and Shanice gasped when they saw it. Shasti and Marta both smacked Rikki on the arms, but Rikki's main focus was on her girl. Bernadette turned toward Rikki, her eyes brimming with tears.

"Yes! Yes, Rikki. Yes, of course, I'll marry you."

The crowd around them burst into applause. Marta took Shanice out of Bernadette's arms, and then Rikki got down on one knee on the painted concrete in front of Bernadette. "I promise to take care of you, my little bee. Forever and ever." She reached into her skirt pocket, pulled out a black box, and opened it.

Her friends and the people around them oohed and ahhed as Rikki slid the diamond engagement ring on Bernadette's shaking hand. Tears were now streaming down Bernadette's face. And even though Rikki had already asked Bernadette to marry her a few weeks before, they'd told no one. This moment in front of their friends and, well, several thousand strangers, made it official.

Bernadette tugged at Rikki's shirt sleeve, urging her to get up off her knees. Once Rikki was standing, Bernadette threw herself into Rikki's arms.

"I love you so much, Rikki." Bernadette's voice hitched with emotion.

"I love you, too, Bernadette," Rikki said. "Thank you for saying 'yes' again."

They kissed to the sound of more "Awws" and exuberant clapping until Madison threw her arms around both of them and said, "Best day ever," making everyone laugh.

The attendee of their section came over and offered her congratulations. She said she'd radioed for the Reds mascot, Mr. Red, to come over for pictures and to bring them a congratulatory souvenir.

After the mascot pictures and receiving two buttons that said, "I got engaged at a Reds game," along with a certificate for two free hot dogs, they finally had a modicum of privacy. Rikki said to Bernadette, "I've spent a long time looking for you, my little bee. I had pretty much given up."

Bernadette's face scrunched up as her tears started flowing again.

"Oh, c'mere." Rikki pulled Bernadette close. The game continued down on the field, but Bernadette seemed oblivious as she hid her face in the well of Rikki's shoulder.

"Can we go now?" Bernadette asked quietly.

"You want to go home?"

Bernadette shook her head. "No, I want to go to Rocco's like we planned, and I want you to call Jaleesa and Tina, Lydia and Pammy, maybe get Brittany on the phone, and I want us all to celebrate the day I officially became your fiancée." She sat up and held her ringed hand above her head. We both watched as the diamond glinted in the bright sunshine. "And then I want to go home and *show* you how much I love you."

"Mmm," Rikki moaned involuntarily. Her little bee certainly had a way of hitting her core. "Anything you want, my love," Rikki said. *Anything at all.*

Shasti stood up, clearly having overheard, and said, "I'll get the phone chain started if you want, Rikki."

"That would be great. Thank you." Rikki turned to Marta and relayed the new plan.

"Sounds good," Marta said. "The Reds can finish this one without us, I suppose."

~~~

Luckily, Rocco's private room was available, and the entire gang was able to drop what they were doing and join in on the impromptu celebration.

Jaleesa seemed the happiest of all their friends and told Rikki privately that even though other people might think the engagement had come a bit too quickly—they'd only been together five months, after all—those people could jump. She also said, quite loudly, that Rikki and Bernadette were a match made in heaven facilitated by an angel on earth named Madison. After that, Madison continually reminded everyone that she had brought the two of them together.

One of the highlights of the celebration, though, was when Brittany and her Domme Skyped in from England. It was late for them, but Brittany insisted on being part of the big news. She had been at Rocco's when Rikki and Bernadette first met. Bernadette held a special place in her heart for Brittany, so Rikki was glad they could make that happen.

Once they finally got home and were back in the house they shared, Bernadette let out a long, cleansing sigh.

"I bet you're tired, my love," Rikki said.

"A bit." Bernadette hung up her keys and Cincinnati Reds hat on the hooks by the front door and then made a beeline for Rikki. She lowered her head and rested it on Rikki's chest. Her arms were smashed to the sides of her body. It was her way of requesting a hug, and Rikki complied. She wrapped her long arms around her now-official fiancée and kissed the top of her head.

"Rikki?" Bernadette said meekly. "I don't have a ring for you."

Ahh, Rikki had wondered if Bernadette might want that for her. "Baby, we agreed that I'm the captain of this ship, right?"

"Mm hmm," she said and nestled in tighter.

"And this captain doesn't need an engagement ring. Wedding ring? Abso-fucking-lutely."

Bernadette giggled. "You sounded like Jaleesa just then."

Rikki released the woman in her arms. "I did, didn't I?"

"We have to set a date, Rikki. And figure out where the wedding will be. And we have to have a reception. Who will we invite? I mean, how big is this thing going to be?" Bernadette's voice was reaching a fever pitch.

"Stop," Rikki commanded. "We have plenty of time to figure all this out, and we'll do it together. But not tonight. Not right now."

"Okay."

The fact that Bernadette physically relaxed made Rikki's heart swell. She truly did trust Rikki.

"For now, let's get you ready for school tomorrow. Coffee set up. Lunch made."

"Okay." Bernadette let herself be led into the kitchen.

"And then I'm going to take you upstairs to that master bedroom suite of ours and undress you for a joint shower. We'll see how we feel after that because we might end up falling right to sleep. But who knows? Best to keep our options open. Right?"

"Right," Bernadette said. "I like when you lead, Rikki."

Rikki's heart filled with love. "I'm glad, sweetie. It's my nature to lead. And it helps that you're an amazing follower." Rikki set up and programmed the coffee pot and then added, "Oh, and by the way, we are ordering a new bed now that the inheritance has cleared. I have one in mind. The frame has all kinds of places to clip cuffs to."

"Yes, please," Bernadette said.

"Absolutely," Rikki said. "And it has a canopy top so we can close the side curtains and be snug as bugs in rugs. But I'm not ordering it until I have a chance to show you and get your approval."

"Me? *My* approval?"

"Mm hmm," Rikki said. "I'm the captain, but I'm not the whole crew. You live here, too."

"*My* approval," Bernadette murmured and went back to making her sandwich. "Hmm."

They made quick work of their tasks and trudged up the stairs. On top of sitting in the sun for several hours, it had been an emotional day. The shower was soothing but in no way made them sleepy, as Rikki thought it might. Quite the opposite. Touching Bernadette's body sparked a flame inside Rikki. The same seemed to be true for Bernadette, and they tumbled into the bed, kissing passionately.

Rikki pulled away first, breathless, arousal pulsing between her legs. She reached up and ran a thumb down Bernadette's cheek and jawline. She kissed her way down Bernadette's body, drinking in the soft moans of contentment as her lover surrendered to her.

Bernadette's earthy aroma told Rikki what she already knew. Rikki kissed the mound reverently.

"Baby," Bernadette said, "I want you, too. At the same time. We haven't, you know, done that in a while."

The urgency in Bernadette's voice sent a shiver of lust through Rikki, who turned in the bed and maneuvered her body face down on top of Bernadette's. She spread her own legs wide, her knees hugging Bernadette's shoulders. Bernadette reached under and around Rikki's thighs, digging her fingertips into Rikki's ass cheeks. She guided Rikki's center to her mouth. A wave of lust ran through Rikki at Bernadette's eagerness.

"Spread 'em, baby," Rikki said, and Bernadette opened her legs wider so Rikki could reach Bernadette's clit from above. Rikki snaked her hands under Bernadette's spread legs, letting her weight fall on her elbows and forearms. She held on to the back of Bernadette's legs, using them for balance as she found the best purchase.

Bernadette moaned the moment Rikki's lips met her flesh. "You taste so good," Rikki said.

"Mmm," Bernadette moaned into Rikki's body, causing Rikki to squirm. Bernadette held her tighter for a moment and then massaged Rikki's ass cheeks in her grasp.

Okay, okay, Rikki thought with a grin, sixty-nine is a cooperative contact sport. Giving oral from on top was always different, but it wasn't hard, just different. Maybe next time, Bernadette should be on top. A butt plug firmly entrenched inside. Ooh, maybe a vibrating plug. Although Rikki was taller, Bernadette had a bigger frame and weighed more, so maybe not.

Bernadette moaned again when Rikki pulled the entire clit into her mouth and sucked hard. With her hands underneath Bernadette's legs, Rikki couldn't reach her pussy for penetration. Her weight was wonderfully distributed at the moment, and she didn't want to alter the balance they had. Bernadette had such an amazing touch that Rikki already felt the spark of orgasm. She let it build while she worked on Bernadette. It wasn't a race. They weren't trying to cum at the same time. Rikki wouldn't allow that nonsense. Cum when your body was ready, *or*, she thought sadistically *when I tell you to.*

Bernadette released Rikki's ass cheeks and reached forward to run her hands and soft fingers down Rikki's back. It was like she was petting Rikki. Or maybe she was urging Rikki on. It didn't matter. It was wonderful. All the while, Bernadette's lips and tongue kept working on Rikki's clit. The soft fingers were replaced with fingernails, lightly scraping down Rikki's back. They ended with two handfuls of flesh in Bernadette's hands.

Rikki lifted her head and moaned her impending release. She undulated her pelvis. Bernadette had to work harder, but Rikki couldn't help it. Bernadette clearly understood that Rikki was close and redoubled her efforts. Rikki was soon rewarded with a mind-clearing, nerve-cleansing orgasm. She shook for a while as Bernadette milked her for aftershocks. She was so skillful. An easy touch when needed, harder other times. She rarely had to be coached any more.

Rikki caught her shuddering breath and refocused her efforts on her little bee below her. Now that she was free to move, she snaked her arm out from under the leg and turned her wrist toward her target. Two fingers plunged inside. Bernadette lifted her pelvis along with Rikki off the bed. Rikki thrust and continued to lick and suck whatever she could reach at this angle. Bernadette's sighs and moans of pleasure spurred Rikki on.

Fingernails dug into Rikki's ass as Bernadette tensed momentarily. She screeched as she climaxed, her body quaking as she did so. Bernadette's legs closed, probably involuntarily, locking Rikki's hand and fingers in between. That was okay. It didn't really hurt.

After a long moment, Rikki nudged the legs apart and pulled her hand out from under her lover. She planted one last sloppy kiss on the sensitive nub below and chuckled when Bernadette slammed her legs closed again with a groan. Yes, her baby often got sensitive after she came.

Bernadette pulled at Rikki's skin, demanding her to turn around and kiss her. Rikki obliged and was rewarded with the softest and most gracious kiss she'd ever received. Rikki made to move into the big spoon position, but Bernadette held on a moment longer.

"I love you, Mrs. Carmichael," Bernadette said.

"And I love *you*, Doctor –"

"Carmichael," Bernadette blurted before Rikki could say the name Garneau.

Rikki sat up. "What?"

"I want to change my name. To yours, I mean. If that's okay." Bernadette's entire face tinged bright red to the roots of her mussy blonde hair.

"Yes!" Rikki said, her heart so full it was overflowing. "Yes, yes, little bee. I am humbled that you want to take my name. I–"

Whatever Rikki was about to say, she couldn't remember, as Bernadette sealed the deal with a hot and steamy kiss that threatened to take them into round two.

# Chapter 9
## Bernadette

**B**ernadette finished the calculus problem and drew a box around the answer. She hated the fact that her hand projected so hugely on the lecture hall screen, but there was no way around it because she liked giving guided notes with the document camera. She never had to turn her back to the class or write out entire problems on a whiteboard.

She looked up from the problem at the forty or so summer Calculus students in the lecture hall and said, "Remember to give an actual coordinate with both the *x*- and the *y*-values." She switched cameras and was momentarily confused when a stranger's image popped on the screen. She almost laughed when she realized that she was looking at herself. *Wow, that shirt looks so good on me.* The gunmetal blue brought out her eyes in a way she'd never noticed before. Rikki really did know what she looked good in. *I need to trust her more. And look at my hair. I love this style. Jaleesa did right by me. They both do.*

"Dr. Garneau?" The remote student's voice sounded tinny over the computer speaker.

Oh, right. She had a solo online student. "Hey, yes, Li Hua. Could you see the presentation well enough? I'm new at this online teaching stuff."

"Yes, it was fine," Li Hua said and then coughed. "I'm new at it, too, and so glad the university let me attend class this way. My asthma is seriously bad in the summer."

"I'm glad we could accommodate you. Honestly, I was surprised when the tech team came to me this morning about setting you up remotely." It was weird having a conversation with one student while forty others looked on.

"Is the current problem set due at the start of class on Wednesday?"

"Yes," Bernadette said to the online student and looked up at the class. "I want them on this desk at the beginning of the class period. Understood? The *beginning*."

Murmurs of agreement filtered through the hall. Several had already experienced the no-nonsense side of Dr. Garneau as points were taken off for late submissions.

"Dr. Garneau," Li Hua interrupted, "my friend Ethan will bring it to you. He's not in the class, but he'll drop it off."

"That's perfect," Bernadette said. "Okay, then," she said to the class, "I think we're done for the day. Remember that I have office hours every day from 10:00 am to noon. They start in half an hour. No appointment necessary. So, if –"

One of the girls in the front row raised her hand. Bernadette consulted her seating chart. The chart thing was something new she was trying this summer. Her students deserved to be seen and acknowledged as individuals, not nameless faces in a crowd. "Yes, Megan?"

"Nice rock," Megan said and smiled.

Bernadette physically tilted her head, trying to figure out what Megan was talking about. She burst out laughing when half the class lifted their hands and pointed to their ring fingers.

"Oh! Oh, oh, oh," Bernadette said with a chuckle. "Thank you. I'm not used to it yet. And, before you ask, yes, I got engaged over the weekend."

A chorus of congratulations rained down from the lecture hall, and even the online student chimed in. Bernadette acknowledged their well wishes and then dismissed the class. This time, though, instead of the students filing out en masse, quite a few came down to her podium to see the ring and ask questions. Obviously, she didn't give every detail, but she did mention the scoreboard message and that she'd gotten engaged at the Reds ballpark that weekend. The students around her, primarily girls, awwed at her and then happily chatted away about how romantic it was and how they would love something like that to happen to them.

Bernadette's heart was full as she stopped at Dr. Wainwright's office. Oh, she wasn't there to see him. No, she hadn't been called in to get the good news about her promotion. Not yet, anyway. *Possible promotion*, Bernadette chided herself. Ahh, who was she kidding? It was in the bag. No, she was there to show off a certain new piece of jewelry to Dr. Wainwright's administrative assistant.

Miss Olga's face lit up when Bernadette darkened the doorstep.

"Hey, stranger. What brings you here?" Miss Olga put down the papers in her hand and stood up to give a quick hug. Bernadette had worked with Miss Olga at the university for five years, going on six now, but only recently found out that Miss Olga was also in *the life*. That was when she found out that Miss Olga and Rikki had known each other for a long time. That bit of information was eye-opening, to say the least.

Bernadette had planned to play it coy by handing Miss Olga a form or something and having Miss Olga notice the ring. Instead, she thrust out her hand and grinned so wide that she almost split her face.

Miss Olga squealed. Yes, she actually squealed and then pulled Bernadette into another hug. "I'm so happy for you, dear," she said into Bernadette's ear. She pulled back and added, "Rikki is a fine person. She is a great match for you. You're a great match for each other."

"I like to think so."

"Her Aunt Tilda would heartily approve."

"Aww, thank you for saying that. I'm sorry I never got the chance to meet her."

Miss Olga smiled, but it was obvious that she was still grieving the loss of her friend.

"Rikki makes me so happy," Bernadette continued. "We don't have a date set or anything, and I don't know if we'll have a vanilla wedding or what, but I want you there, okay?" Bernadette couldn't help the tears that sprang to her eyes. Oh, wow, all of this was becoming super real.

"Overwhelming?"

"Mm hmm." Bernadette swiped at her eyes. "But I'm really happy." She looked up at the clock and said, "I have to get upstairs for office hours."

Miss Olga nodded. "Come have lunch with us today, Bernadette. The ladies mentioned that they haven't seen you in a while."

"I usually talk to Rikki during lunch." Bernadette felt her face get warm. "But I'll text her instead. She'll understand."

"And if she doesn't, then at least stop by," Miss Olga suggested.

"I will."

Bernadette trudged up the stairs with her rolling cart of teaching materials. Really, she should take the elevator, but she liked the challenge. Thankfully, no one was waiting outside her door because she could use a minute to get her thoughts in order. She unlocked her office and stepped inside. How much longer would she have this closet, as Rikki called it? There was barely room for that one student chair. Even if she got rid of the bookshelf, it wouldn't help much. And she needed her books. She ran a finger over the titles and read them out loud. "A History of Abstract Algebra, Discrete Mathematics, Finite Abelian Groups." Yes, she wanted to teach these things, all of them. She was ready to move on from Calculus. Wainwright knew she was ready. The Foundations course she'd developed for the university was proof positive of that. "And there is no way I'm using Baxter's archaic lecture notes."

She plopped in her well-worn chair, searched the university academic website for Baxter's courses, and printed out his syllabi for a guideline. If she was going to take over the courses, she'd better know what they contained. She made mental notes of what she would change in each one but then realized that if she was going to take over those courses, she'd better have her revised outlines finished by the time the fall semester started. Wainwright would probably want to see them well before that. Her wheels were already turning, so she opened a blank document in Word and began outlining the one course she was a shoo-in to take over in the fall.

She had mixed feelings when not a single student showed up for office hours, but she been able to get an excellent start on the syllabus. As usual, the ever-growing stack of problem sets wasn't grading itself, but that was okay. Planning for the future was way more important. Speaking of planning for the future—she lifted her hand to ogle the engagement ring again. She never took herself as someone to get girly goofy over an engagement ring, but here she was doing just that.

Ultimately, Bernadette did have lunch with Miss Olga and the administrative assistants, and it was fun. As expected, they gushed over the new development in her love life. And Rikki completely understood that Bernadette couldn't talk to her during lunch but reminded her in a text that she needed a picture of Bernadette in her afternoon Strengths and Conditioning class the university offered to employees. It wasn't that Rikki didn't trust her to go to the class or that she was micro-managing her whereabouts. No, it was Rikki's way of providing structure for Bernadette and keeping her accountable. Bernadette liked when Rikki did that. It made her feel seen and appreciated. And loved. And taken care of. All of that.

Bernadette spent a couple of hours after lunch grading and sifting through emails. Because she was a woman in a STEM role, she got a lot of emails from women's groups, like yet another one from the Society of Women Engineers. She groaned. *I'm not an engineer. Don't they know that already?* Delete.

The next email was from Human Resources about health, dental, and vision insurance. She should look into getting Rikki on her health insurance policy once they were married. That was something they definitely needed to discuss. As a couple. Especially now since Bernadette understood that she had a say in things like that. She was submissive, *not* a doormat. Not that Rikki ever made her feel like that, but maybe some people here at the university did. But, if all went to plan, that would change once Wainwright gave her the go-ahead. And maybe they would finally give her the Associate Professor designation. She'd earned it by this time, hadn't she?

She glanced up at the clock and schemed that she had just enough time for a tour before packing up and heading to the workout facility. She took the stairs up one flight and worked her way around the halls. The building was pretty empty this late in the afternoon, as she knew it would be. She slowed her gait as she approached Dr. Yang's third-floor office. Good, he wasn't there. She looked with envy through the pane of glass in the door at his large desk. She would kill for that desk. Well, maybe not kill, but she coveted the overlarge surface. That would make her job so much easier. A sizeable circular table sat in one corner of the office with a well-used whiteboard right behind it. Dr. Yang's doctoral candidates spent a lot of time there, going over theory and proofs and probably just hanging out. Bernadette wanted that. Spending time with like-minded people who loved the mathematics that she did. Maybe she should spend more time eating lunch or visiting her colleagues than hiding with the administrative assistants. She vowed to be more collegial once she moved up.

It was dark in Dr. Yang's office, but she noticed the floor-to-ceiling bookshelves. They were built-in and made from real wood, unlike her office's rickety pressed wood piece of crap. Wow. This was going to be great. She would finally be able to bring in and unpack some of her academic boxes.

She knew she shouldn't, but what was the harm? Her hand was already on the knob, anyway. She turned it, but it was locked. Ahh, just as well. She was a rule-follower and didn't want to be accused of anything untoward.

"Humph," she said out loud. *The only thing I'm doing is looking at and planning for my future.*

A thought sprang to mind. What if Dr. Yang was perfectly happy where he was here on the third floor? What if Wainwright was going to shoot Bernadette straight up to the fifth-floor office? Her heart raced as she hurried to the stairwell and up two flights. This time, the office door was unlocked. There was no one around. She quietly turned the knob and let herself inside. She kept the lights off and recoiled at the smell of old paper and musty books. A deep clean would be in order, that's for sure. She went over to the large picture window and sighed at the view of the Myammia Creek meandering its way toward the Ohio River. Ahh, yes. She could get used to this. Baxter had the same furniture and setup as Dr. Yang, but his desk and table were piled high with books, folders, and basic junk.

A noise outside in the hallway alerted her that she needed to bolt. She slid out of the office undetected and made her way to the closest stairwell. Oh, it was the night-time cleaning crew. Still, they hadn't seen her, and that was good. She didn't know how she would explain herself if asked.

She headed back to her office, packed her things, and then busted butt, literally, in the fitness class. She sent Rikki the requisite picture and was in such a good mood after the class that she decided to surprise Rikki at the shop with take-out for dinner. But wait, Dommes typically don't like surprises, so she texted her plans.

BERNADETTE: How about I pick up Chinese take-out and bring it to the shop?

RIKKI: I'm not at the shop. I'm home.

BERNADETTE: Everything okay?

RIKKI: Yes. The plumber came by to give us a quote for the master bath remodel. I also had him give me a quote to put a bathroom in the playroom.

BERNADETTE: Oh, wow. A bathroom down there would be perfect. With shower?

RIKKI: Naturally.

BERNADETTE: Are you staying home? Should I get the take-out?

RIKKI: Y and Y.

BERNADETTE: The usual?

RIKKI: Yes. And thank you, little bee. Love you. Can't wait to hold you.

BERNADETTE: Love you, too, Rikki. The ring got a lot of attention today. I'll tell you more later. Byeee.

Bernadette pulled up at home forty minutes later, the take-out items in tightly sealed bags. She couldn't put her finger on it, but Rikki's texts sounded off for some reason. Maybe she was just tired from the exciting weekend they'd had. Hopefully, nothing weird had happened at the shop or with the inheritance.

She opened the front door, carefully balancing the bags of food and her briefcase. She was about to call out that she was home but heard Rikki talking to someone. Oh, she was on the phone.

"Yeah, just, I don't know, mail the stuff to me, I guess," Rikki said, holding the phone to her ear. She was sitting at the kitchen table with her back to the front door. She didn't seem to hear Bernadette come in, so Bernadette put her burdens down on the small table they kept by the front door, mainly for Bernadette's briefcase.

"Obviously, I'll pay for the postage," Rikki said, slightly irritated. She listened for a while and then said. "Okay, if you don't want to do it, I'll ask Caroline to pop over and get the stuff. She can mail it all to me." Another pause. "Okay, Dad, thanks."

Oh, oh, oh. Rikki was talking to her dad. She never talked about him much, so Bernadette sat as quietly as a mouse on the couch. Oh, no, this was eavesdropping. She should go upstairs. She stood up to do so, but what happened next rooted her feet where she stood.

Rikki put the phone down on the table and hit the speakerphone. "Dad, I met someone. Someone who counts. We're engaged to be married."

"A boy?"

"C'mon, Dad."

"Hey, I had to ask," her father said. He had a pleasant voice, but Bernadette didn't like his attitude. "Would your mother approve?"

Rikki's head fell back as if exasperated by her father's question. "She would. I think she probably maneuvered things to somehow put Bernadette in my orbit."

"That's a nice name. She French?"

"In ancestry only, Dad." There was silence from both sides until Rikki said, "I'll, uh, send you the wedding date once I know it. You don't have to come, but I thought you should know."

"I'll tell your sister. She'll tell your brother."

"Okay, thanks, Dad." Rikki cleared her throat and added, "I gotta go. Something's come up at the shop."

"I'll get your sister to mail that stuff to you," he said.

"Okay, thanks. Bye —" The click as he hung up cut Bernadette's heart. "—Dad."

Rikki flicked the phone away with her fingers.

Bernadette waited for a beat and said, "Up" in her most commanding voice.

Rikki jumped but did as commanded, which actually surprised Bernadette a little.

"Prepare yourself to be boarded," Bernadette said. Rikki's return smile was a wonderful sight. She pulled Rikki into her arms and rocked them both side to side. "You are loved, Rikki."

"Mm hmm," came the response in a high, tight voice.

"It's you and me," Bernadette said and rubbed her fiancée's back. "No matter what they throw at us, we'll handle it. Together." She stepped back and held Rikki at arms' length. "Okay? We'll deal with it. No matter what it is."

Rikki looked deeply into Bernadette's eyes and then reached up to tilt Bernadette's head down and planted a loving kiss on her forehead. "Marta and Shasti and Jaleesa and even Victoria were right. You *are* good for me."

"Wise women," Bernadette said and waggled her eyebrows. "Dinner on the couch? Movie?"

"Yes, and yes."

"Audrey Hepburn, Barbara Stanwyck, or, umm, Judy Garland?"

Rikki didn't answer right away, so Bernadette quickly added, "Or we could totally go old-school comedies. *Monty Python and the Holy Grail*? *Spinal Tap*? Or, or, or maybe I can finally get you to watch *The D.E.B.S.* with me."

"Audrey," Rikki said. "Let me help you with the—"

"Nope," Bernadette said. "Go sit, and I'll bring it to you. If you want, you can load up *Roman Holiday*."

"Oh, good choice," Rikki said. "That's my favorite."

"I know."

Bernadette divvied up the food, got two glasses of wine, and, in three trips, had them set up on the couch. The opening credits to Rikki's favorite Audrey Hepburn movie played, and Bernadette said, "It's okay, you know."

"What's okay?"

"For me to take care of you sometimes."

"I know, sweetie," Rikki said and leaned in for a quick kiss. "And I love you for it."

Bernadette held up her ring and nodded. "I know."

# Chapter 10
## Rikki

Rikki closed the door to her office at the shop and sat in her chair. For some reason, she couldn't bear other people right now. They always wanted something from her. She needed a minute or twenty. Her cell phone rang.

"Naturally," she muttered and picked it up. "Hey, Jon. I didn't expect to hear from you today." Jon was the contractor with the big belly that had amused Madison the night he was there. "Did we get the approval for the handicap spots from the city?"

"Yes, we did," Jon said with a happy lilt to his voice. "And I have even more great news. Believe it or not, the city has given us the green light to get the lot ready for the Fourth of July parade this weekend."

"*This* weekend? Holy shit."

"Yep. If the weather cooperates, that is."

"I hear that."

"We've got the markers in, and I have a crew ready to excavate and get the ground ready for paving this afternoon if you're amenable. We might even start paving."

"No shit?" Rikki said. She hadn't known Jon long, but apparently, he had a way of making her say the word *shit* multiple times. "What do you need from me?"

"The only thing I need today," Jon said, "is for you to be on-site when we first get there to sign the go-ahead and give us the first payment."

"I'm here all day," Rikki said.

"I only need you at the start," Jon said. "But you're more than welcome to hang around."

She wasn't sure how long she was going to stay that day, so she didn't commit one way or another. She went over a few details with him, like making sure the dedicated handicapped spots were van-accessible and that the loading zone designation was big enough but not intrusive. Bernadette was the one who had suggested a loading zone so delivery trucks wouldn't have to block traffic on Market Street anymore. That was her little bee, always thinking, always problem-solving.

After hanging up with him, she put the phone down and felt better about humanity as a whole until her phone call with her father the night before came rushing back into her brain.

"I can't let him get to me like that," Rikki muttered. She was upset that Bernadette had overheard part of the conversation, but the look of compassion in her eyes after she ordered Rikki to stand up had gone straight to her heart. Bernadette's eyes had pleaded. She wanted Rikki to need her. At first, Rikki felt her usual walls going up, but the more Bernadette hugged her and rubbed her back, the more she relaxed and decided it was okay to be soothed. That was hard for her. She was supposed to be the strong one, after all.

"You did something, didn't you, Mom?" Rikki said to her mother's picture. Rikki had meant what she'd said to her father about her mother manipulating the universe, so Bernadette would show up in her world. "Are you and Mrs. Garneau up there scheming?" Rikki said to her empty office.

Without hesitating, Rikki flipped open her laptop and ordered a dozen roses to be sent to Bernadette's office in the Mathematics building. It cost a little more for same-day delivery, but it was worth it. The note read, "I love you, little bee. I'm having an amazing day because you chose to love me back. Yours always, Rikki."

That would put her girl in a good mood, that's for sure. They needed to set a date for the wedding. They would sit down and figure that out this weekend. Bernadette would surely make lists. Oh, how her little bee loved lists. And one of those would be the guest list. Bernadette would want Rikki's family there, wouldn't she? The problem was that Rikki wasn't sure if *she* wanted them there. Her sister Caroline, maybe, but her father? No. Even if she did, he couldn't be bothered, anyway. Not when his third new wife, Gloria, whom Rikki had never met, wanted Rikki's childhood boxes gone so she could set up a home gym. Knowing that the room she had grown up in had stayed pretty much the same after her mom died had given her a lasting link to her mother. It was a link to her life before some idiot shattered it with a bomb and a misguided agenda. It had taken her a long time to forgive herself for encouraging her mother to work at the women's health clinic. Her father never did, blaming Rikki for his wife's death.

Her father had been so deep in his own grief that he wasn't there for any of his three kids. They were all adults, he'd said, and could manage on their own. When they should have come together, they separated, not knowing what to do because the woman who had been the captain of the Carmichael ship wasn't there anymore. Rikki, the youngest at age twenty-four, was left to figure out her grief on her own. She wasn't sure she ever had.

"I need to meet your family," Rikki said out loud as if Bernadette was there. "This needs to happen before the big wedding. They need to know that I will take care of you and that I love you. They need to see that." Her fingers flew over the keyboard on her laptop for airline flights to San Francisco during Bernadette's two-week hiatus in between semesters. She was inches from booking the flight when she stopped herself. "I can't make this decision without her. She needs to have a say." She hesitated for a moment as a realization hit her. "We're in a partnership. It's not just me anymore."

Bernadette had always spoken respectfully about her own father. Her tone was always loving when she mentioned him, but maybe she didn't want to see him or her brother right now, for whatever reason.

She tabled the California trip in her mind and went for another. She opened a map tab and estimated the distance from Denton Heights to Nashville. It was about 280 miles, about four to five hours by car, probably longer with potty stops. Rikki laughed. Does Bernadette call them "potty stops"? She didn't know. They'd never gone on a road trip together, so maybe a trip to Nashville to finally meet Bernadette's online friend Lisa was a good idea. Lisa was the one who had helped Bernadette navigate the early treacherous waters of Bernadette's newfound love of all things BDSM. Rikki wanted to thank the woman in person.

"Maybe we can squeeze in an overnight or two in Nashville before heading to California," Rikki thought. Rikki had told Marta that she just wanted to make Bernadette happy. Maybe a trip like this would.

81

Rikki sat back in her squeaky office chair, her fingers steepled. "Two weeks is a long time to be away from the shop." She stood up, the wheeled chair skittering backward, bouncing into the couch. "It's time."

She headed into the shop and made a beeline for the kitchen. Marta was standing behind Kari, who was mixing a bowl of...something.

"Hey, Boss," Marta said. "Butterscotch brownies. Kari's recipe."

"Oh, great," Rikki said. "That's impressive, Kari. Thank you for your initiative and drive on this. I can't wait to try one."

"Thank you, Ma'am," Kari said, clearly moved by Rikki's kind words.

"Marta, I need to see you in my office when you get a chance."

"Oo-ooh," Kari singsonged. "Someone's going to the principal's office, and for once, it's not me."

The two Dommes cracked up, and then Marta said, "Okay, let me make sure these get in the oven, and then I'll be in. Anything I need to worry about?"

"Not at all," Rikki said. "Quite the contrary."

On the way back to her sanctuary, Rikki checked in with Mark, who was running things out front. She laughed at how big his eyes got when she told him the parking lot job was starting that afternoon.

While waiting for Marta, she ordered supplies for the shop, including those Edison lightbulbs Bernadette was desperate for Rikki to replace in the stringed lights overhead. She would be so happy. And that was Rikki's goal—keeping Bernadette happy.

It wasn't long before Marta knocked on the door. "What's up, Boss?"

Rikki gestured for Marta to sit on the couch. She spun around in the swivel chair and leaned forward, elbows on her thighs.

"Uh." Hmm, where to begin. "Uh, Bernadette and I, you know that we're getting married. A big wedding and all. Or a small one, I don't know. But she deserves a memorable one, my little bee."

"You both do," Marta said. "I'm glad you found each other."

Marta's words went straight to Rikki's heart. She tried unsuccessfully to blink back her insta-tears and ultimately groaned when she failed. She grabbed a tissue and then cleared her throat to get the emotion out of it.

"Boss? What's going on?"

"Blah," Rikki said and then chuckled. "I'm okay. Just emotional. I never thought I would ever get married, and now I'm doing it. I need to meet her family, Marta. I haven't even talked to them on the phone. I want to take Bernadette out there for a week, maybe more. You know, during that time in between semesters."

Marta nodded.

"But there's something that needs to happen before I can do that. Something long overdue." Rikki took a moment to get her emotions under control. "And that is your promotion."

"My what?" Marta put a hand out as if this new information was too overwhelming for her to handle.

"I'm finally getting back on my feet, Marta, and it's time for me to promote you to assistant manager. If you want that."

"Lydia? Mark?"

"They're not leaving as far as I know. There will be three of you. It's time for me to loosen my stranglehold on the shop. You three can handle things. I need to spend time with my girl. And not only for her sake. I've realized a few things recently. I need to spend more time with her for, uh, for me."

"Bo-oss," Marta said, "give me a fucking tissue. You're choking me up with all of this. Jee-zus."

"Sorry," Rikki said. "My brain is moving fast." Rikki then told Marta about the parking lot construction and the designated handicap spots. "Hopefully, it'll be done and open by Sunday's Fourth of July parade."

"Sunday?" Marta was blown away for the second time. "Perfect timing," Marta said. "Shanice and I are picking up the new van tomorrow. Well, it's new to us, but it has very low mileage. The engine is good. I was going to keep looking around, but I thought, why wait? She needs that security now. We both do."

"I'm so happy for you guys." Rikki stood up and held her arms out for a quick congratulatory hug.

"Shanice didn't want me to tell anyone. She wants to practice for a while and get comfortable getting in and out of the van on her own and working the hand controls before we let people know."

"Understandable," Rikki said. "She'll have so much more independence now."

"Things are looking up for my little family of two," Marta said. "And I think I finally have her convinced to start looking at electric wheelchairs."

"Excellent," Rikki said. "She's finally over the fact that an electric wheelchair signifies the permanence of her injuries?"

"Yeah, I think getting her the van has helped. And Boss? I'll take that promotion."

"I'll start you tomorrow. Mark will show you the ropes. You'll be in training with him and Lydia and me for a bit, but I'm sure it'll go smoothly."

"Understood, Boss."

"In your opinion, is Kari ready to be promoted to your job? Or do you think I need to hire someone else?"

"She's ready," Marta said with certainty. "With training."

"I think so, too, but you'll have to train her. Oh, and there's one more thing."

"Yeah?"

Rikki pointed to the door. "Get out of my office."

Marta burst out laughing. "Turnabout is fair play, hmm?"

Rikki nodded and pointed toward the door again.

"I'm going. I'm going."

Before the door closed behind Marta, Rikki heard Mark ask her if everything was okay. Rikki laughed and reopened the door to call him in. She filled him in on Marta's promotion and his role in it. After reassuring him that his and Lydia's hours would not decrease, that only her own would, she sat back down at her desk.

Things were in motion, and she would have felt good about it, but something was nagging at her. It was something Marta had said. 'Why wait? She needs that security now. We both do.'

Rikki took a deep breath, hoping she was about to do the right thing. She looked at the picture of her mother on her desk and asked for guidance. Hearing no objections, she reopened her laptop to determine if it was feasible to do what her head, heart, and soul urged her to do.

~~~

Rikki breathed in calmly and evenly when she heard Bernadette's Prius pull up. Sure and steady footsteps were now on the front porch. Keys jangled, and then the front door opened. Rikki stood up.

"Rikki," Bernadette said with surprise. "I didn't think you'd be home yet. I saw your car out front. Thank you for the gorgeous flowers. They were so—"

Rikki put a finger to her lips to silence her betrothed.

Bernadette was clearly confused, but the gleam in her eye said she was curious about what Rikki was up to. Rikki watched Bernadette's every move as she put her briefcase down and hung up her keys.

"Do you wear my collar?" Rikki asked.

"Yes," Bernadette said and ran a finger underneath the day collar she wore every day. "Yes, I do."

"Which means?"

"That we've committed to each other. A power exchange commitment." Bernadette took a few steps closer.

"And when we get married, that will further solidify that commitment, won't it?"

"Yes, it will, Rikki."

"We will have our big wedding with friends and family, Bernadette." Rikki gestured for her fiancée to sit on the couch. "I promise you that. But I don't want to wait. I don't know why I'm feeling so much urgency around this, but I want to marry you now. Friday. There's an opening at the courthouse. I booked it. Just you and me. Ohio doesn't require witnesses."

"A secret wedding?" Bernadette looked away from Rikki as if trying to wrap her head around this crazy idea. "Friday?"

"Our friends don't have to know. Not even your online friend, Lisa. Okay? I just, I just …" Rikki sat down hard on the couch. "I honestly don't know why I want to do this now. Maybe talking to my dad last night. Maybe thinking about how our moms had so much less time than they thought." Tears filled her eyes, and Bernadette stroked her cheek.

"Let's do it," Bernadette said. "Friday is fine. I'll take a personal day. I don't have classes on Fridays anyway."

"You're okay with it?" Rikki wiped away her tears for the millionth time that day.

"Yes, baby, yes." Bernadette leaned in for a kiss.

It was intended as a small kiss to seal the deal, but then it turned into something much more.

# Chapter 11
## Bernadette

With a moan deep from her toes, Bernadette thrust her tongue deep into Rikki's mouth. Ever since the flowers were delivered to her at the university, she had been aroused. Mightily aroused. Her heart first and then her loins. Rikki sucked on her tongue while she thrust in and out. Rikki demanded equal time, so Bernadette made love to Rikki's tongue instead. Bernadette's fervor must have spurred Rikki on because Rikki's kisses made Bernadette's clothes fall off. Amazing how that worked.

Bernadette sat on her stool completely naked while Rikki was completely clothed. This still turned her on. Rikki kicked the clothes aside and kissed Bernadette urgently. She then abandoned Bernadette's lips and tongue in favor of her nipples, already hard. A hand slid down Bernadette's torso with determination. Rikki thrust two fingers inside Bernadette's warm folds, causing her to lift her pelvis toward the invading digits. She undulated her hips as her lover thrust in and out. Rikki was ravenous for her. That was the only way to describe what happened next.

Rikki pulled her fingers out and grabbed Bernadette by the shoulders, spun her around, and pushed. "On the couch. On your knees. Face away from me." Rikki's voice shook with desire.

Bernadette fell forward, her weight falling on her forearms on the back of the couch, her hands gripping the headrest. Rikki pulled something out of the toy drawer behind them. Bernadette didn't dare turn her head to look. Oh, God, what would it be? Crop? Paddle? Strap-on? Wax? Not those geometric shape thingies. Please, no. She loved slash hated them.

The first clothespin shot white-hot pain through her nipple.

"Yes, baby. Feel it," Rikki said, rubbing her back and ass cheeks. "So good, isn't it?"

"Mmm," Bernadette moaned in response. She couldn't say much more. The sensations were spreading right where she knew they would and right where Rikki intended. The second clip caused the same wave of lust-filled pain.

Rikki let her bask in her clothespin glow while fussing with her own clothes behind her. She then nudged one of Bernadette's knees and shin up and onto the couch's armrest, opening her wide to the warm summer air. Rikki reached in between Bernadette's legs to her slippery mess of desire. Rikki pinched the inner and outer nether lips together on one side and then gently let a clothespin capture them in its jaws.

"Fuck," Bernadette said, hearing the bliss in her own voice, knowing that Rikki heard it, too. A second clip accompanied the first on the other side, and between the two, her lips were spread wide open, ready to receive. Her tangible desire ran down her thighs, and she hoped to God and all things holy that her lover was strapping on something phallic.

Her prayers were answered as Rikki thrust into her without warning.

"Ahh, yes, Rikki," Bernadette murmured, gripping the couch. "I'm yours. Take me. Take me."

Rikki increased the pace and grabbed onto Bernadette's hips. She gripped so tightly that Bernadette was sure to have bruises. She'd wear her lover's marks proudly.

It wasn't long before Rikki moaned. "Fuck," Rikki growled as she slammed into Bernadette. She was cumming and cumming hard. Her thrusting became erratic and then slowed dramatically.

"Please, please, keep fucking me, Rikki," Bernadette pleaded and thrust her body back to encourage her lover to keep going.

Rikki growled and removed the clips from Bernadette's nether lips. Bernadette's moan was part groan as the blood returned to those parts. Rikki began thrusting again, arching her body over Bernadette's. Rikki's hard nipples rubbed against Bernadette's back, and that's all it took for Bernadette's lingering orgasm to rocket home and hit its mark.

"Rikki," Bernadette screeched and then spat an entire string of profanities that would have made her blush if she had been aware of her words. Forgotten was the corporeal world. Forgotten was the other human being in the room. Forgotten was…everything. Everything except the sea of bliss she was floating in. Strong arms held her afloat. It must be an angel's arms holding her aloft in this ethereal place. She heard soft moaning in the distance. It was an incredible sound. It sounded so peaceful and satisfied all at the same time.

Warm kisses showered her face. She opened her eyes, needing to see the angel holding her. Oh, wow. She knew it. The woman who called herself Rikki was that angel. And that angel was hers. Fuck everyone else. "Rikki is mine," Bernadette said out loud.

Rikki chuckled softly. "And you're mine."

"Mm hmm," Bernadette murmured as her eyes closed all on their own.

Bernadette roused when another string of kisses caressed her skin. "Mmm," she murmured. "I love you."

"I love you, too, Bernadette."

They were cuddled on the couch even though Bernadette had no recollection of moving from her kneeling position. "Baby?"

"Yes, love?" Rikki kissed her shoulder.

"Please make a habit of fucking me like that more often."

Rikki burst out laughing.

"I mean, shit," Bernadette said. "I get flowers and then come home to a command to bend over and be fucked. Every girl's dream." She snuggled in closer and gripped Rikki's arms. "Mine," she said.

"Always."

~~~

A secret wedding wasn't exactly what Bernadette had envisioned when Rikki asked her to marry her, but here they were in the courthouse. The documents were examined, the papers were signed, and the payment was given. Even her name change form had been taken care of. The county clerk, a middle-aged woman with amazing erect posture, led them to a small room in a far out-of-the-way corner of the busy office.

Bernadette turned to Rikki with questions in her eyes, but Rikki just shrugged. She didn't know where they were going, either.

"Please stand there and there," the clerk motioned. She had kind eyes. "Hold hands if you wish." Rikki reached for her hand and kissed the back of it. Bernadette had all kinds of weird feelings swirling inside, and that small gesture caused those tears she had been holding back to spring to life.

"Oh, no," Rikki said with a chuckle. "You're okay, little bee."

Bernadette wiped at her tears and said, "I'm fine." She turned to the clerk. "Sorry. I'm just happy."

"We get lots of happy tears in here," the clerk said with a patient smile. "Now, if you're ready, you can say your own vows, or we can use the standard ones I have here." She lifted a book from the podium.

Oh, oh, oh. They were going to exchange vows in this little windowless room.

"We haven't prepared vows," Rikki said, taking the lead as usual. "We'll be having a big ceremony in the fall, and we'll write our own vows then, so go ahead."

Bernadette's heart was so full it almost hurt. For years, she hadn't realized that she wanted someone whose nature it was to take charge. Someone who did the heavy thinking, the heavy lifting. Not that Bernadette needed someone to think for her. Not at all. It was just that she never wanted to rock the boat, whatever boat it happened to be. Lovers, friends, family, school situations, even strangers. She never wanted anyone to think ill of her. And by some miracle, she'd found the one person that helped her navigate those treacherous waters so easily.

"All right then," the clerk said, let's begin. "Do you, Rikki Carmichael, take Bernadette Garneau to be your lawful partner in life, to have and to hold from this day forward, for better, for worse, for richer, for poorer, in sickness and in health, to love and to cherish, till death do you part?"

"Yes, yes, yes. Yes, I do," Rikki said with so much fervor that both Bernadette and the clerk chuckled.

Rikki wrapped an arm around Bernadette's waist as Bernadette listened and then said, "Yes, I do," to the clerk's question.

"Do you have rings to exchange?"

"Not at this time," Rikki said. "At the big wedding."

"All right then. By the power vested in me by the state of Ohio, I now pronounce you legally married as wife and wife." She stepped back and said directly to Rikki, "You may kiss each other."

And they did. Bernadette felt Rikki's loving kiss from her lips to the tips of her toes to the top of her head and everywhere in between. "I love you, Rikki," Bernadette said breathlessly.

"I love you, too."

"Congratulations, you two," the clerk said. "It's nice when two lovely people find each other."

"Thank you," Bernadette said, loosening the death grip she had on Rikki's hand.

"Let's take a picture." Rikki held up her phone for a selfie. She waved off the clerk, who offered to take the picture for them, and that was okay. It made it a truly private moment between them. Rikki made sure to get the cheesy handmade heart hanging off the clerk's podium in the picture, which, for some reason, put the final punctuation on the absurdity of this private wedding in Bernadette's mind.

They left the busy clerk's office and headed to their lunch reservation at a high-priced restaurant in an affluent Cincinnati suburb.

"Madison would like this place," Bernadette said. "White tablecloths. Warm bread and butter." She pushed her plate away. The beef tenderloin had been quite good. It was a bit spicy with the chili infusion and chimichurri salsa, but it was amazing nonetheless.

Rikki raised her glass, "To Madison, that little devil who helped us find each other."

"To Madison," Bernadette said and drank the smallest of sips. She put down her glass. Her stomach was a bit too oogly for much more.

"You okay?"

"I'm fine. Just butterflies still, I think." Bernadette patted her wife on the leg. "Holy shit. I can't believe you're my wife, Rikki."

"I know. I'm a little starstruck over that, too." Rikki pushed her plate away and signaled for the check. "I'm not sure how you'll feel about this, but Jaleesa is an ordained minister and has the legal power to be our wedding officiant."

"No kidding?" Bernadette hadn't known that. "Huh."

"We can discuss it later, of course," Rikki said. "It's been an emotional day. Good emotional. But we will have to decide on our brides' maids and best *men*." She used air quotes around the word best men.

"Maids or Matrons of honor?" Bernadette offered. "That's so archaic. Yuck. I guess it depends on who we ask to fill those roles."

"I know who I'm asking."

Bernadette grinned. "I know mine, too, I think. But let me think on it some more."

"Anything you want, little bee." Rikki downed her glass of wine. "I feel okay to drive, but I'm probably over the limit, so you should, I suppose."

"Okay. I just had the one glass before we ate. And that small sip in Madison's honor."

Rikki nodded and handed her the keys to the Subaru. "You're on my car insurance, and I'm on yours, but we should get all the cars and the house with one insurance company. You know, bundle all that shit together? I'll look into that this week, okay?"

"Sounds like something a married couple would do," Bernadette said.

"Mm hmm." Rikki waggled her eyebrows. "We're adulting, but I like it. And I'm not insuring the Mercedes yet. It's going to sit in the garage until we need it. We don't need three cars in the family."

"Family," Bernadette squeaked. "I like that word."

"You're my family now, Bernadette," Rikki said, her face serious. "Not only does that make me incredibly happy, but I feel grounded or something knowing that someone as extraordinary as Dr. Bernadette Garneau, brilliant mathematician, strong athlete, gifted pianist, the most open and giving soul I have ever known – yes, this person gave herself to me."

Bernadette covered her face with both hands. She never could take compliments.

"Dessert, ladies?" the waitress asked. She pulled out a black book containing their bill from the apron tied around her waist.

"We'll be having dessert at home," Rikki said cryptically and held her hand out for the bill. She checked it over, tucked their new joint credit card under the flap, and handed it back to the waitress, who turned and left.

"Baby," Bernadette said, "I want to learn how to make food like this for us. Maybe I can ask Tina for more help. I mean, she's been great whenever I text her for suggestions."

"I am all for that, baby," Rikki said and rubbed her stomach.

"But there's…"

"There's what?"

"The whole Miss Jaleesa thing," Bernadette said, her worrying hands wrapping around themselves repeatedly. "I mean, making her the wedding officiant, too?"

Rikki put her hand over Bernadette's to stop the movements. "Tell me."

"I mean…" Bernadette sent Rikki a look imploring her to understand the anxiety she felt about fucking another woman's girlfriend. She had no idea if Miss Jaleesa and Tina were married. Somehow, it would make things worse if they were. Rikki's patient expression made it a little easier for Bernadette to attempt to convey her uneasiness. "I mean, Miss Jaleesa is Tina's girlfriend." She hoped Rikki would correct her if the two were married. When no correction came, Bernadette added. "She must hate me, Rikki."

"Tina? Oh, no, she does *not* hate you," Rikki said matter-of-factly. "She likes it when Jaleesa goes elsewhere. Tina is a romantic asexual. It takes the pressure off of her to 'perform.'"

"You used air quotes. Did Tina say that?"

"Mm hmm."

"When?"

Rikki chuckled. "Oh, sometime before my little bee came along. I think it was when Jaleesa started playing with Kari. Before she brought her into the house."

"So, if Miss Jaleesa had gotten to me before you did, I might be one of her subs?" Bernadette didn't let Rikki answer. "No. I wouldn't. I can't stand the thought of sharing." A realization was hitting her. "Rikki, I don't want to share you. I couldn't bear thinking about you with another woman, and, and…" She stopped to get her thoughts aligned. "I will stop lusting after Miss Jaleesa right now. Right here and right now because that is so unfair to you. You must hate me for it. Oh, God, it's so wrong. I'm so sorry, Rikki. Why haven't you, like, punished me for it?"

Rikki chuckled and brought Bernadette's hand to her lips. She kissed the back of it. "Baby, it's okay. I enjoy bringing Jaleesa into our lives this way. She brings out different things in you. And, honestly, it turns me on watching. I like watching you become aroused. Watching you melt under someone else's touch. And I'm not threatened if that's what you think. I'm not jealous. I'm the one that arranges these playdates. Remember? I'm always there with you. Do you understand?"

Bernadette nodded, but when her wife's eyebrows raised up, she knew words were expected. "Yes, Ma'am. I understand."

"Now, having said that," Rikki continued, "you will *not* have intimate moments with Jaleesa or any other woman unless I approve, *and* I am there. I do have limits when it comes to sharing you."

"I would never," Bernadette said, mortified that Rikki would even say the words. "But the minute you don't want this for us, we'll stop. Okay?"

"You got it, baby. And the same goes for you, too. If you want to stop, you must tell me."

"Yes, Ma'am."

The waitress brought them the receipt, and as they stood up to go, Bernadette reached up and took hold of Rikki's upper arm. Maybe to make sure she had Rikki's full attention? There was an urgency when Bernadette said, "I think I want to talk to Tina directly about things, though. I just need to make sure. Especially if I'm going to ask her to help me learn how to cook."

"If that's what you want, we can arrange it, my dear. Now, c'mon, Dr. Carmichael." Rikki pulled Bernadette by the hand toward the exit. "I need dessert."

# Chapter 12
## Rikki

The Fourth of July weekend flew by, and somehow, it was already Tuesday evening. Rikki kissed Bernadette one last time and stepped back from the Subaru. "Baby, I'm so sorry we didn't find time to plan the wedding this weekend."

"Furthest thing from my mind, actually." Bernadette adjusted the seat and the rearview mirror. "Is the shop always that crazy on the Fourth of July weekend?"

Rikki nodded. "It's typically a big day for the shop, and the new parking lot made a nice amount of cash. Mark was out there all day. I'm sure Seamus rewarded him nicely."

Bernadette chuckled, her eyes playful. "I, for one, was still basking in the glow of our secret wedding. The, uh, dessert Friday evening was especially delightful." The tinge on Bernadette's cheeks was positively precious.

Rikki pulled out her phone. "Smile." She took a few pictures of her little bee, who looked so adorably cute. "What time will you be home?"

"Tina said the class starts at 6:00 p.m. and ends at 8:00, so depending on how soon I can get out of there and the Cincinnati traffic, maybe 8:30. I'd say 9:00 at the latest."

"It's a school night for you, so don't dawdle when it's over."

"I won't. Hopefully, I'll have an amazing meal to take home, and we can have it for dinner tomorrow night."

Rikki nodded. Her little bee would do fine in her first-ever cooking class. "You'll text me when you get there and again when you're leaving." It wasn't a question.

"Yes, Ma'am," Bernadette said and saluted. "Too bad Tina and I can't drive down together."

"She works down in Cincy. Easier for her to meet you there."

"Yeah."

"Nervous, little bee?"

"A little," Bernadette said. "What if I don't know how to hold a knife or something? They might laugh at me."

"Let them laugh then. And besides, it's an introduction to cooking class, isn't it?"

"Mm hmm," Bernadette said. "You're right. Hey, are you sure you don't want me to drop you down at the shop? I hate it when my car goes in for maintenance; it takes forever to get it back out."

"I'm fine," Rikki said. "Marta can handle things, and Lydia is right upstairs in the apartment. And, hey, you'll be happy about this. While you're gone, I'm going to make a list."

"A list?" Bernadette's eyes widened. She loved her lists.

"Yep, a list of the things we want for the playroom. A prioritized list."

"St. Andrew's cross," Bernadette blurted.

"Number one." Rikki chuckled and patted the top of her car. "Go on now. I don't want you to be late."

"Bye," Bernadette said and put the car in reverse. "I love you, Mrs. Carmichael."

"And I love you, Dr. Carmichael."

Bernadette waved and then focused on backing out and turning around.

Rikki sat on the porch's top step and watched her wife and car drive away. She was proud of Bernadette for contacting Tina and asking for help with cooking. Tina was the one who suggested they join that beginners' class in Cincinnati together. This was good. The two of them would get to know each other before Bernadette had the difficult talk with Tina. Difficult for Bernadette, not for Tina.

Rikki headed into the house, grabbed the small notebook Bernadette used to make lists and headed down to the playroom. The modular floor mats Bernadette picked out had been ordered and would be arriving soon. They would be laid down on top of the newly stained concrete. The new bathroom would be finished in less than a week, and then the basement flooring could be started. Yep, this whole project was moving right along.

That settled in her mind, she stood in the center of the basement and envisioned her dream dungeon. No, no. It was a playroom, not a dismal, scary-sounding dungeon. She wanted nothing scary for her little bee.

St. Andrew's cross here. Spanking bench there. The queening chair where? Maybe in that corner. Hmm, they'd have to arrange the furniture once it arrived and see what worked best where. Bernadette would probably make a to-scale diagram. All of it still had to be ordered, though. Rikki was a bit apprehensive about spending so much money upfront. The repairs in the shop and the renovations to the old farmhouse were going to be costly enough. But, no, she didn't want to worry about finances right now. She made a mental note to call her lawyer about redoing her will. And Bernadette's. Yes, that had to happen, as well.

But as long as she was dreaming, she could spend as much money as she wanted. "A bondage couch. Yes, yes. *Oh, little bee, you're going to love that.* Maybe a suspension swing, too. And we need a closet or armoire for all my whips and paddles, clips, and cuffs." She was a kid in a candy store. In her mind, anyway.

She made notes on the pad and decided that she didn't want a bed down there but maybe a couch that could accommodate both of them. Bernadette liked passing out after sex, so that might be a good addition. She'd ask Bernadette her opinion. No, no, she'd ask her *wife.*

"Wife," Rikki said out loud. "I'm married now. Holy shit." What date would they use for their wedding anniversary? The later one in the fall from their public wedding, or the one four days ago – the legal date?

"Four days ago, I made you mine," Rikki mused as she walked back up the stairs. That was the day she took her lovely, blushing bride home and literally ate dessert off her body.

Rikki had thrown the mat down on the living room floor and then threw Bernadette onto it after removing her bothersome clothing. Deeply ice-cold vanilla ice cream dabbed onto each nipple melted quickly but did its job hardening the skin underneath. Rikki's tongue lapped at the creamy mess. Her lips sucked the nipples to make sure she'd gotten it all. Bernadette's moans told her she'd been successful. Hot caramel was next, having been heated in a double boiler and dripped from a spoon as Bernadette watched it fall toward her body. Her back arched when the hot syrup hit her now cold nipples. Rikki let her lover bask in the pain she loved so much. Rikki reclaimed Bernadette's nipples and dutifully removed the sticky sweetness.

A hand on the back of her head and a lifting pelvis told Rikki it was time. A pillow strategically placed under Bernadette's ass lifted her up nicely. Rikki dug back into the cold metal bowl and scooped out more of the icy summer treat. She splayed open Bernadette's nether lips and let the scoop fall from a great height. Bernadette instinctually closed her legs just before it hit.

Rikki nudged the legs open again and shimmied between them. With her fingers, she smeared the cold, creamy substance over Bernadette's clit. Funny how that made Bernadette's legs open wider. Rikki was thorough, oh so thorough, licking up the ironically vanilla treat. She stirred the caramel with her spoon and was rewarded with a lovely hot spot. She scooped some out and showed Bernadette, who squirmed and arched her back. She groaned as the hot substance hit her clit. She sucked air between her teeth as she succumbed to the pain.

"Ride it out, baby."

Bernadette's groans turned to slow moans, which was Rikki's cue. A liberal amount of whipped cream completed her sundae, and Rikki ate and ate and ate her human dessert until the vessel beneath her smashed her loins against Rikki's face and screeched her release.

Arousal scorched through Rikki at the memory. "Best dessert ever," she muttered to the empty house. She sighed. It was so noticeably lonely without her little bee.

She glanced at one of the many clocks Bernadette had in the house. Huh? It was well after 6:00 pm. Rikki checked her phone. Nope. No text or missed call. Well, Bernadette had probably gotten caught up in the excitement of the new class and forgot.

Rikki set about packing lunches for her and her little bee for tomorrow as a surprise when Bernadette got home. Her phone dinged just as she'd put the finishing touches on Bernadette's sandwich—turkey and cheese with mayo, no tomatoes, please. It was a text from Tina.

TINA: Miss Rikki – Bernadette is on her way, right?

RIKKI: Yes. She left a little after five.

TINA: It seems like it's taking forever. The class has already started.

Adrenaline shot through her. She slammed closed the text chat with Tina and opened her phone app. She called Bernadette's phone, but it went to voicemail immediately. She tried again. Maybe she'd gotten a flat tire and was dealing with that. No answer. Shit.

"Track her phone," Rikki said out loud and opened the tracking app. She willed herself to breathe while the app took its damn fucking time finding a signal. *No location found.* "Fuck." She closed the app and tried again. She got the same infuriating message.

Rikki put both hands out and willed herself to be calm. She breathed deeply through her nose and let it out slowly through her mouth. *Think. Think.* What to do? Maybe Bernadette stopped by the college first.

A quick text to Olga said that she hadn't seen her, but she'd zip over to the university campus to see if Bernadette or the Subaru were anywhere to be found.

Realizing she'd left Tina hanging, she reopened the text window.

RIKKI: I can't locate her using the app. You stay there in case she shows up. I'm going to …

*Fuck, fuck.* What *was* she going to do? Call in the troops, that's what.

RIKKI: I'm going to drive down there. I know the route she would have taken.

TINA: Okay.

TINA: Give me the license plate number. And the make and model. I'll get Jaleesa to call the highway patrol. Maybe she broke down on the side of the road or something.

TINA: We'll find her, Miss Rikki.

RIKKI: Thanks.

Rikki opened another text chat with Shasti.

RIKKI: Bernadette's missing. She didn't show up for a class in the city. I have no car. I need to look for her.

SHASTI: I'm on my way.

RIKKI: Bless you.

SHASTI: Gather up your wallet, keys, phone. Snag some pictures of her. The framed ones in your living room. Bring anything that might be helpful.

RIKKI: Okay.

SHASTI: I'm in the car.

SHASTI: Put on shoes. Take a sip of water. Bring a paper bag – you know why. Bring a couple.

RIKKI: Okay.

Rikki did as bidden. There were advantages to having a Mommy Domme as a close friend. Rikki gathered the items and threw them in her bag. She put their marriage license in the bag, too. She didn't know why. It was a comforting link to Bernadette, maybe.

She locked the front door and sat on the top porch step, waiting. *We need rocking chairs out here*, Rikki thought and wondered why that had entered her mind. Her stomach churned. *Fuck*. She made a beeline for the house and fumbled to get the front door unlocked. She made it to the toilet in time to unload the contents of her stomach. She dry-heaved for a while until finally getting herself under control. Obviously, her body was going where her mind refused to.

Her little bee was okay, wasn't she? Rikki looked to the ceiling, silently calling on her mother's reassurance. She sobbed as the pain of loss hit her all over again. "No, no, no, no, no," she cried. "Please, God, no. Let her be okay. Let her be okay." She fell to the bathroom floor when her legs gave out.

Shasti helped her up and made her rinse her mouth out and splash water on her face.

"You need to be strong," Shasti said as they walked to her car. "We don't know what we're going to face, Rikki. It could be nothing or require the most strength you've ever had."

Rikki rubbed her nose. She heard the words, but they weren't really registering. They weren't registering because there was some weird time-lapse delay in her foggy brain.

"I've got you, Rikki," Shasti said as they pulled out of the property in Shasti's car.

The fog continued to shroud Rikki as she gave Shasti directions. She sat up straighter when they reached the highway and frantically looked for the Subaru. Was she in a ditch? Unable to respond?

Oh, God, she couldn't breathe. Shasti yanked the car off the road and then shoved a paper bag in Rikki's face. Rikki breathed into the bag to Shasti's soothing words.

"Breathe slowly. Yes, good. Breathe into your belly. Hold it. Again. Easy, easy."

Rikki heard the far-away ding as a text came in. She reached for her phone, but Shasti told her she would look and reminded her to breathe. Rikki turned her head slightly to read the text. She focused on breathing and on not alerting Shasti that she was spying.

TINA: Miss Rikki? Jaleesa might have found her.

RIKKI (SHASTI): Shasti here.

RIKKI (SHASTI): I have Rikki. We're driving toward Cincy. On the hwy now.

TINA: Let's switch to your phone, okay?

RIKKI(SHASTI): Okay.

Rikki focused on breathing as Shasti opened her own phone. Shasti's fingers flew fast and furious. She said to Rikki, "Bernadette's at Northside General. She's in the Emergency Room."

Rikki's stomach heaved again. She threw open the door but had nothing to give. Shasti's soothing hand was on her back.

"Take a sip," Shasti shoved a water bottle in her face. Rikki sipped.

"C'mon," Rikki said, finally finding the strength. She shut the car door and pounded on the dashboard. "Let's go. Let's go. Let's go." The small part of her rational mind reasoned that if Bernadette was in the emergency room, then she wasn't dead.

Shasti eased back onto the highway and didn't go fast enough for Rikki's liking, but Rikki didn't fuss. She practiced breathing and not letting her stomach have control.

Both Rikki and Shasti flew out of the car in the parking lot and ran inside. Tina was waiting for them.

"We have a room here," Tina said. "A family consult room." She led the way and punched a code on the door. "The advocate nurse will be back in a minute to give us an update."

Why wasn't Tina telling them anything? How bad was it? It was bad, wasn't it? Rikki couldn't ask. She couldn't power her way through this. She had to let her friends think for her until she found her footing.

A door on the opposite side of the room opened. A middle-aged woman with a gentle expression came in, and Rikki shot to her feet. "I have a progress report," the woman said. "The car accident was severe enough to land her here. She is fairly stabilized now. But due to HIPPA laws, I can only speak to family members at this point."

Shasti spoke first. "Rikki is her fiancée."

"Ahh, Dr. Balakrishnan," the woman said, sounding uncomfortable, "you know that's not good enough. I am so sorry. Are you her primary—"

"No," Rikki interrupted. "She's my wife."

"Rikki," Shasti warned. "You can't. That's not legal. I can go in as her general practitioner."

"She's my wife," Rikki insisted, knowing she sounded crazy. "Here." She shoved the bag into Shasti's hands. "In here. Find it."

Shasti opened the bag and rooted around, and finally, after a hundred hours, unfolded the four-day-old marriage certificate. "Whoa! They *are* married." She handed the certificate to the advocate.

"That changes things," the advocate said. "I'm not supposed to do this, but I don't care. I'm going to take you back there. And we'll find out firsthand what the latest updates are."

"We'll be here, Rikki," Shasti said, taking the marriage certificate back. "This is the best place for her to be right now. They'll take care of her."

Rikki held out her hand, and Shasti knowingly handed her a fresh brown paper bag. Rikki still had tunnel vision, but at least her stomach was cooperating. For now. In a far distant place, she heard Tina crying and Shasti consoling her.

Rikki barely registered the fast-moving things around her and followed the advocate through winding hallways until they got to a triage room. The woman led her to one side of the big room, where at least four people were fussing over someone.

"There she is," the advocate said. "We'll go to a spot where they're not working. Just don't get in the way."

Rikki had to blink several times to register what she was seeing. Her Bernadette. Broken. Attached to machines. Two separate medical teams worked on different parts of her body. One machine was helping her breathe. Its rhythmic sound was not soothing. Not soothing at all. There was a tube coming out of the side of her torso. The tube had blood in it. Blood. Two doctors were washing out a huge gash. Rikki saw meat and bone. Oddly, her own body didn't react to the carnage. Two other doctors were wrapping up Bernadette's left arm. Rikki scanned for all the limbs. All there. Feet, too. Hands, yes.

Rikki's gaze made its way up to Bernadette's face, a place she hadn't dared look at first. The swollen features, the tube in her mouth, the bandage around her head—This was Bernadette? No, no. How could this be Bernadette? Rikki blew out a breath and put her fist to her mouth.

"This is not a good time," one of the doctors growled to the advocate, who simply nodded but did nothing to move Rikki away.

Rikki stepped closer and put her hand on the back of Bernadette's. She didn't want to grab it in case something was broken.

"I'm here, baby. It's Rikki." She rubbed the hand. "They're taking good care of you. Be strong. I love you. Let them take care of you. I'll be here the whole time. I love you. I love you." And then her lungs couldn't find air. Somebody pulled her away and led her toward the door. She barely registered the sob as she clung to the doorframe and then looked back at her girl.

"We're going to let them work now, Rikki."

Rikki looked back at the advocate. Yes, that was best.

"Take a deep breath." She did. "Let's hit up this restroom before I fill you in. After that, I'll take you back to your friends."

The advocate gratefully left her alone in the restroom, and Rikki somehow got her lungs working, and her stomach settled. She splashed water on her face and, when she finally had herself settled enough, headed out and joined the woman in a small consultation room.

"Rikki, it's a lot, and I need you to be strong," the advocate said, opening a folder.

Rikki nodded and looked down at nothingness.

"She has two collapsed lungs and at least five broken ribs. She has a nasty bump and cut to the head and is most likely concussed. The eyes are responsive and seem fine, but that, too, will need to be determined. A broken left forearm and a fractured left kneecap. You saw the open gash on her left leg. That will need surgery, I'm told. But there is some good news."

Rikki scoffed.

"Scans showed no injuries to internal organs."

Rikki looked up.

"Somehow, no squishy parts were damaged," the advocate said. "And that is really, really, really good."

"Squishy parts," Rikki repeated. What an odd way to phrase that.

The advocate nodded. "I'm sure you have a million questions, but I want you to absorb that news first, Okay?"

"Okay."

"C'mon, let's take you back to the family room. With your permission, I can fill in your friends if you want me to."

"I, uh," Rikki started and took a breath. "Yes, thank you. I don't think I can do it. This is overwhelming."

"The way I see it, you have great support out there, especially with Dr. Balakrishnan in your corner. And your wife? With all that love surrounding her, she has everything to live for."

Rikki couldn't help the unbidden tears that welled up. She took a few halting breaths and then got herself back under control. She nodded and let herself be led back to the people she needed most right now.

# Chapter 13
## Bernadette

Blue. Sky. Fluffy. Clouds. Float. Peace. Peace. Weight. Heavy. Under water? Under ground?

~~~

Bright. No, no. Eyes shut. Voice far…Voice close.
"I'm here, baby." Kind voice. Nice. Soothe. "Be strong."
Okay.

~~~

Hand. Squeeze. "Hi, baby." Kind voice.
Squeeze back.
"She squeezed my hand. I'm here, sweetie. You're okay."
Eyes open. Bright. Eyes shut.
"Turn off that overhead light." Urgent voice.
Trust. Eyes open. Okay. Ceiling.
Hand squeeze.
Squeeze back.
"Baby, it's Rikki. I'm here. I've been here every day."
Eyes move. Left. Right. Up. Down. Blurry. Can't find. Eyes close.
Hand Squeeze. Hand gone. No!
"Hi." Kind voice. Soft. Closer.
Eyes open. Blink. Focus. Kind face. So pretty. Angel?

"It's me, little bee." Angel voice. "You had your surgery. They stitched up that gash on your leg, and you have a cast for your knee and your arm. No complications. They said you're strong and making great progress every day."

Mouth full. Throat closed.

"No, no, baby. Don't try to talk." Angel touch. Cheek.

"That's an excellent sign, Rikki." Far voice.

Rikki? Rikki? Think. Think. Yes! Rikki! Love. Reach. Can't. Stuck.

"Shasti, does she have to be strapped down like this?" Rikki voice.

"Yes, so she doesn't claw at the stitches. I think she wants to hold your hand. She's reaching for you."

"I've got you." Rikki hand squeeze.

Squeeze back. Five times. Prime number. Ha! Push Rikki hand flat. *Tap, tap, tap, tap.* Wait. *Tap, tap.*

"She's tapping her index finger on my palm." Rikki confused. "She's trying to say something. Is she in pain or something?"

Learn. *Tap, tap, tap, tap.* Wait. *Tap, tap.*

"Is she tapping out a code, like the alphabet?" Far voice. Also kind. Gentle.

"It's four, then two. So, like D then B?"

No. No. No. Wipe Rikki hand. Erase.

"She said not that." Rikki voice. Excited. "She's communicating with me, Shasti. She understands."

"Don't start crying again, Rikki. Stay with her. I'm asking for help in the group chat. One of these geniuses might understand what she's doing."

Learn. *Tap, tap, tap, tap.* Wait. *Tap, tap.*

"Same message. Dang it. I'm sorry, baby. We're a little slow on this end. Give us a minute to figure this out." Rikki squeak. "She gave me a thumbs-up. Holy shit. My baby is still in there, Shasti." Rikki cry.

Rub Rikki palm. Soothe Rikki.

"Aww, I think she's trying to reassure me. Oh, my God." More Rikki tears.

Wave.

"Hi, baby. Shasti, she waved at me." Hand leave. Face above.

Blink. Blink. Blurry.

"There you are. Your pretty blue eyes looking back at me. No, no, don't try to talk. You might choke. They have a tube down your throat to help you breathe. They'll take it out soon. Maybe tomorrow, they said."

"Rikki, Madison thinks it's Morse code." Kind far voice. "She sent a link. If this is right, Bernadette was tapping out 'Hi.'"

Thumb up, up, up.

"You were saying, 'hi'?" Rikki laugh. "Oh, my God. You're incredible."

Smack bed. Four times. Perfect square. Ha!

"Okay, Okay," Rikki say. Stroke forehead. Love. "I'll move back." Rikki hand flat.

*Tap, Slide, Slide.* Wait. *Tap, Tap, Tap, Tap.* No. Too fast. Erase.

"Shasti, grab that pen and paper. Can you take dictation?"

"Yes, of course." Shasti voice close.

Shasti? Who? Fuzzy.

"Put the code on the bed here." Rustle. "Okay, little bee, have at it. We're ready."

*Tap, Slide, Slide.* Wait.

"W."

*Tap, tap, tap, tap.*

"H. I know that one now."

*Tap.* Wait.

"Oh, just one? Uh, E."

*Tap, slide, tap.*

"R"

*Tap.*

"'Where'? Are you asking where you are?"

Thumb up.

"Oh." Rikki sigh. Big. "Baby, you're in the hospital. In the ICU."

Taps. *Why?*

"You were in a car accident. You have some injuries, but the great news is that you're going to recover and be just fine."

Thumb up, up, up.

Taps. *Others?*

"Others, others." Rikki thinking. "I think you're asking whether or not there were other people in the accident. No, the pickup truck that hit you was the only other vehicle involved, and he is fine."

Thumb up, up, up.

"Until I sue his ass, that is." Rikki angry.

"She's worried about other people right now," far voice say.

Taps. *Who*? Point far voice.

"Oh, that's Shasti. Dr. Shasti Balakrishnan. Madison's mistress."

Oh! Oh! Oh! Thumb up, up, up. Frantic wave. Beckon.

"Oh, looks like she wants to talk to you, Shasti."

"Here I am, Bernadette." Warm hand on hers.

Point Rikki. Okay sign. Palm up – question?

"I think she just asked me if I thought you were doing okay, Rikki."

Thumb up, up, up.

"She obviously doesn't trust you to tell her the truth."

Thumb up.

Laugh. "Rikki is doing fine. Okay, she's sort of a mess, but we're taking care of her."

Taps. *Sleep? Eat?* Point Rikki.

"Oh, she's on to you big time, Rikki." Shasti laugh. "Yes, after a fashion. She's staying at Tina's parents' house. They live three miles from the hospital. She goes there when they kick her out of your room at 9:00 p.m., and then she comes back at 6:00 a.m."

Thumb up.

"Yes, Bernadette, your wife is doing fine."

Taps. *Wife?* Palm up – question.

"Yes, baby," Rikki say. Take hand. "I made you my bride one week ago today."

Wife? Wife? Fuzzy. Wait. Courthouse. Yes! Dinner. Oh! Dessert!

Taps. *Dessert.*

Rikki burst. Laugh.

"Do I want to know?" Shasti ask.

"No," Rikki say. "But it means that she remembers now."

Push palm flat. Taps. *Happy Anni—*

"Happy anniversary?" Rikki laugh. "Yes, baby. Happy one-week anniversary." Hand squeeze. "Oh, Shasti. She's in there. She's going to be okay." Rikki tears.

Stroke hand. Soothe.

"Time for meds." Different voice. Boy voice.

Taps. *Love Rikki.*

"I love you, too, my little bee."

Point Shasti. Reach hand. Squeeze.

"I think she's saying thank you and that she loves you, too," Rikki said.

Thumb up. Heavy. So heavy. Falling.

Hand on forehead. Soothe.

Under water? Again?

~~~

"Rikki," Bernadette called. Her voice was hoarse, practically non-existent.

"I'm here." Rikki's beautiful face appeared above her.

"I love you." Bernadette's voice was mostly air.

"I love you, too." Rikki stroked her forehead. "They extubated you early this morning, sweetie, so your throat will be kind of sore for a while. They said you had been breathing mostly on your own!"

Bernadette smiled. She tried to reach up but couldn't. She grunted.

"I'm sorry they have you tied down," Rikki said. "It's only fun when I tie you down, right?"

Bernadette laughed, but it quickly turned into a cough and then pain. Oh, such pain.

"Clutch this with your upper arms as best you can," Rikki said, placing a small pillow on her chest. "Hold it tight when you need to cough. I'll try not to make you laugh again, okay?"

Bernadette gave her a thumbs-up.

"How are you feeling, baby?" Rikki asked. "Besides the broken ribs."

Bernadette tried to look down but couldn't. Something was preventing her. "What's this?" She pointed toward her neck.

"Oh, that's the cervical collar. They had to leave that on while you had the breathing tube. But now that it's out, I'm sure they'll take it off soon."

"Okay," Bernadette croaked.

"And I won't make a joke about you wearing someone else's collar, okay?"

Bernadette gave her a thumbs-up and tried to swallow. Her mouth and throat were so dry.

"I've held your hand every day, little bee."

Bernadette smiled, sure that the love she felt for Rikki shined bright in her blurry eyes. "How long? What day?"

"It's Sunday, so you've been here in the ICU for six days. Shasti says you're making amazing progress."

"Shasti is great," Bernadette said in her best gravelly voice.

"Yeah, she's been making sure I take care of myself."

"Mommy Domme." Bernadette's smile faded, and tears sprang to her eyes.

"Oh, no," Rikki smoothed her forehead. "Are you in pain? What happened just now?"

"Madison?"

"Madison is upset like we all are, but we're taking care of each other. She has Shasti, don't forget."

"Mommy—" Her throat was so dry.

"Mm hmm," Rikki said. "Mommy Domme. Madison stays at Jaleesa and Tina's when Shasti's here with us."

"Say hi from Prof—" A slight coughing fit started, and she clutched the pillow Rikki had given her. Broken ribs sucked, she firmly decided. Rikki held her hand throughout the fit. "Sorry." It was mostly a whisper at this point. Her throat was dry and uncooperative.

"What in the world are you sorry for?"

"You have…" She had to rest for a moment. "…to take care of me."

"It's what I signed up for," Rikki said. "'For better or for worse. In sickness and in health.'" She did a little tap dance. "Tada!"

"Kiss me," Bernadette demanded in her best whisper

"Oh, oh," Rikki stammered. "Let me see if I can maneuver my lips over your collar." To her advantage, Rikki was tall and could lift herself far enough and high enough to land her lips on Bernadette's.

Bernadette moaned. To her own ears, it sounded like, "I'm finally home." Hopefully, Rikki understood that. She must have because she kissed Bernadette again. Bernadette wanted it to develop into something a little more but had to pull back as she started to cough again. Rikki bolted out of the way.

"Clutch your pillow, little bee."

Bernadette nodded and did so., even though it was hard to do with her one arm strapped down.

"We'll keep practicing," Rikki said. A gleam in her eye said she was here and wasn't going anywhere. "I have a feeling we'll be back to sexy time in one form or another soon enough."

Bernadette, coughing fit over, sent her lover a look that she hoped would be construed correctly.

Rikki fanned herself. "Is it getting warm in here?"

Message received loud and clear.

Rikki cleared her throat and said, "Sometime today, you're getting a swallow test. I'm not sure how they do that, but if you pass, then you can start having real food. Yay!"

Bernadette gave a thumbs-up but had to close her eyes. She didn't mean to, but she groaned. Her whole body ached. Everything felt so weird.

"Aww, I know you need to sleep, sweetie, but I want to tell you what's happening. They said tomorrow you're going to get that other chest tube taken out and start respiratory therapy. If that goes well, you move to the step-down ICU for a little while. Once they're sure you're stable, it's off to a rehabilitation facility for you."

Thumbs-up.

"I argued to take you directly home from the hospital, but Shasti talked me down off that ledge. You need more care than I know how to give you right now."

Bernadette patted Rikki's hand and said, "Rikki?"

"Yes, baby?" Rikki held her hand.

"The car? The shop? Tell me."

112

"That old car? It's totaled. It was insured. I won't miss it, and we have a sweet Mercedes convertible waiting for us in the garage back home."

"Sorry."

"About what? The car? I don't care about the car. *You* are the only thing I care about, baby." Rikki squeezed her hand. "The insurance company needs your statement about the crash, but we'll wait until you can talk."

"Don't remember."

"You don't remember what happened?"

"No."

"You know what? That's a good thing. A very good thing."

Rikki squeezed her hand and fell silent for a moment. Bernadette wasn't sure but thought maybe Rikki was trying to get her emotions under control.

"Um, they have several eyewitness testimonies, baby," Rikki continued. "All of them said you were driving fine and that the driver of the pickup truck changed lanes too soon and pushed you off the road into the concrete overpass."

Bernadette turned her palm up to indicate she didn't remember.

"It's okay if you don't remember. Oh, hey, Marta picked up your Prius from the shop. It's at home in the driveway."

"Mmm," Bernadette said. She was so sleepy, but she didn't want to leave Rikki. "My family? School? Shop?"

Bernadette tried to stay focused on Rikki's words, but it wasn't easy. Her body, aching in all kinds of weird places, kept stealing her attention, but she did get the basic idea that the three assistant managers were running the coffee shop just fine. Miss Olga had everything handled at the university, and Rikki had spoken with Bernadette's brother for a long time about the accident.

Reassured, she let the fog take over.

~~~

"She's awake now," Rikki said. "Her eyes are opening."

"Oh, great," the nurse said way too cheerfully. "Just in time for your bath." She was middle-aged and clearly a veteran in the step-down ICU. To Rikki, she said, "She got her collar off, did you see?"

"Yes, I was here when they took it off this morning. She can finally look around. I'm just relieved there weren't any neck or spine injuries."

"Very lucky. The ribs and the rest? Not so lucky." The nurse turned to Bernadette. "Time for your pain meds, Miss Garneau. And then your bath, new linens, and a clean hospital gown."

"Okay," Bernadette said, but inside, she cried, *No, no, no. No more meds that make me foggy and sleep. I don't want to get addicted, either.* She didn't know where her strength came from, but she blurted, "No!"

"No to what? The bath or the meds?" The nurse asked.

"No meds."

"No meds? Are you sure?" The seasoned nurse eyed her as if weighing her sincerity. "We absolutely do not want to get behind this pain—five broken ribs, broken left forearm from shielding, left kneecap fracture, laceration on the left thigh, two chest tube wounds healing, head laceration, diagnosed concussion with the loveliest purple knot on the forehead, and a glorious black eye. And I'm sure I've forgotten something."

A young female nurse's aide came into the room and set up supplies for the sponge bath.

The nurse looked Bernadette in that black eye and asked again, "Are you absolutely sure you don't want pain meds right now?"

"I'm sure," Bernadette answered, voice firm. "Not right now."

"Mash that call button at the first inkling you'd like relief," the aide said. "Don't wait. Don't try to be Supergirl."

"You've been through a lot," the nurse added. "I'll check with the doc about lowering your doses, okay?"

"Yes. Please," Bernadette said.

The nurse looked toward Rikki for confirmation.

"Yes, yes. If that's what she wants," Rikki said.

The nurse nodded and turned back to Bernadette. "Let's get you bathed and prettied up for your wife, shall we?" She turned back toward Rikki and said, "And that's your cue to go down to the cafeteria and grab some dinner. Dr. Balakrishnan's unofficial orders."

"I know. I know. Baby, I don't want to leave you, but you're in good hands. Literally."

Bernadette squeezed Rikki's hand, happy that she didn't have to be strapped down in the step-down ICU. "I love you, Mrs. Carmichael."

"I love you, too, Dr. Carmichael. I'll be back soon."

Once Rikki left, Bernadette let herself be manhandled by the nurse and the young aide. With expert skill, they rolled her on her good side, which hurt like a mofo, but she tolerated it because getting washed and getting clean sheets made her feel so much better. They washed her neck, back, ass, legs, and whatever else they could reach. As they washed her, she repeated the list of injuries in her head so she wouldn't focus on the pain. Rikki kept telling her it could have been much worse. Bernadette supposed so. She could still think pretty well, and they said when the bones and sprained ligaments in her ankles healed, she would walk in time. Did that mean she'd be in a wheelchair until then?

"What happened to my clothes?" she blurted.

"From what I understand, they had to cut them off you. I believe your wife told them to toss everything," the nurse said. "Too much blood, probably."

"Blood?"

"Head wounds bleed a lot."

She didn't care about the clothes. It was her day collar she was concerned about. The one that said she belonged to Rikki. And her ring. "My ring? Where's my ring?"

"Your wife has it," the nurse said as they lay her back down and did some crazy Houdini act of getting the old bottom sheet out and a new one on. She thought about the logistics of that while they washed her front and private parts. "Your wife showed us the ring. It's gorgeous. I wish I had someone as dedicated to me as she is to you. She's been here every day."

"I'm keeping her."

"I would!" The nurse cackled and then put her in a fresh gown. "All done, my dear. Pain meds now, perhaps?"

Bernadette shook her head.

"Here's the call button. I'll check on you in a bit."

"Thank you for helping me. Both of you."

"You're welcome, dear."

The last thing Bernadette heard before falling asleep was the young aide say to the nurse, "Those two should be, like, the poster people for gay ladies."

The nurse cackled again as the door shut, leaving Bernadette in blissful silence.

# Chapter 14
## Rikki

Rikki grimaced when the transport team lifted Bernadette roughly off the stretcher and deposited her unceremoniously onto the bed at the rehabilitation facility. Bernadette grunted as they adjusted her, and it took everything Rikki had not to intervene and do it herself. Being at the mercy of so many other people had been trying on her. She was used to being the one in control, the one making the decisions, the one taking care of Bernadette. She had to trust that the professionals around her knew what they were doing.

After the transport team packed up their things and wished Bernadette good luck, Bernadette whispered, "Are they gone?"

"Yes," Rikki said with a laugh.

"They hit every stinking bump on the way here from the hospital. Did you feel it?"

"I did." Rikki adjusted Bernadette's sheets just the way she liked them. Not too tight over the knee cast and loose over the feet. One doctor or another, there had been so many, told her that it was a miracle she hadn't broken an ankle. They were surprised that she hadn't torn any ligaments either. Yay. Fewer things that needed to heal.

"I have my own private room?" Bernadette looked around at her new digs at the rehabilitation facility. "How much does this cost?"

"I have a feeling Dr. Balakrishnan pulled a few strings. She sends a lot of her patients here. I'm grateful that we're so close to home now."

"Good, because you're going home at some point today. Take a shower in your own house. Get fresh clothes."

"No, I'm f—"

"You're *not* fine," Bernadette interrupted. She put up a finger to stop Rikki's retort and added, "I'll get Jaleesa to pick you up and carry you home. Don't test me. I'll do it."

Rikki clamped her mouth shut. Bernadette's feistiness was a thing to be celebrated.

"And besides, I'd like you to bring me back a few things," Bernadette said, her tone softer. "I have no clothes. No shoes. Just this." She pulled at her hospital gown. "I'll make a list. Look, Rikki, you've been positively amazing with me. I can't do this without you. I'm so proud to be your wife, but as your wife, I'm ordering you to go home. In the least, check on the house. Register the Mercedes. You never know when I'll suddenly be able to drive again, and then, bam, we'll need two cars." Bernadette smiled, a sad sort of smile. "I love you, Rikki. I—" Tears filled her eyes as she struggled to get her emotions under control.

"Aww, baby," Rikki said, reaching for Bernadette's hand. "You're okay. You're just tired."

"No, it's—" Bernadette took a deep breath and let it out. "You've sacrificed so much for me."

"It isn't a sacrifice."

"Agree to disagree." Bernadette adjusted in the bed and groaned. "When can people visit me?"

"Not for a few days yet," Rikki said. "You're still on infection watch, and we don't want to chance it. So how about we just get settled into our new place?" She stroked the uninjured part of Bernadette's forehead. Every day, she and Bernadette discovered more parts of her body that could be touched without discomfort. And for the moment, Rikki's lips replaced the fingers. The soft kisses made Bernadette sigh. Rikki moved her hand lower. Her fingers wandered to lovely places unmarred by her lover's trauma. She stroked Bernadette's neck and shoulders, planting kisses here and then there. She gently touched Bernadette's chest, careful to avoid the still-healing chest tube wounds on her sides, the broken ribs, and the deep bruise on one breast from the seatbelt.

Bernadette purred at the physical attention. "I've missed this, Rikki." Much of Bernadette's entire right side was fair game, so Rikki moved down Bernadette's body, kissing lovely spots. Sometimes her lips touched skin;

other times, the flowery cotton hospital gown. She looked up to find Bernadette's eyes filled with … what? Love, lust? Both?

"Foot massage, baby?" Rikki asked. "I'll be gentle. I have your favorite lotion in one of these bags."

"I'd rather you massaged somewhere else, Rikki." Bernadette's lusty whisper shot delicious tendrils of arousal through Rikki's body. The involuntary tilt of Bernadette's pelvis made her own needs known. "But I know we can't."

As if to validate her statement, the door burst open, and the rehabilitation facility doctor and two nurses came in. They fussed over Bernadette, adjusting her IV and going over the meds list. Rikki had to correct them twice because Bernadette wanted lower doses of everything. When the doctor raised his eyebrow in disbelief, Rikki quipped, "She can take a fair amount of pain."

Bernadette burst out laughing and had to clutch her pillow against the pain in her fractured but healing ribs. The pillow, Rikki noted, had been "borrowed" from the step-down ICU unit at the hospital. Oh, well. They'd never see it again.

The doctor acquiesced and said that once she was settled, they would be taking out the IV, and she'd be on oral meds. After the examination, the team left them alone, and at Rikki's suggestion, Bernadette called her brother in California. They switched over to an app that Bernadette's sister-in-law Cathy suggested so that they could see each other. It was heart-warming to see Bernadette's countenance brighten when she talked to her family. And it was officially the first time they saw Rikki "in person." It was uncanny how Bernadette favored her father, an engineer at the latter end of his career.

Rikki participated in the family call and added details about the accident and recovery that Bernadette either didn't know or had forgotten. Collectively, they concluded that her family didn't need to make the trip out right now and that waiting to visit until the wedding in the fall would be fine with Bernadette. They did, however, agree to check in with each other more often and set a date and time for the next group video chat.

After closing the app, Bernadette scooched over on the bed and patted the space next to her. "You. Here." She beckoned Rikki with her finger.

"Me? There?" Rikki tried to figure out how to navigate the hospital bed. She lowered the railing on one side and then had Bernadette lower the entire bed itself so Rikki could gently crawl in without jarring any of Bernadette's hurts.

Bernadette reached for Rikki's hand and entwined their fingers. "I love you, Mrs. Carmichael."

"I love you, too, Dr. Carmichael." Rikki rolled on her side, facing Bernadette, and snuggled up as close as she dared. She lay one hand on Bernadette's chest but moved it to her stomach when the weight was too heavy on the ribs.

"Rikki?" Bernadette said, her eyes closed, her voice sleepy.

"Yes, sweetie?"

"They took away my day collar."

"I know. Do you want to wear one?"

"Yes," came the quick answer in a voice not as sleepy.

"That can be arranged."

"Good. And Rikki?"

"Yes, love."

"Nap with me."

"Oh, yes. Happy to oblige, my dear." Rikki stroked Bernadette stomach. She was one hundred percent sure she'd stay awake, lying quietly, listening to Bernadette's breathing while she slept. That didn't happen.

Sometime later, they both woke to the visiting neurologist entering the room. Rikki was tsk-tsked by the nurses for being in Bernadette's bed with her, but they didn't press it, and Rikki didn't care anyway. Bernadette needed intimacy and cuddling as much as she needed stitches, casts, and bandages.

~~~

Ever since Bernadette got moved to the rehabilitation facility, Rikki spent each night home alone. She hated every minute of it. For the last eight nights, she endured lonely showers and poor attempts at sleeping in their bed. She clutched Bernadette's Pooh bear nightly, but he just wasn't cutting it without Bernadette attached to it. Despite being the middle of summer, the quiet house was cold, and when Rikki woke that Monday morning before sunrise, she decided to give up on sleep and head over to the facility.

She swept the enormous pile of ignored mail into two canvas shopping bags. Madison had been commissioned to fetch their mail from the box and check on the house while Bernadette was in the hospital, and Rikki stayed down in the city. Shasti had asked Madison to flush toilets, run water in the sinks, and make sure there were no raccoons in the pantry.

Yes, all that mail needed to be dealt with starting today. Rikki was sure there was an equally large pile at the coffee shop, but she couldn't bring herself to abandon Bernadette and actually go to work. Lydia, Mark, and Marta gave her daily reports, which was good enough for now.

Bernadette had been in the facility for a week and a day at his point, and each day Rikki brought in something Bernadette wanted. One day, it was the laptop. Another day, it was some loose clothing and some snacks. A handheld grabber came next, and today, Rikki was bringing a large analog clock that Bernadette had been jonesing for. Rikki also stashed a small clit vibrator in her pocket. Who knew if they'd ever get a private moment to use it. She staged everything by the front door near Bernadette's briefcase and made two to-go coffees — one for her and one for Bernadette.

Rikki showed up at the facility well before visiting hours, but they let her in any way. There was a reason for that. One week into her stay, Bernadette had already become a staff favorite. Rikki knew it was because she thanked them and was sincerely grateful for the attention and care they gave her. Kind of like the attention she gave her students, her friends, and Rikki, too.

Rikki dumped the bags of mail on the floor and dove into the bed with her girl. They slept for another hour or so until a nurse woke them up to start Bernadette's day.

At the pre-ordained time, a soft knock sounded on the closed door to Bernadette's room.

"How do I look, Rikki?"

"Uh, baby," Rikki said, "there are a million ways to answer that. You look good."

"Thank you." Bernadette reached up and ran her fingers along the stretchy fabric of her day collar. "How does my hair look?"

"Fantastic, baby."

"Come on in," Bernadette called, her voice strong.

Madison came into the room first, followed by Shasti. Madison was uncharacteristically quiet and stopped at the foot of the bed, her eyes down as if she were afraid to look at Bernadette.

"Hi, Madison," Bernadette said gently. "Is that for me?"

"Mm hmm." Madison handed her the over-large Pooh bear. "Mistress thought you might need a friend to keep you company when Miss Rikki goes home." She inhaled sharply. "Oh, hi, Miss Rikki. Sorry. Oh, shoot."

"You're fine," Rikki said and winked at Shasti.

"I love this Pooh bear," Bernadette gushed. Rikki could tell she was being sincere. "He is so adorable. Thank you so much."

Madison nodded but kept her eyes down.

"You can look at me," Bernadette encouraged. "I'm doing so much better now."

Madison looked up. "You look kind of broken on this one side."

"Yep. The leading theory is that I either turned in the driver's seat before impact or was thrown to the side on impact."

"Impact," Madison repeated.

"Mm hmm. I just need some time for my bones and other things to heal."

"Oh, wow, is that how you pee?" Madison pointed excitedly to the catheter bag partly filled with urine hanging off the side of the bed.

Bernadette laughed. "Yes, I'm not able to get up on my own yet. Fingers crossed they'll be removing that today."

"What if you have to poop?" Madison asked, her eyes wide.

Bernadette laughed again and squeezed her new Pooh bear so it wouldn't hurt. "It's called a bedpan, but I'll let your mistress explain that whole process to you later. Okay?"

Although Shasti didn't speak, her grin and wide eyes said, "Thanks a lot, Bernadette."

Madison moved closer and reached for Bernadette's hand. It was quite endearing. "Are you okay, Professor? I've been so worried."

"I am on the mend," Bernadette said. "Your visit is doing wonders to keep my spirits up. And I hear that you checked up on my house and that you mowed the lawn. Thank you."

"You're welcome. And you don't even have to pay me."

"Of course, we'll pay you." Bernadette looked at Rikki with questions in her eyes, asking if Rikki could please make that happen. Rikki nodded.

"Guess what, Professor?"

"What, kiddo?"

"You have over eight hundred members of the 'Fans of Dr. Garneau' group on the University website."

Bernadette raised an eyebrow at Rikki, who shrugged. "What group is this, Madison?" Rikki asked.

"I got Miss Olga's help, and Shanice and I set up a group page for the professor so that people could send their good wishes, and we could update them as to your progress. Mistress examines all my posts before I put them up, so there's nothing too personal on there." She leaned closer and whispered, "Like no one will know about the bedpan stuff, Miss Bernadette."

Another coughing fit ensued at that moment, just as Shanice and Marta came in.

"Baby girl," Bernadette cried to Shanice as she recovered her breath. "Why are you crying?"

Shanice simply shook her head and handed Bernadette a bunch of colorful get-well balloons. Rikki tied them to the bedframe out of the way.

Tears continued to stream down Shanice's face.

"I'm going to be okay, Shanice," Bernadette said.

"Mama, please," Shanice implored Marta and pointed to Bernadette's sheets.

"I'm sorry, Bernadette," Marta said. "She wants to see your legs and wants you to move them. Would that be okay?"

"Oh, of course."

Rikki lowered the bed to the height of Shanice's wheelchair and then gently pulled down the sheet to expose Bernadette's unshaven, pasty-white legs and socked feet. Bernadette wiggled her toes on command and then lifted her good leg fairly high. Even Rikki was impressed. The limited physical therapy they had started in the step-down ICU had definitely helped. Bernadette apologized that the cast and bandaging on her left leg made it too heavy to lift. She wiggled her toes instead.

Shanice ran her hand on Bernadette's shin. "You can feel that, Miss Bernadette?"

"Yes, I can."

Shanice finally looked up and sighed. "Oh, good."

"Did I pass?" Bernadette asked, a definite twinkle in her eye.

"You did. Thank you." Shanice tapped Bernadette's shin again and said, "You are really white for a white lady, Miss Bernadette."

They all burst out laughing while Marta scolded Shanice for her impudence. Bernadette, meanwhile, clutched her new Pooh bear as she succumbed to the pain in her ribs caused by laughing.

Marta helped Rikki pull the sheets back up and said, "She's been worried sick. We all have."

"I've felt the love, Miss Marta."

Madison looked ready to burst. "Guess what, Professor?"

"What?"

"Shanice helped me make that group page. She's a whiz at computers. She thinks really fast. Too fast for me. OMG."

Shanice laughed. "That's because you can't slow your own brain down for two seconds to focus, Madison."

"Truth in that," Madison acquiesced.

Shasti nudged Madison away from the bed and said, "The two of them have worked tirelessly to do this for you, Bernadette. Before we leave, they'll show you how to access the website. I'm sure the group would love a message directly from you. It's abundantly clear how much your students love you."

Rikki choked up, watching Bernadette choke up. The entire room became quiet – quite an incredible accomplishment for this particular group.

A big booming voice entered the room before the body attached to it did. "Is it true our lovebirds got married without us?" Jaleesa led the parade of her self-selected family into the room. Tina, Kari, Dana, DeShawn, Harriet, and even Bailey followed her in.

"Oh, you brought the puppy?" Bernadette gushed. When Bailey heard that, he lifted his arms and let his wrists and hands fall as he panted his pleasure. Funny how a puppy could walk on two feet.

"I brought the whole fam-damly," Jaleesa said as Tina ushered them to an open space in the large room. Jaleesa's countenance changed and became serious. "So, seriously, you two. Did you get married?"

Bernadette looked to Rikki to answer.

"We did," Rikki said to a cheer that went up in the room. "But don't worry, we're still planning the big wedding with a certain tall, very loud, former college basketball player as our officiant."

"I'm not loud," Jaleesa said, followed by a room filled with howling laughter and disbelieving scoffs, most of them from her own family members.

"It was such a lucky thing we were married," Rikki said, "because I had to sign for Bernadette's surgery, procedures for treatment, business office stuff, car insurance claims, her health insurance, and just everything."

"You did all that, baby?" Bernadette asked. "You didn't tell me."

"I don't want you to worry about those things," Rikki said. "I think these friends of ours will back me up when I say that your job right now is to heal that body of yours."

General murmurs of agreement filled the room.

"Yes, Ma'am," Bernadette said, her cheeks tingeing wonderfully pink as she fingered her collar.

*The collar soothes her,* Rikki thought. *Good. Kneeling also soothes her, but she won't be doing that for a long time, if ever again.*

Rikki stepped out of the way as Jaleesa's family members approached Bernadette. Harriet was silent but cried tears of concern as Bernadette consoled her. The retired art teacher rubbed Bernadette's forearm and nodded her understanding.

Dana asked if she and DeShawn could go over to the house and plant some pretty summer flowers and trim bushes and trees, to which Jaleesa threw out an off-color comment about Dana trimming her bush. Tina added that Bailey would help by picking up sticks. Both his and Bernadette's faces brighten at that. Rikki was proud of her girl for being so present.

Kari filled Bernadette in on the softball goings-on with wins and losses and the triple she'd hit using Bernadette's advice about hitting – something about an aggressive mindset.

Rikki beamed as she watched Bernadette interact with their friends. They were all here for her. Tina and Jaleesa approached next. The all-kidding-aside look of concern on Jaleesa's face and Tina's teary-eyed countenance made Rikki see Bernadette as they did – a broken thing. A treasured thing that they'd almost lost.

A firework of adrenaline burst in her chest and spread to her heart, lungs, head, stomach, and bowels. She bolted out of the room and dove into the closest restroom. She couldn't breathe and felt like puking or having diarrhea or both. Skirt up, she sat on the bowl and tried to get her breathing under control.

The restroom door opened. A paper bag was thrust under the stall. "What do you need?" Shasti asked.

Even though she was sitting on the bowl with her skirt tucked around her waist, Rikki unlocked the stall door. Shasti peered in. "Use the bag." Rikki followed Shasti's calm instructions and finally calmed her breath to a reasonable rate. The urge to have diarrhea passed, followed by the urge to empty her stomach.

After washing her hands, she sat down hard on the bench in the restroom. Shasti sat next to her. "Who puts a bench in a bathroom?" Rikki asked.

"It's for people with compromised ambulatory skills."

"Ahh," Rikki said and took a deep breath. "I wish my body wouldn't do this to me. It comes on so fast. I hate it."

"What set this one off?"

"Nothing. Everything. Just the totality of her accident and all the work that's yet to come. Shasti, she groans in her sleep. I don't know what to do to help her. I, we, all of us, we could have lost her."

"Slow down," Shasti advised. "Breathe."

"You know, Bernadette said to me one time that no matter what life throws at us, we'd figure it out together."

"She said that?"

Rikki nodded. "Before the accident. It was right after I gave her the engagement ring at the ball field. I thought I'd always be the one who figured things out and that Bernadette would just follow."

"Not so much now?"

Rikki shook her head.

"So, then you'll figure things out together." Shasti patted Rikki on the knee.

"This one is bigger than me, Shasti. It's bigger than both Bernadette and me."

"We're all here to help, Rikki. You have a lot of people ready and willing and able to help. Seriously, you need to read the posts on that group page Madison and Shanice set up. Her university community is really stepping up. The messages are incredibly heartwarming."

"Will it make us cry?"

"It will."

"I'll have tissues ready," Rikki said, attempting humor.

"A few suggestions," Shasti said, her Mommy Domme voice loud and clear. "For you personally, I mean."

"Hmm?" Rikki leaned back against the wall, trying to feel like a person brave enough to handle life with all its many twists and turns.

"Regular exercise and meditation for you. Breathing exercises, too, like the ones Bernadette is doing religiously with her spirometer. Those things might help lessen the severity of your attacks. And you're not going to like this last one."

"I'm not?"

"No, sorry," Shasti said with a grin. "Lowering caffeine intake might help."

Rikki chuckled. "I own a coffee shop. That's not going to be easy." She folded the used paper bag and stashed it in her skirt pocket. "You know, I'm supposed to be the strong one. The one who guides the ship. I might need a lot of help navigating this one."

"Permission to come aboard, captain?" Shasti quipped.

"You're already here, Shasti. You're already here."

# Chapter 15
## Bernadette

The coffee was heavenly. Hot and real, unlike what passed for coffee at the rehab facility. "Thank you, Rikki," Bernadette said and took another sip. She set her to-go cup on the adjustable table. "I'm glad you had a chance to go to the shop this morning."

"Me, too," Rikki said. The dark circles under Rikki's eyes concerned Bernadette, but she'd fuss at her later. All of this was hard on Rikki, too. "I've got my laptop and am prepared to pay bills—yours, mine, and ours."

A light knock sounded on the closed door as if the person knocking didn't want to disturb the occupants inside. Clearly, it wasn't one of the nurses or staff. They tended to barge right on in. Rikki stood up to open it. "Hey, Madison."

"Morning, Miss Rikki." Madison bounced into the room. "Hi, Professor Garneau. I'm ready to be your office assistant."

"Look how cute you are. You got all dressed up for me?" Bernadette pointed out Madison's tucked-in button-down shirt, vest, and smart bowtie to Rikki. "So handsome, isn't she, Rikki?"

"She is."

"Mistress said I looked like a sexy secretary and that if she gets a good report from you guys, she'll have me for lunch."

"Have *you* for lunch?" Bernadette asked. "Not a sandwich?"

"Mm hmm," Madison said with meaning. "So, I have to leave by 11:30, okay?"

"Let us not stand in the way of afternoon delight," Rikki quipped. She was about to sit back down when there was another knock on the door. "Looks like I have a part-time job opening doors." She reopened the door and said, "Oh, hello," obviously not knowing the person who walked into the room.

"Warren," Bernadette said. "Nice to see you again."

"You as well, young lady," Warren said to Bernadette. Warren was an older Black man with an assortment of white whiskers on his face. He totally had the kindly grandfather vibe going for him.

Bernadette turned to Rikki and said, "Rikki, this is Warren. He is the oh-so-helpful maintenance man who replaced those broken blinds this morning. Now they should lower all the way to the sill and block out that morning death ray of sunlight."

Rikki chuckled and said, "Nice to meet you, Warren."

"Warren, Rikki is my wife," Bernadette said to him.

"I know. I heard you were a newlywed."

"How?"

"Nothing is secret in this place," he said with a shake of his head.

"Oh, wow," Bernadette said. What else did they all know about her and Rikki? "Um, what's all this?" She pointed to his hands.

"Your gal Friday here commissioned a table and chair so she could be 'efficient' while helping you."

"Way to make things happen, kiddo," Bernadette praised. "Or, since you're my new secretary, maybe I should call you *Ms. Kim*?"

Madison nodded vigorously.

Warren asked Madison where she wanted everything, and once things were situated to Madison's, err, Ms. Kim's approval, Bernadette thanked him.

He left with a smile and nod for each of them.

"Guess what. Guess what?" Madison said before sitting down.

"What?" Bernadette asked, lifting the top part of the adjustable bed so she was in a quasi-sitting position. Her ribs protested, so she lowered herself a bit. Better.

"I'm fostering a turtle."

"And your mistress approves of this?" Rikki asked with a slight Domme tone to her voice.

"Mm hmm," Madison said, bouncing from one foot to the other. "If this goes well, then Dr. Addison might let me foster a puppy."

Bernadette exchanged a glance with Rikki and then said, "Assuming your mistress okays that."

"Of course. Of course."

"Will you ever foster kitties?" Bernadette asked. "If so, invite me over. We always had kitties growing up. I wanted to get one when I moved here, but then I met Jen, and she didn't want pets. 'Animals should be kept outside,' she always said."

"Even in the cold and rain?" Madison asked. A mixture of anger and sadness battled across her face.

"I guess, but she's no longer in my life, so maybe…" Bernadette looked at Rikki with puppy-dog eyes.

Rikki just chuckled and said, "Perhaps when we're a bit further along with all of this, we can discuss it." She twirled her finger around to indicate the entire room. "And on that note," Rikki plopped a bag filled with mail onto Madison's table. "Cards and mail for you to open, Ms. Kim." She picked up a letter opener and started to show Madison how to use it, but Madison blurted that she knew how. "Oh, good. Bring the opened cards to Miss Bernadette and the bills and the rest to me."

"Yes, Ma'ams," Madison said, bent her head, and got to work. It lasted two minutes, tops.

"Professor?"

"Hmm?" Bernadette looked up from the 'Fans of Professor Garneau' group webpage on her laptop.

"What's with this paper-drawn clock on the wall?"

Bernadette chuckled. "Rikki hung that up there. It was part of my neurological exam. Dr. Broward asked me to draw a clock set to 2:30."

"Why is the little hand not on the two?" Madison's brows were knit. Was she worried that Bernadette wasn't completely right in the head?

"He asked me the same thing, funny enough," Bernadette said. "It's because when the big hand moves around the circle, the little hand is also moving, but at a slower rotational frequency. So, at 2:30, the little hand is about halfway to the three."

"Whoa," Madison said. "You are so brilliant."

Bernadette laughed. "That's not exactly what the doctor said, but thank you, Madison."

Madison frowned.

"Oh, please excuse my manners," Bernadette apologized. "Thank you, *Ms. Kim.*"

Madison perked up and dug back into the mail with fervor. For about thirty seconds.

"Oh, and your friend Lisa on *Kinks* has been leaving you messages on your chat page. I don't think she knows about your accident."

Bernadette grimaced. "Dang this concussion. I have to text her. Thanks for letting me know."

Madison nodded, looking pleased with herself, and then attacked the mail once again.

Bernadette grabbed her phone and sent Lisa a semi-long text starting with the words, "I'm okay! I'm on the mend!" She conveyed the details of her accident in broad brush strokes and promised to call her when things were "less hectic." She didn't wait for a reply and powered down her phone. She could get caught up in a thirty-minute text exchange easily with Lisa and decided to be present with the people in the room with her instead.

She flashed Rikki a smile and then went back to the 'Fans of Dr. Garneau' webpage. The posts made her tear up for the millionth time. There were so many 'get well soon' messages, but there was also a fair number indicating that she was their favorite professor or that she had been the one to help them like math again. It felt good to see such tangible proof of the effectiveness of her teaching. One post used the wording 'tolerate math.' She showed Rikki, who smiled and then went back to paying the shop's bills, or maybe she was doing the payroll. One of the shop's assistant managers, Lydia maybe, had called Rikki to say that everyone had been patient about the late payroll, but they were getting rather antsy. They, too, had bills to pay, so Rikki made a special trip to the shop that morning to check things out and pick up what she needed. It was the first time she'd been back since the accident, and it had been three whole weeks already.

*She is such a beautiful woman,* Bernadette thought as she basked in Rikki's orbit.

Rikki caught her looking. "Are you okay, baby?"

Bernadette smiled coquettishly and nodded. She looked Rikki up and down lasciviously and waggled her eyebrows. "Mm hmm," she murmured suggestively.

Rikki simply winked and went back to whatever she had been doing.

Madison stood up and delivered a stack of opened greeting cards to Bernadette. "They're organized first by color and then by size."

"A girl after my own heart," Bernadette said. "Thank you, Ms. Kim."

"There's one from Victoria in there," Madison said, warning Bernadette.

"Ahh, okay. Thank you," Bernadette said. "Bills, next?"

"Yes, Ma'am," Madison said. "I'll separate what looks like possible junk mail. I do this for Mistress, and she says it's very helpful. She gets happy when I help, and when she's happy …" Her cheeks turned bright red.

"You're such a good helper, Madison. Rikki and I will give a favorable report to your Mistress."

"Thank you, Ma'ams," she said and bounced back to her workstation.

They settled into a lovely routine, and when Rikki changed over to their house bills, Bernadette taught her how to access the online accounts. She had to teach Rikki the algorithm for the various passwords. Bernadette thought Rikki was going to lose her mind when she explained the Fibonacci sequence scheme she used. The amazing thing? Rikki eventually caught on.

After a while, Rikki groaned and plunked the bill in her hand back on the pile. "I can't do another single one of these right now." She stood up, stretched, and then leaned down to kiss Bernadette. "I love you, little bee."

"I love you, too." The second kiss heated up nicely, and Bernadette moaned into Rikki's mouth.

"Brrng, brrng," Madison said.

"Shit," Bernadette muttered. They'd forgotten that Madison was in the room.

Madison stood up. "Ima just get going now. It's almost time, anyway. And these are pretty much done. Just this junk mail here left to sort."

"Take a breath, Madison," Bernadette said with a laugh. "Thank you so much for your help this morning, Ms. Kim. And a big, big, big thank you for setting up that group page with Shanice. That was so thoughtful."

"Welcome, Professor." Madison gathered up her things. How she managed to get so spread out with her belongings was a mystery to Bernadette and must be the bane of Miss Shasti's existence. "I'm going now," Madison singsonged. Under her breath, she added, "Bow chicka wow wow."

Bernadette burst out laughing. "That kid is something else."

"That *kid* is twenty-five and very grown up in many ways," Rikki said. "Let me text Shasti that Madison is on her way home. I'll give her that good report, so lunch at the Balakrishnan-Kim household will be, err, *delightful*." Once she was done, she placed her phone on her closed laptop and looked at Bernadette with a hungry expression. Rikki's gaze ignited some lovely places on Bernadette's body.

"C'mere, Mrs. Carmichael," Bernadette said, her intent clear. "Lunch won't be here for another hour at least."

"Physical therapy?"

"Pfft. Not until 3:00."

"Doctors' visits?" Rikki asked as she lowered the safety bar on the bed.

"Done. Seven-thirty this morning." Bernadette moved over, proud of herself for being a bit more agile.

Rikki reached into her pants pocket, pulled out something purple, but shoved it back in.

"Is that an eggplant in your pocket, Mrs. Carmichael? Or are you just happy to see me?"

Rikki answered by smothering Bernadette with a steamy kiss and then adjusting her body to Bernadette's without disturbing too many bruises, bangs, or brokens.

Bernadette leaned toward Rikki, not even close to being on her side – the ribs were not allowing that at the moment and said, "I consent."

"Oh, do you, now?" Rikki reached under the sheet, pulled up Bernadette's hospital gown, and gathered it around her neck. Breasts wonderfully exposed, Rikki feasted, carefully avoiding the heart monitor leads. She brushed her lips over the seatbelt bruises on Bernadette's breast and then graced each nipple with a soft kiss, hardening them. Bernadette pressed the back of Rikki's head to her nipple and arched her body. Or she tried to anyway. The ribs protested, and she groaned, but not in a good way. Rikki was undeterred. She lessened the pressure and moved her way down Bernadette's body, landing kisses on Bernadette's stomach and hips. She even kissed the top of the cast encasing her knee.

Bernadette was embarrassed that she wasn't shaved down below, but Rikki didn't seem to mind. Kisses adorned her mound, and Rikki lifted her head, her eyes a lusty green, and listened toward the door. No sounds. Bernadette moaned. She knew what was coming.

Rikki locked her gaze on Bernadette's as she got out of the bed and then pulled the good leg away from the other. She listened again and then lowered her head. A fleshy-lipped kiss hit Bernadette's clit, making her clench her core at the contact. Yes, it hurt, but she didn't care. Her good arm reached down and petted the head in between her legs. It had been so long.

"Make love to me, Rikki," Bernadette implored her lover.

Rikki sucked Bernadette's labia into her mouth like she was starving. Her tongue dove inside, pushing the warm folds apart. Her warm breath made Bernadette's muscles tighten and ribs protest. She didn't care.

She lifted her pelvis in time to Rikki's tongue strokes. "Mmm," Bernadette moaned in pure bliss. "Yes, baby, yes."

Rikki hummed into Bernadette's center, causing the most delicious vibrations.

A noise. Rikki bolted up and covered Bernadette with the sheet expertly. Bernadette groaned at the loss. They couldn't see the small windowpane in the door from the bed, so Rikki snuck over to check.

"All clear." Rikki pulled the small clit vibrator back out of her pocket. "I'll keep my finger on the off button, just in case."

"Okay," Bernadette said as nervous arousal coursed through her body.

Rikki lay by her side again and held the vibrator in her hand. At Rikki's request, Bernadette placed her hand over Rikki's to guide her, and together they maneuvered the toy under the sheet.

Rikki turned it on and then off. "See? I'm on it."

Bernadette chuckled. "You're out of practice, baby." She moved the vibrator to her clit. "Now, you're on it."

Rikki smiled and flicked the vibrator back on. Bernadette's hips lifted as far as her broken body allowed. It was so intense. She moved Rikki's vibrator hand around her clit, enjoying the slow buildup of sensations. There had been so much pain and fogginess that she welcomed this release. Rikki moved the head to the opening of Bernadette's center. She circled the opening.

"So good," Bernadette moaned.

With Bernadette's guidance, Rikki moved back up to Bernadette's nub. "Oh, fuck, Rikki." Bernadette's hips undulated. "Right there, right there, right there." She held Rikki's hand and the vibrator tight against her clit. Her pussy pulsed in pre-orgasm. Oh, shit, it was one of those. Everything—time, sound, space—stopped. Until it didn't and roared back through her body. "Fuck!" she screamed. Rikki's hand clamped over her mouth, muffling the torrent of curse words. Rikki held the vibrator tight until they'd milked out every last pulsing spasm. Rikki turned off the vibrator and pocketed it.

"Holy mother of fuck me, Rikki," Bernadette gasped and let Rikki kiss her. Rikki settled down next to her, adjusting Bernadette's gown and the sheet, erasing the evidence. "I love you."

The door burst open, and the day nurse came in. "Your heart monitor is going crazy." She took in the scene before her and wordlessly adjusted something on the machine. "Ahh. I understand the sign on the door now."

"The what?" Bernadette asked.

The nurse retrieved the sign, and in Madison's unmistakable handwriting were the scrawled words 'Do Not Disturb.'

Bernadette pulled the covers over both their heads.

"Newlyweds," the nurse grumbled good naturedly and left them in blissful peace.

# Chapter 16
## Rikki

Rikki meandered around the tables in her coffee shop, pleased with the way her managers and the staff had handled things during her continued absences. The only reason she was there that Sunday morning was because Bernadette insisted. Yes, her girl could be quite the force when she wanted to be. It was no wonder Madison had thought her former Calculus teacher was a Domme.

Rikki looked up overhead. Every single one of the hanging Edison lights was working properly. Bernadette would be pleased. She sent a picture to her girl, hoping to brighten her morning. She also sent a picture of the plants framing the front picture window. Somebody had worked magic because they looked healthy and vibrant, not haggard and dying the way they usually did. She'd have to find out who to thank. And the customers certainly seemed happy that morning. That was probably the most important thing.

Rikki found herself gravitating toward Bernadette's favorite couch. She plopped down, keeping her promise that she wouldn't hole up in her office and lock the door.

"Hey, Boss," Marta said and sat in the chair to Rikki's left. "You wanted to see me?"

"Just to touch base," Rikki said. "You're a natural at this managing thing."

"Well, shit. Lydia and Mark have been amazing teachers, and the minions—"

Rikki chuckled. "You call my employees 'minions'?"

"They like it," Marta said. "Anyway, the minions have been amazingly patient with me. Even *they* have been schooling me."

"I appreciate you, my friend," Rikki said, surprised at the tears that popped up uninvited.

"She's going to be okay," Marta said gently. "Your business, too. You've been so good to everyone over the years, Boss. It's our turn to take care of you."

"I don't think I know how to be taken care of." Rikki wiped at her eyes, appalled that she was having such a weak moment in the middle of the shop.

"You've both been through a lot. It's okay to be human every once in a while."

Rikki laughed. "I hear that." She took a cleansing breath, blew it out, and then added, "They're teaching Bernadette how to transfer to a wheelchair this afternoon."

"Milestone day. I remember that day well with Shanice. It wasn't easy. She wanted to give up so many times, but I wouldn't let her. And hey," Marta smacked Rikki on the thigh, "why the hell are you even here? We've got this."

"Bernadette made me." Rikki knew the smile reached her eyes.

"You are so whipped!" Marta teased.

"Can you blame me?"

"Not at all." Marta leaned closer and said in a low tone, "You know, Boss, there are ways to, uh..." At Rikki's perplexed expression, Marta added, "In a wheelchair. Ways to be intimate."

Rikki's eyebrows shot to the sky. "I hadn't thought about that." What she didn't tell Marta was the many ways she and Bernadette had found to give each other pleasure undercover—pretty much literally under covers—since Bernadette had been in the rehabilitation facility. The fact that Bernadette wanted to use the clit vibrator to give Rikki pleasure was a pure testament to her loving and generous nature. Rikki leaned in closer. "Do tell. But, err, try to keep the personal details out if possible."

Marta gave a few suggestions in broad brush strokes, which got Rikki's mind whirling. Most of those things wouldn't be feasible in the rehab facility, but at home—absolutely! An odd thought struck her.

"Bernadette had that ramp built at the house for Shanice."

"We thought about that, too," Marta said. "Isn't it weird how shit like that happens? Shanice says it's all part of the energy flow. Karma or something."

Rikki nodded. Shanice had become highly spiritual since her own accident a year ago, and Marta went along with it. Asking a spiritual healer to sage Bernadette's house before she moved back in after the ex-girlfriend moved out was Shanice's idea. Who knows if it got rid of stale and unwanted energy? All Rikki knew was that she needed to get her little bee home as soon as practically possible. And right now, she needed to help her learn how to get in and out of a wheelchair.

"I need to go." Rikki stood up abruptly.

"Yes, you do," Marta said. "We're fine here. I've got Lydia right upstairs if I need anything. And you're just a phone call away. But Boss?"

"Yeah?"

"We're not going to call you."

"Humph," Rikki said, not quite knowing how to take that. With so much going on in her life, she decided that, yes, she needed to accept the help from her friends. Why was that so stinking hard for her? "Thank you," she said. "Now get back to work."

Marta laughed, and they hugged briefly. Rikki headed to the front counter to get two coffees. One of them would be decaf.

~~~

Rikki entered Bernadette's room quietly, just in case she was sleeping. She needn't have worried because Bernadette was awake and talking to Olga on her laptop. Even odder was that she was also sitting in a wheelchair with Shanice by her side.

"Hi, Miss Riri," Shanice whispered and then waved. She pointed excitedly to Bernadette's chair.

Rikki nodded and smiled, knowing that the smile didn't reach her eyes this time. She set Bernadette's coffee on the table near the laptop.

"Is that Rikki I see behind you?" Olga said from the computer screen.

"Hey, Olga," Rikki said succinctly.

"You look tired, dear."

Rikki shrugged. Her tiredness was understandable, right? What she couldn't understand, though, was why she had missed the milestone event.

"What's happening here?" Rikki said with more aggression than she'd meant to show.

Bernadette looked up at her sheepishly. Her expression spoke volumes. Things were happening that Rikki hadn't been privy to.

Bernadette opened her mouth to answer, but Olga blurted, "She's going to teach tomorrow. Remotely. With Dr. Wainwright's approval, that is."

"What do you mean?" Rikki said. "What's going on?" She did *not* appreciate being blindsided like this.

"He's ready to join the meeting, Bernadette," Olga said, ignoring Rikki's question.

"Okay." With a grunt of real effort, Bernadette leaned forward toward the laptop. She greeted her department chair, switched cameras, and proceeded to mimic teaching a math lesson of some kind. The free-standing camera captured the equations on a notepad. Her handwriting was a bit shaky, but it was legible.

Rikki motioned to Shanice that she would be stepping out during the demo. She bypassed her favorite restroom and headed out the facility's front door. The heat of the July afternoon hit her, but she barely noticed. She walked past Bernadette's Prius, the car she'd been driving because her Subaru was now in a heap at the junkyard. She walked past the first wing of the facility and increased her pace past the second. Her flats weren't exactly the best walking shoes, but it was all she had. She had no idea where she was going, but she walked until her legs ached and she was out of breath. She set her sights on a bench near the parking lot and plopped in a heap once she got there.

Shasti recommended that she get more exercise, so there you go. But that wasn't why she was walking, and she knew it. Oh, no. It was because she was positively furious and had to channel it somewhere. She didn't know where to direct her fury, which made it even more maddening.

"I've been there for everything. Ev-er-y-thing," she said, enunciating every syllable. "Why was I left out? The fucking wheelchair transfer? Teaching? When the fuck did that become part of the plan? Have I not been here every day and been part of every decision when she was unconscious and even when she was conscious? Haven't I been taking care of things, little bee?" She breathed in deeply as Shasti had coached her. She relaxed her shoulders like Bernadette always reminded her. She had a bag in her pocket, but she refused to need it. "Don't I get to be part of your successes, too? Why was I left out?" She looked to the sky and asked, "Mom? Aunt Tilda? What's happening? I don't understand."

Rikki knew she had issues with her need to control things, but she refused to believe *control* was the only concern at hand. "It's more than that," Rikki said, her heart breaking a little. "I wasn't allowed to be part of it. I wasn't invited."

She wiped the sweat from her forehead and refused to let any tears come. She was too hopping mad for that. She stood up, straightened her spine, and marched back into the facility. She stopped at her favorite restroom to splash her face and neck with cool water. Feeling somewhat refreshed, she headed back to Bernadette's room.

She wasn't prepared for the flurry of activity that greeted her when she entered.

"Is this Nicky?" a short, stout woman with badly dyed hair asked. Her nametag said *Sylvia, Head of Occupational Therapy*.

"Rikki." She did not extend her hand. She shot a glance at Bernadette in the wheelchair. She looked tired. Rikki's heart melted a little.

"Got it," Sylvia said. "Bernie was so excited to show you how good she is at transfers. Isn't that right, Kevin?" she asked the young therapy technician.

"Mm hmm," he said, sounding bored.

"She kept saying, 'Nicky will be so proud of me,' didn't you, Bernie?"

"Mm hmm," Bernadette said noncommittally, sounding like Kevin.

"Okay, Bernie, let's go. You've been in the chair for an hour and a half. Thirty minutes longer than intended. You must be exhausted."

Bernadette, or was it 'Bernie' now, nodded.

"Nicky, come over here and watch how we help. She'll do most of the work, but since she's non-weight bearing on that left arm and leg, we need to help that side."

Rikki didn't bother to correct the therapist about her name and instead focused on her girl. She didn't like Bernadette's color. Yes, her girl had overdone it.

Once Bernadette was back in bed and adjusted comfortably, Rikki thanked the therapists as they left. She kissed her girl on the forehead and then wheeled Shanice out to her new van. Shanice excitedly showed her the way she maneuvered the wheelchair onto the ramp, raised herself up and into the van, and then locked it into position to drive. The hand controls seemed simple enough, and Shanice said she'd gotten the hang of things pretty quickly. Rikki was glad for her independence and told her so.

Once back in the room, Rikki quietly made her way to the chair she had claimed as hers and sat down.

"I'm sorry," Bernadette said meekly.

"Oh, hey, baby." Rikki got up and stroked Bernadette's forehead. "I thought you were sleeping. How are you feeling?"

"Oh, God. Not good." She still looked pale. "I'm sorry I didn't tell you they changed the therapy to this morning. I wanted to surprise you when you got here."

"Yes, I was surprised."

"And not in a good way." Bernadette looked away. "I saw it in your eyes. I hurt your feelings, and that kills me." She patted the bed and scooted over. "Please lay with me. It's the only thing that makes me feel normal."

Rikki complied and adjusted herself to Bernadette's body. She lay her arm across Bernadette's middle possessively.

"I just wanted you to see me be good at it," Bernadette said. "I wanted to make you proud. I wanted to surprise you."

"I'm not fond of surprises. You know that."

They lay quiet for a moment, each probably remembering the last time Bernadette tried to surprise Rikki by opening and arranging her mail at the shop. It was an understatement to claim that Rikki had overreacted badly. She had almost lost her little bee because she'd been so paranoid about another round of identity theft.

"I am proud of you," Rikki said. "I'm not sure I would have the strength to go through what you've been dealing with. But I think there's something else going on with you, and I'm not sure what it is. What's with this whole thing about teaching tomorrow? Why didn't we discuss that together?"

"I'm sorry," Bernadette said and then lay quiet. Rikki thought she'd dozed off, but then Bernadette's thoughts came out in a torrent. "I don't want the University to think I'm a burden, that I'm not capable, that I can't hold my weight anymore, that I'm not good enough."

"And you don't want *me* to think you're a burden, either," Rikki said, understanding dawning on her. "You're not and never will be."

"I don't want Wainwright to give away Baxter's 8000-level courses to someone else because he thinks I'm not well or can't handle it after my accident. I wanted to show him that I could do it. That I'm competent."

"And you wanted to show me the same things?" It was a question this time.

"Yes."

"I want him to know that I'm smart enough to teach at that level. I want him to find value in me."

*And she wants* me *to find value in her as well.* Her little bee was hurting, both inside and out.

Rikki sat up and kissed her girl on the forehead. So much was going on inside her. "I value you, baby. You know that. I obviously need to tell you more often. You don't need to prove anything to me."

Bernadette shrugged.

"Oh, no, no, no, no, no," Rikki said, peppering Bernadette's forehead and hands with kisses. "I love my little bee the way she is. Please don't change her."

"I need to show everyone that I'm strong and can work hard and can be the best."

Be the best? The *best.* Did her girl feel she had something to prove? To Rikki? To her boss? When she played the piano that day at Jaleesa's, she was upset that it wasn't *perfect.* How in the world could Rikki make Bernadette understand that there was no such thing as *perfect*? How could she show her that *perfect* was a very subjective concept? And that striving for this perfection could be as debilitating as those broken bones she had.

All Rikki could do at the moment was reassure her girl that all was well between them. She did, however, need to address Bernadette's misconceptions. And maybe, just maybe, she'd take a look at her own misconceptions, too.

"I already committed to teaching tomorrow, Rikki," Bernadette said. "Can you be here with me?"

"It would be my honor to finally see Dr. Garneau teach." Rikki kissed her girl on the lips chastely. "I'd kiss you proper-like, but you always seem to compromise my virtue whenever I get in this bed with you."

Bernadette chuckled and pushed Rikki away half-heartedly.

"Naptime, *Bernie*?" Rikki hoped Bernadette would smile at the nickname and was rewarded with a sly grin.

"Yes, please, *Nicky*," Bernadette quipped.

*Yes, there's my little bee.* As they drifted off, Rikki made some tentative decisions about things going forward. One thing was for sure. It was time for her little bee to remember who her Dominant was.

# Chapter 17
## Bernadette

Bernadette knew this moment was coming. The moment when the party was over. Not that being laid up flat on her back with broken bones, unable to roll to either side, was a party, but the free pass for sweets and comfort foods was coming to an end.

"No. Absolutely not. No more of this shit." Rikki tossed the small snack pack pudding from Bernadette's breakfast tray to the counter near the door. "Someone else can have that. You will tell them you no longer want this crap on your tray. No muffins or Danish or whatever other BS they're trying to put in you."

Bernadette nodded without speaking and knew instantly that was a mistake. Would she ever learn? Rikki's face was suddenly inches from hers. "Do. You. Understand?"

Other people might witness their exchange and think Bernadette was being harassed or even abused. Quite the contrary. This was Rikki's love language. A little thrill went through Bernadette's body. "Yes, Ma'am," Bernadette said. "I should have told them at the start."

"Yes, you should have," Rikki said and stepped back. "And no more sodas or fruit punch. You'll ask for water or something without sugar."

"I will. Yes, Ma'am." Oh, God. Saying the words sent another thrill throughout her entire body. It made so little sense that Rikki's Dominance would both turn her on and settle her simultaneously. But this, exactly this, is what she'd signed up for. She hadn't realized how much she missed it in the long weeks she'd been recuperating. Was Rikki feeling the same way?

"And when you're teaching today, if you get too tired, you will stop and let those TAs take over. You said they were more than capable, right? Bianca and Eashon?"

144

"Yes, they're students in my new Foundations class, and apparently, they volunteered to help with Calculus."

"And?"

Bernadette wasn't sure what more Rikki wanted from her.

Rikki grabbed Bernadette's chin and lifted her head. It was so gentle that Bernadette barely felt the Dominance she craved. *The concussion. That must be it. She's being gentle in order to take care of me.* "And if you get tired?"

"Oh, yes, yes, Ma'am. I'll stop and let them take over."

Rikki bopped Bernadette's nose with her index finger. "Good girl."

"Rikki, oh, my God, please kiss me." Bernadette squirmed.

"What's this?" Rikki said softly. "Is my little bee turned on?"

Bernadette nodded.

"Is she wet? Ready to spread her legs for me?"

Bernadette's moan was her only answer.

"Not enough time, baby. But I think we have a nice clear window this afternoon after lunch. Tina's joining us for lunch, by the way, so you two can finally talk. And since the gang isn't coming until 6:00 for movie night, it looks like we have a nice block of time."

"Okay," Bernadette said. She could hear the dejected tone in her voice. The only thing she really heard was that Rikki wasn't going to kiss her.

"Aww," Rikki said. "Let me at least kiss those lips I married."

Bernadette threw both arms, even the broken one, around her lovely Domme's neck and pulled her tight. "I love you, Rikki," she said in between kisses. "My Domme," she murmured.

"Mmm," Rikki said. "I love you, too, Bernadette." Rikki moaned and then pulled out of the embrace. "You slay me. Every time."

"Good," Bernadette said with a mischievous grin. "I think it's time to get me dressed and in the wheelchair. I need to look over my notes."

They made quick work of the clothes. A bra was out of the question with the broken ribs, so a loose blue button-down shirt and a new day collar, a gift from Rikki, to match the shirt. Loose dark-colored shorts down below since the camera would only focus on her upper half. Bernadette thought it was a bit naughty teaching commando, but then she remembered that Victoria had her do just that while wearing skirts. Bernadette groaned. She wanted to forget the fact that she'd ever been with Victoria, even if it was only for a very short time. Victoria had written a nice note in the get-well card she'd sent, which was confusing. Bernadette wanted nothing more to do with the woman, but she was Rikki's long-time friend. She hoped Rikki hadn't asked Victoria to come by for movie night. She just didn't have the strength to pretend to be okay with it. She was supposed to forgive and forget. Unfortunately, both things seemed impossible to do right now.

The occupational therapy team came in and took her mind off Victoria as they manhandled her body into the wheelchair. They didn't let her or Rikki help much. That was frustrating because she wanted to practice the transfers on her own—well, she still had to have some help because of her stupid broken arm, but still. They left just as quickly as they came. Fine. Whatever.

A knock on the door signaled Madison's arrival. Madison asked if she could help since Shanice had a big project to finish for work and couldn't be there.

The setup for the class was seamless, and after a brief thank you to her students for being patient and another public thank you to the amazing TAs, Bernadette got into her lesson. She was not surprised when she saw Dr. Wainwright walk into the lecture hall after the class got started. Even though these were odd circumstances, she got lost in her work and completely forgot that she was in a wheelchair. She forgot she had a concussion and broken limbs. She forgot that the accident had almost taken her life and left Rikki a widow after four days of marriage. No, she didn't think about any of those things as she basked in the subject she loved so much. And it wasn't just the mathematics she'd missed; It was the interactions with the students, too. That was an interesting revelation. One she'd have to examine later.

"So, remember that the original function needs to be one-to-one or monotonic if it has a viable inverse. Limiting the domain, as we did with the sine function in example two, is one way to handle that." Bernadette snuck a peek at the students on her split screen. A hand had gone up. She consulted her seating chart that Madison had graciously fetched from her office. "Hold that thought, Zahair," she said. "I just need to finish mine before I forget. I'm sensing that trig is a bit of a stumbling block for us, so next time, we'll do a short review of trig functions, including the sixteen-point circle."

Bernadette laughed when the class of forty or so students groaned. "Aww, such babies. Seriously, that review will make the calculus easier. And that's what we want." She took a breath. God, she was tired. Beyond tired. "Umm, okay, Zahair, what was your question?"

"You answered it."

"I did? The trig stuff?"

He nodded.

"I'm a mind-reader now." The class chuckled good naturedly.

Another hand went up. "Megan?" Megan, yes, that was her name. She'd remembered from the last time. "Dr. Garneau, you should record these lectures and put them online. I know about a million Calc students that would watch them."

"That's a lot of Calc students," Bernadette said with a chuckle. "But I'll think about your suggestion. Thank you." And there was no way she would ever put herself out there like that. So open to criticism. No way.

She shivered. The stupid rehab room was cold. She breathed a small sigh of relief when two things happened—Wainwright left the lecture hall, and a sweater went around her shoulders. She looked up at Rikki and smiled. "Thank you," she mouthed.

"Is that your Boo?" Megan asked.

Bernadette smiled. She didn't usually share personal information, but these were extenuating circumstances. "Yes, this is my partner."

"Can we see her?" Megan asked. Nosy, that one.

Bernadette looked up at Rikki and shrugged, indicating it was up to her to lean down so her face was in the camera shot. Rikki lowered herself and smiled at the students. "I'm taking care of your teacher so she can get back to you as soon as possible," Rikki said.

A chorus of "Awws" went up in the room. Bernadette laughed when she heard a few students, female voices included, say, "She's hot" and "Dr. G scored."

Rikki laughed and moved out of camera range with a shake of her head. Behind the camera, Madison lifted a piece of paper with the number five written on it. That meant there were five minutes left to the class period.

"Okay, let's wrap things up here. Again, thank you for being patient with me. And thank you for the beautiful and uplifting notes on the 'Fans of Dr. Garneau' webpage. Your messages elevated me at a time when I needed them the most. Thank you."

"We love you, Dr. G," someone called. "Heal quicker," someone else quipped, causing laughter. "We can't learn without you," another said. "Your girlfriend is hot," came another.

"I agree," Bernadette said to the last one and then laughed. "Umm, let's see. Oh! Your problem sets were delivered to me here by courier, and I'll get them back to you as soon as I can. Meanwhile, Bianca and Eashon will fill you in on their office hours."

Bianca and Eashon spoke to the class, and then Bernadette dismissed the students. As prearranged, the TAs stayed behind.

"You must be exhausted," Bianca said as she stepped in front of the classroom camera.

"I am, but I've been told there's a nap waiting for me somewhere around here."

Bianca laughed and told Bernadette that they had everything handled on their end, but they'd need a copy of next week's unit test.

Bernadette said she'd send them a copy later today or sometime tomorrow. Thank God she was organized and already had it written. "How has the Foundations class been going?" Bernadette asked.

"Oh, please, Dr. Garneau," Eashon broke in and stepped into the range of the camera. "You're the only one that knows how to teach around here. We had to start up the study group again."

"But we're ecstatic that you'll be back tomorrow," Bianca added. "And, um, Eashon and Marty and I want to ask you something."

"Oh?"

A pair of firm hands came to rest on her shoulders. It was Rikki's way of telling her it was time to power down.

"With Professor Baxter retiring, we need a dissertation adviser. We were hoping you could be ours. I mean, we have to run our ideas by you individually, of course, and put in the formal request and all of that, but—"

"I would love to do it." The hands on her shoulders squeezed tightly. "But I'm not one hundred percent yet. I have to be sure I don't overdo things." The grip on her shoulders relaxed. Taking on all of those 8000-level courses she was sure to inherit from Baxter would take up a lot of her free time. At least she'd get to ditch the Calculus classes. Mentoring doctoral candidates was something she had always wanted to do, too, but no one had ever asked her. Probably because they thought she was only a professor of calculus to undergraduates. To be able to dig into mathematical theories and help further the subject she loved by helping others contribute, yes, that was the ticket. And maybe she could find time to write her own articles. Yes, yes. That's what she always wanted.

"Well, thanks for thinking about it, Dr. Garneau," Bianca said. "I'll see you tomorrow, this time as a student. Oh, hey, that courier you mentioned. She wouldn't be sitting in that room with you, would she?"

Madison's face lit up. "Can I?" She gestured toward the camera.

Bernadette nodded and pushed the wheelchair back using her one good leg.

"There she is," Bianca gushed. "Hey, nugget!"

Bernadette exchanged a confused glance with Rikki.

"Hi, Miss Bianca," Madison said and waved frantically.

Uh, oh. Another one of Madison's crushes was manifesting right before their eyes.

"How's Thomas doing?" Bianca asked.

"She's awesome. She likes those disgusting vegetables you suggested. Like collard greens and kale."

"Excellent. You are the best box turtle fosterer this side of the Mississippi."

Madison squirmed at the praise.

"That one there," Bianca said to Bernadette. "That nugget? She sat outside your office door in between her classes. What was it, *mi tesora*? The days you had Pharmacology and Philosophy?"

"You remembered."

"Of course I did." Bianca looked over at Bernadette and said, "She's been your little ambassador, telling people office hours were now with Eashon and me in the graduate lounge for Calculus and with Dr. Wainwright for Foundations. She even hung up a sign."

"Thank you, Madison," Bernadette said. "Your signs are always so helpful." The hands were back on her shoulders and pressing hard. "Okay, listen, I'm fading here." She thanked Bianca and Eashon for their help and closed the group meeting window after saying their goodbyes. She then turned to thank Madison.

"You are one special little angel, kiddo," Bernadette said. "I think my mother sent you here from heaven just to help me."

For once, Madison was quiet. Until she wasn't. "Thank you, Professor. I thought the same about you. Except my mother is still here. Well, in Columbus. Mistress is helping me understand that maybe I'm *not* stupid and maybe I'm *not* worthless." She clamped her lips together, obviously trying not to cry. Rikki pulled Madison into a hug and soothed her with positive affirmations. Bernadette reached her good arm around and joined the hug.

After a few moments, Rikki asked gently, "Are you okay to drive, Madison?"

Madison nodded and gathered her belongings, which once again had become spread out on every surface in the room. Keys, water bottle, Chapstick, mints, a second brand of mints, phone, and a whole array of things that had been stuffed in her pockets. As Rikki was leaving to walk Madison out to her car, she said to Madison, "You all set for this evening? You've got the goods?"

Bernadette was too tired to wonder what the heck those two were up to. She only had the strength to power down the electronics and then wheel over to the bed. She wanted to crawl in it so badly, but she couldn't. Everything hurt. She had passed on the meds that morning because she needed to be clear-headed to teach the class, but it was painfully obvious that she still needed them. She didn't have the strength or the healed bones to manage getting into the bed on her own, so she hit the call button attached to her bed, hoping someone would come soon. Sometimes it took them forever to get to her room, which really sucked when she had to go to the bathroom. She'd learned to hit the button when the first inkling of need hit her. But sometimes, they'd put her on the bedpan, and she couldn't go. Not out of shyness or anything. She'd long gotten over that for survival. Apparently, inactivity combined with all the medications could cause constipation. Great. Another wonderful thing to deal with. Broken bones, concussion, cuts, and bruises— those weren't enough. Well, thank you so very much. And worst of all, Rikki had started asking her for the pee and poop report every morning and pushing more and more water on her. Ugh.

Rikki came back just as one of the morning nurses came in. Together, they helped Bernadette onto the toilet, and even though she tried and tried, she still couldn't do her business. It was so damn frustrating, but fuck it, she was too tired to care. She wanted her bed. The nurse supervised while Rikki helped her off the toilet and back into the wheelchair. Bernadette's heart swelled. If Rikki could do this on her own, then she was one major step closer to going home. Rikki got her back in the bed without any help or correction from the nurse. The nurse then administered the pain meds Bernadette desperately needed. One was a muscle relaxer. She wasn't sure what the others were. Rikki snuggled up to her to nap. In what seemed like no time, Rikki was shaking her shoulder to wake her up.

"Tina's here, baby," Rikki said softly.

"Mmm?" Bernadette opened her eyes, one at a time. She yawned so big that both Rikki and Tina chuckled. "Mmm, hi, Tina," she said sleepily. Her senses were waking up but slowly. "That smells good. You brought lunch?"

"Indeed," Tina said. "Turkey club courtesy of the Indigo Café. Are you awake enough to eat?"

Bernadette was groggy, that was for sure, but she enlisted Rikki's help in sitting up in the bed to eat. She didn't have the strength or energy to attempt to get back in the wheelchair.

"Thank you," Bernadette said and reached for Tina's hand. "That was a lot of effort."

"You're worth it." Tina's smile was genuine.

Bernadette felt her cheeks get warm.

"Miss Rikki," Tina said, "my parents wanted me to tell you that they got your flowers and the restaurant gift cards. They said that totally wasn't necessary, but they sent their thanks."

"That doesn't even begin to cover the enormous thanks I owe them for letting me stay at their house near the hospital. If I had to commute every day to see my baby, I would have lost it."

"We all understand," Tina said. She turned toward Bernadette. "They and I want an update on our little patient here. Tell me how you're doing. Are you in much pain? Are you managing your pain meds?" There was an urgent edge to her voice that confused Bernadette.

"She weaned off the narcotic meds early on," Rikki answered quickly. "She's only on a couple of mild pain relievers now."

Tina visibly relaxed, which made Bernadette relax as well. "And I'm trying like hell to get off those other two," Bernadette said in reassurance. Maybe there was a history of narcotics abuse in Tina's family. She'd ask Rikki later. Not that it was any of her business.

"Do you remember what happened?" Tina placed a comforting hand on Bernadette's forearm.

Bernadette answered as honestly as she could and was surprised when Tina started crying.

"I'm sorry, Bernadette," Tina said. "It's my fault. If I hadn't asked you to go to that stupid cooking class, none of this would have happened." Tina hid her face in her hands.

"That's the silliest thing I've ever heard," Bernadette said.

"What do you mean?"

"Tina, it was an accident. It could have happened anywhere. Anytime." Bernadette reached for Tina's hand and held it. "C'mon. Please don't blame yourself. I don't. I never even thought that once. Rikki doesn't either."

"Tina," Rikki said, "No one, least of all us, blames you for anything. We appreciate that you've been hurting, too. We all have. But she's going to be all right. Aren't you, baby?"

Bernadette nodded. "Mm hmm. With the love and support from all of you guys, I can't miss."

"Bernadette and I have this saying," Rikki said. "'From this point, forward.' We can't keep going back over the woulda, coulda, shouldas. It's counter-productive, gets us nowhere, and can't change anything. We're not time travelers. So, my girl and I would like you to join us here, right now, in helping her get better," she paused for a moment and then repeated, "from this point forward."

"I will," Tina said, wiping at her tears. "Thank you for hearing me."

Rikki just smiled and then opened her sandwich, clearing the way for Bernadette and Tina to get to know each other better.

They made small talk while they ate, chit-chatting about softball and the goings-on in the Jaleesa-Tina household. When they were pretty much finished eating, Rikki stood up. "I can vacate if you wish. I have a good book on my e-reader and am happy to give you two the room."

Tina spoke first. "I'd like you to stay, Miss Rikki. If it's okay with Bernadette."

"Stay, baby," Bernadette said.

Rikki did stay but moved her chair back and out of the way.

"Tina, I…" Bernadette started, but she wasn't sure what to say. How do you, on the one hand, apologize for screwing someone's girlfriend and, on the other hand, ask permission to keep doing it?

Tina took over. "Oh, honey, I know that Rikki arranged to meet today because she wants us to clear the air about Jaleesa." She sat taller and lifted her chin. She exuded confidence in almost everything she did, so it was kind of surprising that she was a submissive. On the day of the team barbecue at their house, it was obvious that Tina was the one who ran the household. "I understand why you might feel you need to talk to me about Jaleesa, and I really appreciate your concern for my well-being. Let me be very clear when I tell you this. Bernadette, I have absolutely no issues with Jaleesa seeing you for sex and affection. You're a beautiful, attractive woman with the spirit of a saint."

Bernadette groaned. Why could she never take a compliment? "Thank you."

"Now," Tina continued, "Jaleesa and I have an understanding that she's never broken. I expect her to come home to me every night, to sleep in our bed with me. You know I mean actual catching some z's, right?"

"Yes, I get the picture."

"I also expect her to tell me where she's going and who she's seeing. If she's playing with Dana or Kari in their rooms or the dungeon, that's fine. We all give them their privacy, but she has to get up when they're done, wash up, and come back to me."

"What about Harriet?" Bernadette asked.

"She doesn't have sex with Harriet. Basically, just impact and aftercare."

"DeShawn? He's the only male in your house. Well, except for Bailey."

"Bailey's a goofball," Tina said with obvious affection. "He doesn't live with us and probably won't. We just do pet play together—non-sexual pet play. I know it seems weird—BDSM without sex, but it helps him decompress and destress. It helps me, too, I suppose. I enjoy helping him that way."

"That kind of makes you a switch, doesn't it?"

"Yeah, I guess so," Tina said. "Now, DeShawn? He's a gay man. Jaleesa took him in when he wasn't thriving over with Seamus's clan. They are kind of rough over there. Humiliation is a big thing for Seamus, but DeShawn is such a gentle soul. Jaleesa takes care of him. She's not bisexual, and neither is he, but they somehow manage. I think he just needed a firm but gentle hand and the occasional release, if you know what I mean. I think she cages him often."

"You've been in the cage, too, haven't you?"

Tina laughed. "Oh, you thought I meant the human cage. Uh, yes, she cages me sometimes when I've messed up. Usually, because I run my mouth, but I accept her discipline, just like you accept Miss Rikki's, I'm sure." She patted Bernadette on the arm and clarified, "I meant she cages his privates so that erections are painful, and since she's in charge of those, he can't have one without her approval."

Bernadette thought that sounded kind of harsh but didn't say so. She may not care for or like someone else's kinks, but she knew enough not to judge. "I feel so bad that we haven't talked about this before," Bernadette said. "I mean, I obviously trusted Rikki and Miss Jaleesa when they implied that our playtimes were okay with you, but it kept eating at me."

"Polyamory is unconventional, for sure," Tina said. "And there are times when I'd rather she cuddles with me while we watch a movie or something instead of going to the others, but I get what I need. Occasionally, she supervises my mandated self-care routine. She says it's a good physical release for me. I suppose so." Tina gathered the wrappers from the to-go meal and stuffed them in the big bag. "Miss Rikki told you that I'm a *romantic* ace, right? I want the cuddles, kisses, and affectionate pats on the ass. I'm just not that interested in sex. Ask me if I'd rather have a turkey club from the Indigo Café or have sex, and I'm pretty much asking for the mayo and a side of chips."

Bernadette chuckled. She squeezed Tina's hand. "You are delightfully one of a kind, Tina. You're so generous with your thinking and with your time. You two make an amazing couple."

"I think so, too," Tina said. "I like to think that I ground her in some ways. Like in a good way, not a time-out way."

Rikki nodded her agreement but stayed silent otherwise.

"What we have works," Tina continued, "so please don't think you're interfering. She tells me everything. Oh, not *everything* everything." Tina laughed. "The look on your face."

"This is new for me," Bernadette said meekly. "All of it."

"Yeah, understandable," Tina said. "Hey, listen, I should get going. I'm taking Kari to her first piano lesson this afternoon." She winked and then stood up. "She's even going willingly. Imagine that."

"Miracles do happen," Bernadette said.

"We'll be back later for the movie. And just so you aren't weirded out, Jaleesa informed me that Dana is her official date tonight. Dana has been, what's the word, *needy*, I guess. So, I encouraged Jaleesa to make special time for her. And, just so you know, those two like to kiss a lot, especially in public, so be ready for those shenanigans."

"I appreciate the heads up," Bernadette said. She tried to sit up as Tina leaned down for a hug, but her ribs protested.

"Get some rest, honey," Tina said. "And when you're ready, we'll have our own cooking classes, okay? Just you and me. For once, you can be the student."

"I would love that. Thank you." Bernadette lay back down. She closed her eyes for a moment. She was so tired.

"I would love that, too," Rikki said. They spent another five minutes saying their goodbyes until Rikki finally said to Tina, "Here, let me walk you to your car."

The only thing Bernadette could do was close her eyes again and wait for Rikki to come back. It wasn't like she could get up and go for a walk or anything.

When Rikki returned, she closed the door, walked to the bedside, and cupped Bernadette's chin. "Are you mine?"

"Yes," Bernadette croaked out, cleared her throat, and tried again. "Yes, Rikki. I'm yours. You're my Domme."

"Good." Rikki leaned down and kissed Bernadette's mouth with a passion that spoke of promises and unwavering commitment.

# Chapter 18
## Rikki

Without a word, Rikki moved away from Bernadette's bed and closed the blinds. She picked up a bag, reached in, and pulled out a box with Bernadette's diamond engagement ring. "That collar you're wearing and this ring you'll wear once we get home are public articles of possession. *My* possession. They send a message to you and to everyone else that you belong to me." She tucked the ring safely into the outer pocket of the bag. "And when we exchange rings in the fall, I will wear your ring, symbolizing your possession of me."

"I get to possess you, too?" Bernadette sounded surprised.

"Indeed," Rikki said. She reached back into the bag and pulled out a dozen or so clothespins. "All of these will be used on your body this afternoon because I want that. These items are also reminders that you belong to me, and I can do with you as I please. But, as always, little bee, you have the right to say 'no' by using your safe words." Rikki bopped her girl softly on the nose with a fingertip. "Of course, if you literally say the word 'no,' I'll stop and check in anyway."

"Thank you, Rikki."

Ahh, yes, that was her girl. Always eager to please. "You like being appreciated, don't you?"

"Umm, I guess."

"Everyone does." Rikki commanded her to pull her hospital gown up, breasts exposed. Rikki leaned down and kissed the breast farthest from her, luxuriating with the soft flesh. One of Bernadette's hands wound through Rikki's hair. She didn't apply pressure. No, it was the equivalent of petting or saying thank you for paying attention to me and for loving me. Rikki was glad to oblige. She pulled back and blew softly on the nipple, hardening it while visible shivers bumped along Bernadette's skin. A clothespin, designed to give the perfect tension, hovered near the distended nipple. Anticipation was sexy. Anticipation was foreplay. The clip latched on, causing a deep intake of breath from the woman on the bed. "Yes, yes. That's my girl." Rikki stroked her lover's forehead. "Take the pain I offer you."

"Mmm." Bernadette's sigh was part moan.

When her breathing evened out some, Rikki said, "I saw your joy this morning, working with your students. They appreciate you." *You need to be needed, don't you?*

"Mm hmm," was apparently all Bernadette could say as Rikki gave her other breast the same treatment.

Rikki popped the clip on the nipple and watched Bernadette writhe in the pain-to-pleasure cycle. A deep need grew in her own core. One of possession certainly, but it wasn't just that. The passion she felt might also be described as compassion. The woman lying below her had been through something no one should have to experience. She was strong and fighting the good fight, but she needed to feel more than her injuries and brokenness every day. Rikki wanted Bernadette to feel alive and to experience some much-needed release.

Several more clips bit into each breast, and then the rest left a trail down Bernadette's body. "My girl is wet for me," Rikki said, dipping a finger into Bernadette's center. Oh, how Rikki wished she could put on a strap-on and enter her girl slowly. Slow strokes at first to get into a nice calming rhythm, faster yet as friction fired up nerve endings, but no, no, no. They couldn't do that. Rikki reined in her thoughts. They were arousing her too much. This was all about Bernadette. The only relief Rikki would get was knowing that she'd helped her little bee.

Two fingers now dipped inside, and Bernadette squirmed. Rikki reached up and flicked the clothespins one by one as she pumped her fingers. She snickered at Bernadette's frustrated groans. *In good time, little bee. In good time.* They actually didn't have the luxury of time, but Rikki also didn't want to rush. No, she had a reason for what she did next.

She reached into her bag and pulled out three items. Bernadette's eyes grew big.

"Baby," Bernadette said, fear in her voice, "I'm not cleaned out."

"I'm aware. Now, hush." Rikki grinned as Bernadette clamped her lips tightly together.

Rikki donned disposable gloves. She placed a towel-covered pillow, the small pillow permanently borrowed from the ICU at the hospital, and slid it underneath Bernadette's bottom. Ahh, yes, much better access. She lubed up Bernadette's rosebud and inserted one then two fingers. She hoped no one would decide to check on Bernadette at this moment because it would be hard to cover her quickly.

"My baby loves all things anal," Rikki said, getting her girl ready for the plug laying on the sheet.

"Been so long." Bernadette's words were breathy. Rikki made them more so by flicking a few clips.

Rikki pulled her fingers out and applied a generous amount of lube to the plug, the smallest one in Bernadette's arsenal, and twisted it at her entrance. "Relax, my love. Relax. You will like this."

"I'm not cl—"

"Hush. I know. I'm fine with it." Rikki pushed with a twist and slowly gained ground on the resisting knot of muscles. Once the plug was fully inserted, Bernadette sighed one of the most blissful sighs Rikki had ever heard. Excellent, that was what Rikki was after.

Rikki leaned down and gave Bernadette's clit a sloppy wet suck. Just one. Bernadette groaned at the betrayal. Rikki just laughed, took off the gloves, and flicked the clothespins again before taking them off one at a time. Watching Bernadette writhe in sensation as the blood flowed back to those spots was priceless. She wanted this relief for her girl. Bernadette would get her release for sure. Rikki wasn't that sadistic, but the release wouldn't be right now.

Rikki rubbed the clip marks, knowing these marks on Bernadette's body were temporary. In a bit, she would add a few longer-lasting marks of possession. She pulled Bernadette's gown down, covering her body, and then pulled the sheet up. After a quick wash of her hands, she leaned down and kissed her girl's forehead. "I'll be back in a few minutes."

"Oh, God, Rikki," Bernadette cried. "You're just leaving me like this? The plug. What if—"

Rikki moved so quickly that it shut Bernadette up. "Did I ask you to question me?"

"N-no. No, Ma'am."

"I'll be back in a few." And with that, Rikki left the room without a backward glance. Once she was in the hallway, she grinned. There was a lot of trust between them at this point, but Rikki liked it when Bernadette questioned her. They had made progress in this area. Bernadette had been a far-side-of-the-pendulum submissive when they first met, falling to her knees on their first date. Well, fine. Rikki told her to get on her knees, but everything about their first official interactions screamed Bernadette's submission. No, it was good that Bernadette questioned things now instead of blindly accepting them. Even professors of mathematics could have moments of growth.

Rikki stopped at the nurses' station and asked one of the aides for a cup of ice water to be delivered to her girl. And, as if an afterthought, she asked for a cup of ice, just ice, for herself. That done, she headed to her favorite restroom and relieved her bladder. She washed up and then sat on the bench. She remembered how Shasti helped her manage her panic attack that day everyone came to see Bernadette. That was one week ago to the day. Shasti had always been there for her in times of need. When Aunt Tilda had the stroke and then passed. When Eileen stole her identity and wiped out her bank accounts. When Victoria mistreated Bernadette. And now, during this whole car accident thing. So, asking Shasti to be her best man or maid of honor or whatever they would call it was the absolute right thing to do. Bernadette had agreed to the choice and was also one hundred percent sure of her own pick, too. Rikki had already asked Shasti, who gave a resounding, "Yes!" They'd ask Bernadette's pick after the movie. Or maybe before.

Rikki checked her watch. Nah, a few more minutes. She opened the e-reader app on her phone and found the book Madison had loaned her. It was about a bunch of billionaire lesbians and their submissives. "I bet billionaires have problems just like the rest of us," Rikki murmured and read a few pages.

Another check of her watch told her it was time to head back.

She entered Bernadette's room to see her girl's face flushed red.

"Are you okay, little bee?"

"Kelly came in here," Bernadette whispered in hushed tones. "She asked me if I needed the bedpan. Oh, my God, Rikki, why did you leave me?"

"Did you use the bedpan?"

"What? No!"

Rikki shrugged like it was no big deal, like her girl didn't have a big ole butt plug stuffed inside her for the aide to see. "You got your water, I see."

"I didn't ask for it."

"I did."

Bernadette's sharp intake of breath told Rikki that Bernadette had caught on. "You sent her in here, didn't you?" Her tone was pure accusation.

"I can neither confirm nor deny that," Rikki said calmly and held the straw to Bernadette's lips. "Drink." Bernadette drank.

"And she brought ice for you."

"Mm hmm." Rikki took the lid off the Styrofoam cup of ice and reached in. She pulled a cube out and grinned at Bernadette's dawning comprehension.

Rikki ran the ice cube across Bernadette's closed lips and grinned wider when Bernadette licked the melted water off. She loved intimate moments like this. She yanked the sheet off her girl.

"Lift your gown for me."

Using both hands, Bernadette reached down and pulled the gown up her body. A fresh cube lazily traced its way over Bernadette's now-exposed breasts, avoiding the nipples. The melted ice water ran down Bernadette's sides and onto the sheet. It could be avoided, but it wasn't a concern for Rikki at the moment. Bernadette squirmed, knowing what was coming.

A fresh cube. An already erect nipple. A perfect match. When contact was made, Bernadette's low moan and tightening stomach told Rikki all she needed to know. The second nipple received the same treatment. Rikki's lips replaced the ice as she sucked the soft flesh of Bernadette's breasts, leaving ownership marks. The hickeys would fade, yes, but Bernadette would have these marks as a reminder of who owned her. Who owned her body. Bernadette would get comfort seeing them later. What Bernadette would say to the aides at her next sponge bath? No, Rikki wasn't concerned with that.

Ice traveled down Bernadette's torso, stomach muscles clenching as the ice moved. The meandering glacier traveled lower and lower. Once that cube was completely melted, Rikki used her hands to stroke and massage Bernadette's stomach and lower abdomen.

"Baby, c'mon," Bernadette pleaded. "Please, I need you lower. I need release." Bernadette's good leg moved away from the bad, opening herself up in invitation.

Rikki said nothing but leaned over and kissed the cast encasing one of her girl's broken parts. A fresh cube traced a path over Bernadette's mound. Another was fetched to run a route down and around her nether lips, outer first, then inner. The ice melted quickly in this region. Another was fetched and tucked inside, only to melt practically instantly. The towel underneath her soaked up the cold water.

Rikki's tongue traced the path her ice cubes had taken, building up more tension in her girl's body. She opened Bernadette's legs wider and sucked the tender skin of her inner thighs, leaving more visible marks of ownership there. She kissed her way back up and stopped at Bernadette's clit to lay a chaste kiss on top. Virtuousness was not the order of the day, so she forked her fingers to spread the folds away from Bernadette's growing nub. Rikki flicked the top with the tip of her tongue. Two hands grabbed Rikki's head but didn't push down. They didn't insist. They knew.

Rikki gave her full attention to the bundle of nerves, sucking and licking and flicking. When Bernadette's breathing changed, Rikki stopped all movement. Bernadette groaned her dismay. Rikki reached under Bernadette's leg for the lube she'd stashed there and squirted an overly generous amount around the butt plug. She twisted it. Bernadette's melting moan was reward enough, but Rikki didn't stop. She pulled the plug out to its zenith, twisted it, and then shoved it back in. Bernadette's pelvis lifted. Her good leg moved farther away, inviting Rikki in.

Rikki maneuvered the plug twice more and then wiped her hands on the towel underneath Bernadette. Using the other hand, she snaked out a now-melting ice cube from the cup and ran it around Bernadette's clit, slowly at first and then faster. She held the cube directly on top while Bernadette writhed beneath her, senses overloading.

Time to do it. Rikki tucked the almost melted cube into Bernadette's center and then shoved a clean, dry washcloth in Bernadette's hand. She placed it over Bernadette's mouth.

"Bite on this baby. It's a self-inflicted gag."

"Okay," Bernadette said and did as she was told.

Rikki speed-kissed her way back down Bernadette's body and then rubbed Bernadette's clit with her fingers. "Cum for me, baby. Cum now. You've earned this. Such a good girl." Rikki peppered her with encouragement, although she was sure Bernadette didn't need any. Bernadette arched her pelvis, held her breath, and then convulsed in orgasm. Her body turned to the side slightly as her hips bucked.

Bernadette ripped the cloth out of her mouth and pulled Rikki to her. The kiss was so passionate that Rikki's own body spiked with arousal. She was glad she could do this for her girl.

Bernadette pulled away, murmuring, "Rikki." Just the one word. It was a one-word statement of gratitude, love, and devotion.

Rikki kissed her girl's forehead and held her hand until her breathing evened out. She waited a moment more for the long sigh of contentment she knew would come. When it did, she reached below and gently pulled out the plug. She wrapped it in the towel and cleaned up her girl as best she could with a fresh washcloth and towel she'd had at the ready. She shoved everything deep into the hamper and then cleaned off the plug and the clips in the room's private bathroom.

"Rikki," came an urgent plea. "I have to go."

"What, baby?" Rikki asked, rushing out. "Go where?" But she knew. It was what she had hoped for. She shoved the plug and clips back into the bag and tossed it on her chair.

"I have to, you know, go to the bathroom."

Yes! Mission accomplished. "Let's do it."

Bernadette was a bit shaky, but Rikki managed to get her into the wheelchair fairly seamlessly and then on to the toilet. She shut the door so Bernadette would have privacy but chuckled when Bernadette groaned in much needed relief.

This was married life. For better or for worse. She'd take it.

# Chapter 19
## Bernadette

A second nap followed the mind- and colon-blowing orgasm, and Bernadette woke refreshed and ready for company. She didn't let on that she was awake so she could take a private moment and take in all that was Rikki. How had she gotten so lucky? This beautiful woman loved her so much. See? There was a reason she had gotten stuck teaching Calculus to first-year students for so long. She had to wait for Madison to be her student. It was a divine intervention. But she was more than ready to move on to the higher-level courses.

"Oh, hey," Rikki said, putting her phone down.

"Hi," Bernadette said, still floating from afterglow and her second nap of the day. "I love you, Mrs. Carmichael."

"And I love you, Dr. Carmichael." Rikki got up and kissed Bernadette's forehead. "Feeling better?"

Bernadette rolled her eyes. "Yes."

There was a knock on the door. "You ready for company?" Rikki asked. "Do you have to go to the bathroom or anything?"

"I'm fine, and yes, I'm ready."

Rikki opened the door, and Miss Shasti came in first.

"There she is." Miss Shasti had such a strong, no-nonsense, confident way about her. All the Dommes in Bernadette's life did. Jaleesa and Marta, too. Even Victoria. It was something innate in their makeup. "You have great color in your cheeks, dear." Shasti got right up in Bernadette's space and put the back of her hand on Bernadette's forehead. "Very good. And how is the leg? The staples, I mean."

"I would like them out, thank you."

Miss Shasti lifted the sheet and made a quick check of the bandage. She grunted in satisfaction. "Getting itchy?"

"Sometimes."

"Do not, whatever you do, scratch or sneak peeks at them. That's how you introduce infection."

"Thanks, Miss Shasti," Bernadette said. "Where's kiddo?"

"She's right here." Shasti turned toward the door. "C'mon in, peanut."

Madison walked in carrying a large box. The turtle. It had to be. Bernadette was about to greet Thomas when the box meowed. Her eyes grew wide.

"What did you bring?" Bernadette looked from Madison to Rikki to Miss Shasti and back to Madison.

Madison, uncharacteristically, still hadn't said a word and put the box on the bottom of Bernadette's bed. She carefully opened the top, reached in, and pulled out a fluffy black and white kitten.

"Aww," Bernadette gushed. She made grabby hands toward the kitten. "May I hold her?"

"Yes," Madison said and handed the squirming bundle of fur toward Bernadette.

"You are precious," Bernadette said to the kitten. She placed the furball on her chest and scritched her behind the ears. "Come see her, Rikki." Before Rikki could get close, a second kitten with similar coloring was placed on Bernadette's bed. "Two? Are you kidding me?" Bernadette placed the second kitten next to the first, and the purr storm that erupted made them all chuckle.

"Both girls?" Rikki asked.

"Yes, you can tell by the—"

"We know," Rikki interrupted. "You did good, kid."

"Thank you, Miss Rikki. I'm sorry I forgot to greet you."

"No worries," Rikki said. "Much more important things are happening here." She gestured toward Bernadette.

"Come, Rikki, pet them," Bernadette said urgently. "Aren't they cute?" The kittens were nuzzling into Bernadette's neck, probably looking for warmth. She pulled her sheet tightly around them in the crook of her good arm. Rikki petted Bernadette's face before reaching down to pet the purring wonders.

"Madison," Bernadette said, "you moved up to fostering kittens?"

Madison nodded and then shot a look at Rikki.

Bernadette didn't know what to make of the exchange, but she hoped everything was okay in Madison's world.

"Baby," Rikki said, "these little guys—"

"Girls," Madison interrupted.

"Madison Kim," Miss Shasti reprimanded.

"Shoot. I'm sorry for interrupting you, Miss Rikki."

"This is a special day, so it's okay," Rikki said. "Please be mindful in the future."

"Yes, Ma'am."

"These little *girls*," Rikki continued, "are yours if you want them. I am one hundred percent on board."

"To keep?" Bernadette clutched the kittens tighter. "Oh, Rikki. Yes, yes, yes. Are you sure?"

Rikki nodded.

"Thank you, baby. And thank *you*, Madison. This is so sweet. What are their names?"

"I didn't name them. I figured you and Miss Rikki would do that." Madison's already pink cheeks turned even brighter. "I'll foster them until you come home, and we get a plan."

"Sounds like something, Miss Shasti would say."

"She did." Madison reached for Miss Shasti's hand.

"Sounds like you all have this worked out," Bernadette said and looked up with gratitude at Rikki. "So, yes, we'll take them. I need to figure out names, don't I." She picked up the fuzzier one, but nothing came to her. "I have to see their little personalities come out before I can name them."

"Sounds good, baby," Rikki said.

Another knock on the door sent Rikki over to answer it. Tina entered first, carrying a crockpot of something. Oh, wow, was that real food? Kari was next, followed by Jaleesa holding hands with Dana. Dana was positively glowing. They were so cute together. It was fascinating how love and attention brought out a glow in a person. People must see that in her whenever she held Rikki's hand.

Marta and Shanice entered next, and the room got loud with joyful greetings and excited conversations. Everyone petted the kittens, who mostly slept tucked in Bernadette's arms. She wondered if Madison had brought food or a litter box for the babies. She must have. Miss Shasti wouldn't let details like that be overlooked.

"Rikki," Bernadette said softly to the woman who wouldn't leave her side, "is that everyone?"

"Mm hmm," Rikki said. "Why? Were you expecting someone else?"

Bernadette shook her head so fast that Rikki narrowed her eyes. "Tell me."

Bernadette groaned. "I just, um, wasn't sure if you'd invited Victoria and Alyssa."

"I did not." And that was it. No further explanation and no further inquiry as to why Bernadette had asked. Rikki must know. She must understand.

Bernadette found herself relaxing. She hadn't realized how much the thought of their presence, well, just Victoria's, was a source of anxiety. Pretending to have forgiven Victoria would have taken more energy than she knew how to give at the moment.

"Hey, Bernadette," Tina called, "how much chili would you like?" She held a ladle over the crockpot. Bernadette indicated a small amount with her fingers. "You got it."

Kari delivered the meal and waited while Bernadette moved the kittens to her lap and adjusted the bed into a semi-sitting position, as much as she could tolerate anyway.

"I had my first piano lesson today, Miss Bernadette," Kari said, her voice excited. "My teacher is a college student, and she's younger than me, but she's pretty—"

"Pretty, huh?"

"Yes," Kari said, lowering her voice. "She sits up so properly, it's funny. She has these soulful eyes that suck you right in. And her skin is smooth. Her color is, like, somewhere between Jaleesa's lighter tone and Dana's darker."

"Nice. What'd you learn?" Bernadette took a small spoonful of the chili. "Oh my God, this is so good."

"Tina is an amazing cook," Kari said. "I've been helping her. Harriet usually does, but Harriet has been staying in her room more."

"Is she okay?"

"Jaleesa says she is. She says that Harriet goes through periods of solitude like this from time to time." Kari reached down and petted one of the kitties. "Their impact sessions have increased, I've noticed."

"Well, please tell her I'm thinking about her."

"I will. Jaleesa asked me to check in on her every so often. Oh, I learned to play a C major scale today with one hand. That whole thumb underneath maneuver is hard."

"You'll get it. Learn the proper techniques. Make sure the absolute tips of your fingers come down on the keys, not the pad. Like your bone is making contact."

"My teacher said something like that."

"And be patient, Kari. You'll get there. It will just take time."

Kari nodded her understanding and then excused herself to continue helping Tina dish out the food. Bernadette's heart smiled as she listened to the room bustle with the excited chatter of her friends enjoying each other's company. She had once called them Rikki's friends, but Rikki corrected her and said they were also hers. Rikki was right.

Even though Rikki and Madison had scrounged enough folding chairs for everyone, Jaleesa and Dana sat on a blanket on the floor in the corner. Jaleesa leaned back against a pillow, and Dana sat between Jaleesa's knees, her back to Jaleesa's front. It was cute how affectionate they were. Bernadette was surprised that she felt no jealousy. She picked up Rikki's hand and kissed the back of it.

"What was that for?"

"Just because."

Rikki tapped her on the nose and smiled.

"Hey," Bernadette said, "can I get everyone's attention, please?"

The room quieted down fairly quickly until Shanice said, "She's got that commanding teacher voice, doesn't she?" which made everyone chuckle.

"Umm," Bernadette started, "thanks for coming, you guys. I love this. So, what do you get when you put, uh, four Dommes, five submissives, and one switch in a room together?"

167

"Tell us, Bernadette," Miss Jaleesa said.

"A family."

A series of "Awws" went up in the room, and Marta asked for a tissue, making everyone chuckle. Everyone knew she was a softy, but in a good way.

"Movie time?" Shanice asked. When there was a general consensus, she wheeled over to the DVD player and screen she had set up upon arrival and hit the start button.

"What are we watching?" Bernadette asked Rikki quietly.

Rikki didn't answer. She just pointed to the display.

"No way," Bernadette gushed. "D.E.B.S. is awesome." Only Tina had seen it before, so Bernadette said, "It's a silly movie, kind of campy, but so much fun."

They ate in relative silence as the movie rolled on. The best was when Shanice gasped and said to Marta, "Mama, look, a Black girl!"

"And she's the leader, too. How about that?"

Shanice sat up taller and wiggled happily in true *little* fashion.

"And there's an Asian girl, too," Madison added and bounced in her seat like Bernadette had seen her do a million times.

"Whoa," Kari said when Lucy Diamond, the gorgeous main villain, appeared. "She's hot."

Jaleesa let out a belly laugh. "I might be having a threesome when I get home." To that, Dana smacked Jaleesa on the shoulder. "Or not."

The group chuckled, but their attention went back to the story on the screen. It wasn't long before Rikki nudged Bernadette and silently told her to look over at Jaleesa. Jaleesa and Dana weren't watching the movie anymore. Dana had turned around in Jaleesa's lap, and they were locked at the lips. Jaleesa's hand had snaked down Dana's shorts, and it was clear that she was stroking her.

Bernadette was fascinated. Normally, she would have looked away out of embarrassment. And she was about to when Jaleesa broke off the kiss and looked in their direction. She made direct eye contact with Bernadette and grinned. Dana writhed in Jaleesa's lap, close to orgasm, it seemed. And then Jaleesa stopped all motion and pulled her hand out of Dana's shorts. Dana's groan made Bernadette grin. She noticed several other grins in the room, Rikki's included. Oh, yes, everyone was well aware of the amorous activity in the corner. It seemed like poor Dana would be denied until they got back home.

The movie played on, and Bernadette was happy that her friends seemed to be enjoying it. This was going to be a good memory. She'd made so many happy ones with this group already. Sometimes, it takes a while to find your people, your tribe, but she'd found them.

A sob escaped from deep inside before she knew what was happening.

"Baby, what's wrong?" Rikki was up and standing over her instantly, soothing her forehead. "Are you in pain?"

Bernadette shook her head, but the sobs kept coming. The kittens were wide awake now and crawling all over the bed. Madison, a stricken expression on her face, scooped them up and put them back in the box for safekeeping.

The movie in the background stopped playing, and all eyes were on her.

"What's wrong?" Rikki asked again.

"I want to go home," Bernadette cried. She saw the compassion in her friends' eyes. "I want to sleep in my own bed. I want to roll over and be the little spoon." Her friends chuckled softly. "I want to get up on my own and go to the bathroom. I want to be able to get you coffee and kneel at your feet." The tears kept flowing. "I want, I want to play piano with Kari and go to Miss Shasti and Madison's and meet Thomas, the girl turtle. I want to see Shanice and Miss Marta's new van, play darts with Miss Jaleesa, and worry about Tina home in a cage." A bigger chuckle went up in the room. "I missed the bird-watching hike with Miss Jaleesa's family. I want to see Dana and DeShawn's beautiful flowers, learn to cook with Tina, and play softball again." She groaned and said, "I want to take a fucking shower." Her tears turned into hitching sobs.

A firm hand, not Rikki's, gripped her wrist. "Breathe," the voice commanded. "Look at me." Oh, it was Miss Shasti. A cool washcloth was applied to her wrist. The cool cloth made its way to Bernadette's forehead, face, and neck. Another cloth appeared, and the other wrist was wrapped in cool relief. "All of these things will happen, little one," Miss Shasti said. The washcloth began another round. "You will need to be patient and strong and determined. With the help of this family surrounding you, you'll be able to do all of those things you mentioned and more." Miss Shasti's laser-focused but compassionate gaze held Bernadette's. "Do you understand?"

"Y-yes. Yes, Ma'am." Bernadette took a shaky breath and then cleared her throat. She realized Rikki was holding her right hand. Madison was holding her left.

Madison said, in all seriousness, "Washcloth therapy is awesome, isn't it, Professor?"

Bernadette couldn't help chuckling. "Yeah, it is." She looked up at Miss Shasti, whose presence was still large in Bernadette's space. "Thank you."

Miss Shasti nodded and then looked over to Rikki. "First thing tomorrow morning, I'll check on those adjustable beds I ordered for you."

"Plural?" Bernadette said.

"I'm not sleeping without you anymore," Rikki said to more "Awws" from their friends. "We'll be setting up shop downstairs in the *littles'* room. I'm sure they won't mind."

"Go for it," Madison said, and Shanice agreed.

"Rikki," Bernadette said, "when I'm all better, and we move out of the *littles'* room, can we finally put in those bunk beds with the, what's it called?"

"Trundle bed?"

"Oh, yes. Put in bunk beds with the trundle for the *littles'* room?"

"Of course we can, little bee," Rikki answered gently. "When you're all better."

"Rikki, when can I go home?"

"You've made such amazing progress," Miss Shasti answered. "It's really your call. But I recommend you wait until the beds and reclining wheelchair arrive, and we get things set up for you at home. Like home health care which I'll check on tomorrow as well."

"That gives me so much hope," Bernadette said. "Thank you. Thank you, everyone. I'm sorry I melted down like that."

"Completely understandable," Jaleesa said to murmurs of agreement.

"Miss Bernadette," Shanice said from across the room, "I have a Reiki healer on standby once you get home."

"Thank you, Shanice," Bernadette said. "I don't know what that is, but I'm sure it will help."

"You want to tell them, baby girl?" Marta asked Shanice quietly.

Shanice nodded but then shyly tucked herself into Marta's side and wouldn't speak, so Marta took over. "The doctors said she is healed and strong enough to get fitted for prosthetics."

A huge cheer went up in the room, and Bernadette started crying again. "Happy tears. Happy tears," she said when Rikki looked concerned. "Tissue, please."

"Tissues all around," Jaleesa boomed as she and Dana stood up to give Shanice hugs.

"That is amazing, Shanice," Rikki said. "We are all here for you." She looked down at Bernadette. "Looks like maybe the two of you are going to learn how to walk at the same time."

Marta started crying again and said, "Fuck you, Boss," and gestured for the tissue box, making everyone laugh again. But it was a relieved laugh. Things were going to be okay in their collective world. Several other hands went out, and the tissue box made the rounds again.

Rikki looked at Bernadette, eyebrows raised in question. Bernadette nodded. Yes, it was time.

"Hey, everybody, as you all know," Rikki said, "Bernadette and I are going to have our big wedding in the fall. We'll get you that date as soon as we can. It'll be based on my little bee's progress. But I want to thank Jaleesa for agreeing to be our officiant." Cheers went up around the room, and Jaleesa, obviously moved, didn't respond with a typical booming retort. Tina moved to Jaleesa's side, grabbed her hand, and then kissed her on the cheek. She whispered something in Jaleesa's ear, to which Jaleesa nodded and pulled Tina into a side hug.

"And I'm not sure if you all know," Rikki said, "but I've asked Shasti to be my best man. We've got to find a better word for that."

"How about best *woman*?" Madison offered.

"Maybe."

"Can I be, like, the flower girl?" Madison asked, bouncing on her toes.

"No," Bernadette answered quickly.

The fallen look on Madison's face was priceless. "We'd love for Shanice and Pammy to be our flower girls."

Shanice's face lit up, but she didn't say anything as she glanced at Madison's crestfallen expression. Marta patted her girl on the back. Shanice nodded, saying that she would be honored to do so.

"Madison," Bernadette said, "would you bring me the furballs?"

"Okay." Madison's voice was so dejected that it almost broke Bernadette's heart.

Bernadette held up the calmer of the two kittens and said, "I'm naming this one RJ for Rikki Junior." Rikki looked at her with surprise. "Because if Rikki can't be with me, then her namesake will."

Marta reached for more tissues, which caused a chuckle to go around the room. Even Madison laughed.

"And this feisty little one I'm naming MJ in honor of the person I'd like to be my best woman."

Miss Shasti clapped Madison on the back, but it was obvious that Madison hadn't caught on yet.

"Her name is Madison Junior, in honor of the girl who changed my life by being so kind and insistent that I meet her friends at Rocco's that cold January day."

"Me?" Madison looked from Bernadette to Rikki and then to her Mistress for confirmation. When Miss Shasti nodded, Madison gasped and said, "Yes, yes, yes. I'll be your best man or best girl or whatever. What do I have to do? Wait! I know. Bachelor party-y-y-y!" She announced in full Madison voice and subsequent hushing from her Mistress.

"So that's a 'yes'?" Bernadette asked.

"Yes!"

"Come give me a hug." Hug complete, Bernadette said to Madison, "We have so much to plan. Like what I'm wearing and what you're wearing and what flowers I should carry."

"That's a lot, Professor. I'll start a list."

"A girl after my own heart," Bernadette said and began a rousing game of thing-under-the-blanket with the now wide-awake, rambunctious kittens.

"Here's to wedding days and walking," Jaleesa said and raised her water bottle high. Bottles were raised, and the sentiment echoed. Dana whispered something in Jaleesa's ear, hiding her mouth behind her hand. Jaleesa's eyebrows raised up comically high, and she said, "Okay, back to the movie. I got a date promising to do naughty things to me later."

Bernadette chuckled with her friends as a rush of warm feels like nothing she'd ever felt before settled in her heart.

# Chapter 20
## Rikki

The bell on the coffee shop door jingled, and Rikki looked up. She watched her handsomely androgynous friend Victoria, or Daddy Vic to her subs, come in and head to the counter. The shop was relatively empty this time in the early afternoon, so Victoria was able to get her beverage quickly. It would be coffee, black. No cream, no sugar, no froth, no nothing.

*Always the same*, Rikki thought, *even after all these years.* She waved her friend over to the couch where she had set up camp for the day. It was Bernadette's couch, of course.

"Hey," Victoria said simply. She was dressed down and apparently hadn't come from work. She still looked badass, though, in her tight button-down shirt, black jeans, and steel-toed boots. And the short butch hair was impeccable as always. Victoria got a lot of second looks from potential submissives. Bernadette had been one of them.

"Thanks for coming, Vic," Rikki gestured to a seat, but Victoria took a different one. *Always have to be in charge. Grow up, Victoria.*

"How is she?"

*Can't say her name?* Rikki waited a beat and then said, "Bernadette's home. For about a week now. Healing nicely and happy to be out of that rehab facility."

"I bet."

"We're going to the ortho doc in the city on Friday for x-rays, and if all looks good, the casts will come off and the staples in her leg removed."

"That's good." Victoria's sentiment seemed genuine.

"I'm taking her to the university on Wednesday for the first time since the accident."

"Yeah?"

Rikki nodded. "She wants to give her Calculus final exam in person. She doesn't want her students to think she's completely abandoned them."

"That's, uh, that's cool." The disinterest in Victoria's voice was clear and palpable.

"She also has a department meeting she doesn't want to miss," Rikki continued, knowing Victoria didn't care. "Did you know Shanice got a wheelchair-accessible van?"

"Nice."

"That's how we got Bernadette home from the rehab place."

"Why did you summon me here, Rikki?"

Rikki sighed. *Get straight to the point, why don't you?* "You make it sound like I'm a mafia boss or something." Before Vic could interrupt, she added, "Look, we want to invite you and Alyssa to the wedding."

"Alyssa and I broke up."

"Oh, shit, Vic. I'm sorry. When?"

"Doesn't matter." Vic looked toward the shop's front window and took a sip of coffee. She swiped away a tear and then gestured to the lush greenery surrounding the shop name in the front window. "Dana did a good job with those plants. They don't look half dead anymore." She turned to look back at Rikki. "Look, just don't send Alyssa an invitation."

"Understood." Rikki took a sip of water, letting her friend have a moment.

"You know," Victoria said, "I always pictured me at your side when you got married." She didn't make direct eye contact. "You know, as your seneschal? And you by mine if I ever got married."

Rikki started to say that's why she had asked her to come by. She wanted to talk to her about that in person, but Victoria cut her off. "Look, I know you already asked Shasti. Rowena told me. It's okay. We've grown apart, and I'm sure your sub doesn't like me much."

*My 'sub'?* "She has a name, Victoria."

"You're ready to settle down, Rikki," Victoria said, ignoring Rikki's statement. "Me? I don't know." Victoria shook her head as if trying to stave off her emotions. "I'm moving. I have a cousin in Indianapolis who will let me stay with her until I get on my feet. She owns a security company, so…"

"Shit, Vic."

"I'm leaving this weekend. I've been packing ever since Alyssa went back to her asshole Dom. I need a fresh start. There's a big BDSM scene in Indy. I'm going to do things better this time around, Rikki." She looked up and finally made eye contact.

"What do you need?" Rikki asked.

"Need? Who the fuck knows? You want the equipment back?"

"Aunt Tilda's stuff?"

Victoria nodded. "Dominique said she'll take whatever you don't want."

"Let me ask Bernadette, and I'll get back to you."

"Seriously? You have to ask your submissive?" Victoria scoffed. "I think you've gone soft, Rikki."

Rikki stood up. "And I think you need to show more respect for my wife."

"You have to decide on the equipment soon."

"We'll pass," Rikki said.

"Okay then." Victoria stood up. "I'm going. I wish you well, Rikki. Both of you. Feel free to tell everybody that I'm leaving. I consent." Victoria laughed like she'd made some kind of inside joke, but Rikki wasn't sure what the joke was.

"Good luck, Vic."

Victoria turned away and strode toward the exit. She hesitated before opening the door and looked back at Rikki. She smiled and then nodded, basically saying thank you in her own way. For what, Rikki wasn't sure. Victoria wiped at the tears in her eyes and pushed open the door.

"Shit," Rikki said. She had hoped to sit with her friend for a while, catch up, and tell her about Bernadette's progress. She wanted to tell her how Bernadette could practically get herself in and out of the new adjustable bed and into the wheelchair on her own. She wanted to tell Victoria how she had arranged for someone to be with Bernadette during the day when Rikki was at the shop. Tina was over there right now, giving Bernadette a cooking lesson. The result was going to be dinner tonight. But that part of her relationship with Victoria was over, apparently. And that made Rikki sad.

She hated that Victoria had stubbornly distanced herself from the group and never outgrew that old-school way of thinking. What did Madison spout from her philosophy class the other day? Some people come into your life for only a season or something like that. Rikki stood for an extra beat, mourning a friendship that had apparently run its course. With a sigh, she headed into her office to distract herself with paperwork.

~~~

Rikki entered the house quietly, just in case Bernadette was sleeping. She set down the box that had been sitting on the front porch. It was from her sister Caroline. Her father obviously couldn't be bothered to send it. And it wasn't a big box, either. She doubted another one was on the way. No, they had probably tossed most of her childhood stuff out. Whatever. She hadn't been back home in years, anyway. She'd open the box another day. Or maybe never.

"Oh, hey, Miss Rikki," Tina said. "I think cooking wore her out." She pointed to the *littles'* room turned downstairs master. "She's napping."

"Thank you," Rikki said. She hung up her keys and put the mail in the basket. "It smells so good in here."

"We made cottage pie. Yours is warming in the oven. It'll keep for quite a while." Tina turned to get her bags. One of them probably contained her own cottage pie to take home to her big family. "You know, I got choked up this morning when I got here."

"How come?"

"The ramp." Tina sighed. "She put that in for Shanice, and then she ended up…" Tina's emotion closed her throat.

"I know. I thought the same thing." Rikki patted Tina on the shoulder. "Thanks for today. Anything else I should know?"

"Oh, the home health nurse said Bernadette was looking good. She said she would not be surprised if Bernadette got the casts off on Friday. And she said those staples have got to come out immediately. The skin is starting to close over them. But all in all, Bernadette had a good day. She had good energy."

"Fabulous," Rikki said. "Thank you for being here."

"Bernadette is so polite," Tina said. "She didn't want to seem rude, so she fought the nap for quite a while. When I told her she needed to be rested and refreshed for when you came home, she said, 'Good night,' and then I helped her to bed."

Rikki chuckled. "I'm going to let her sleep. Sleep brings healing."

"So does intimacy," Tina said suggestively.

"No worries in that regard," Rikki said. "I have plans."

"I should go," Tina said. "I'm glad you asked me to help out. I'm enjoying getting to know your wife better."

Rikki smiled and thanked her again.

After Tina left, Rikki checked on her sleeping girl. She looked peaceful, so Rikki stole up the stairs to freshen up and change into something more comfortable for lounging.

"Rikki?" came a sleepy voice from down the stairs.

"I'll be right down." Rikki threw on some slippers and bounded down the stairs. "Hi, beautiful."

"Oh, I am not," Bernadette said, smoothing down her bedhead hair.

"People pay a lot of money at Jaleesa's salon for hair like that."

"Stop," Bernadette said with an amused lilt to her voice.

"Your scar completes the look." Rikki ran her finger over the pink wound on her forehead. "It's sexy." Later on, she would rub some healing vitamin E oil into the tender skin so it wouldn't scar too much.

Bernadette didn't answer verbally. She put out her arms, asking for help getting into the wheelchair.

"Do you need to go to the bathroom?" There was a porta-john in the room for emergencies, but Bernadette had been using it less and less, preferring to be wheeled to the actual bathroom.

"No, I just want to be with you." Bernadette glanced at the big clock that had made its way back from the rehab facility to the *littles'* room wall. "We can eat now or wait. Whatever you want."

"We'll wait," Rikki said with a devilish smile. "Stay right there."

Rikki left the room and laughed when Bernadette called after her, "Like I have much of a choice?"

When Rikki came back in, Bernadette's eyes opened wide, but she didn't say a word. Ahh, yes, that was Rikki's trusting girl.

"Why are you wearing clothes?" Rikki asked in all seriousness.

Bernadette smiled. "Because I was hoping you'd take them off me?"

"Good answer." Rikki nodded and helped relieve Bernadette of her bothersome t-shirt and shorts.

"Open your legs," Rikki said simply.

"Why, how very forward of you, Mrs. Carmichael. I'm a married woman."

"And don't you forget it," Rikki said. "Lower the top of the bed so you can lay back a little. Ass up." She put a towel-covered pillow under Bernadette to raise her up.

Rikki squirted shaving gel into her hand and rubbed it generously over Bernadette's mound and outer labia. She showed Bernadette the shaving razor and then got to work. She applied more gel where necessary and rinsed the razor in a small bowl of water she'd brought in. During the process, it became obvious that Bernadette was getting turned on. Oh, it wasn't anything overt, just the subtle opening of her legs and the softer breathing. The murmured, "Thank you, baby," was the real clue.

"Madison sent another video of RJ and MJ playing," Bernadette said. "They are so cute. When can we bring them home, Rikki?"

"Once you can walk on your own."

"Oh." The dejected tone in Bernadette's voice almost broke Rikki's heart.

"Which will be soon," Rikki added. She used a washcloth to rinse off the last of the shaving gel and then kissed Bernadette's mound, but nothing else.

"Tease," Bernadette said.

Rikki took a few moments to clean up the supplies. Bernadette would have been unhappy if she'd left a mess. Yes, pleasing Bernadette had become a priority in their young marriage. It was something Vic had yet to learn about relationships and submissives. Rikki decided to hold off telling Bernadette about the visit with her ex. It would keep.

"Ready?" Rikki said and held out her hand. They had the wheelchair transfer routine down to a science at this point.

Bernadette tried to use her non-weight-bearing arm to help, and Rikki admonished her. Maybe she'd work a punishment for that into their scene. Yes, definitely.

Once in the wheelchair, Rikki wheeled Bernadette to the living room. She walked over to her phone and opened her music app. She found one of

Madison's playlists she'd sent to everyone. This one was called "Ooh La La" and perfectly set the mood for intimate time.

Rikki wordlessly took off Bernadette's stretchy day collar and buckled on the purple downstairs play collar.

"Really, Rikki?" Bernadette said, her voice kind of breathy. She loved her purple collar. It was unique, like her relationship with Rikki.

"I like you naked," Rikki said, evading the direct question.

Bernadette reached up and touched the waistband of Rikki's shorts as if suggesting that Rikki should become as naked as she was.

"Did you or did you not try to use your bad arm getting in the wheelchair?"

"I did. I'm sorry," Bernadette hung her head. Nope, she wasn't in submissive mode. Not yet, anyway.

"Was that the right thing to do?" Rikki walked over to the drawer of kinky supplies and pulled out several zip ties. She also pulled out the safety scissors and laid them on the coffee table.

"Is this the arm you tried to use?"

"Yes, Ma'am." Nope, still not in submissive mode.

Rikki positioned the offending arm and zip-tied it to the armrest. She checked to make sure it wasn't too tight.

"Rikki?"

"Did I ask you to speak?"

"No, Ma'am." Ahh, her submissive mindset was getting closer.

She showed Bernadette the other zip ties as a warning. Misbehave, and the other limbs would get the same treatment.

"Be good," Rikki said.

Bernadette nodded. Good, if she'd spoken, her casted leg sticking straight out would have been zip-tied. Not that the zip tie would have mattered since she couldn't really move it anyway.

Rikki lowered the back of the reclining wheelchair slightly and then lifted the armrest on Bernadette's good side out of the way. She slid the footrest further away, opening up Bernadette's center. Ah, yes, that's the ticket.

Rikki leaned down and pressed her lips lightly against Bernadette's. Ahh, they were hungry for attention. Rikki slowed down Bernadette's eager mouth and then pulled away. Bernadette groaned at the loss. Rikki stepped between Bernadette's open legs and bent at the waist. She kissed two erect nipples she found on her way further down. Two fingers splayed open a growing clit, she also happened to discover. Two fingers swept through Bernadette's arousal—wow, her girl was wet—and then lightly coated the erect nub. Rikki stroked the clit lightly. Not meant to bring on an orgasm. Not yet. The strokes were simply meant to tune her girl's body to the soft, sultry music playing in the background. Bernadette's right leg tried to close on Rikki's hand but bumped against Rikki's leg.

Rikki pulled away to another frustrated groan from her girl and reached down for a second zip tie. She secured Bernadette's good leg to the wheelchair, thereby keeping her legs open wide. She zip-tied the broken leg to its rest as well. Not really needed, but Bernadette liked symmetry. Oh, the possibilities now.

Rikki leaned in, kissed one erect nipple, and then sucked it until Bernadette moaned. She moved to the other and did the same. Rikki reached over and pinched the first nipple. Funny how that caused Bernadette to tilt her pelvis. Hmm. They must be connected. What would happen if this nipple got twisted like a radio knob and the other continued to be sucked?

A grunt followed by a hand grabbing the back of Rikki's head resulted. Rikki chuckled and pulled back to more frustrated groaning.

"Rikki, Rikki, Rikki," Bernadette said with a long sigh.

"Hmm," Rikki grunted, not liking what she was hearing. She stood up and walked back to the supply drawer. One ball gag installed later, and they were in business.

"Mumph," was all Bernadette could say for some reason.

Rikki considered zip-tying down the good arm, but she'd wait. Bernadette was about to give her just cause soon enough. Rikki went back to the drawer and pulled out the newly purchased item Marta recommended. Bernadette hadn't seen or even heard about its existence yet. Hmm, should she use a blindfold? No, no, she needed her girl to watch.

Wordlessly, Rikki moved in front of the wheelchair but didn't make eye contact. The woman in front of her was a plaything—something to be used for Rikki's pleasure. Rikki secured the thigh-strapped dildo to Bernadette's good leg. The dildo stood straight up. The confused look in Bernadette's eyes was almost comical. That is until Rikki slowly slid her shorts down, kicked them aside, and positioned herself over the dildo. She lowered her body slowly until the tip was at her entrance. Penetration wasn't her go-to means of self-pleasure, but it would be today. She let the head of the dildo push at her wet entrance. No lube was needed, that was for sure. She reached toward Bernadette and put both hands on the back of the wheelchair for stability.

With a soft, satisfied moan, she lowered herself to the hilt. Without any regard for Bernadette, she raised herself up and then thrust down on the dildo, her ass making contact with Bernadette's thigh. She made sure not to come down too hard, though. She didn't want to smash her girl's good leg to bits. She pulled up and plunged down, establishing a nice, slow but steady rhythm. She leaned back away from Bernadette and pulled up her own t-shirt. She gave her girl a show by squeezing her own breasts and pinching her nipples. Bernadette's eyes were riveted on the scene in her lap. Her right hand flew down and gripped Rikki's hip as if guiding Rikki's movements.

Rikki grinned. Ahh yes. *That's* what she had been waiting for. *That's* what she knew would happen. She slowed her thrusts and grabbed the carefully placed zip tie stashed within reach. She continued to fuck herself but managed to zip-tie Bernadette's loose arm to the raised armrest. It comically looked like Bernadette was raising her hand to ask the teacher a question. Nope, this *teacher* was not currently entertaining questions. Nope, this teacher would use her submissive's body until she came.

Rikki squeezed her girl's breasts and tuned Bernadette's radio with the convenient nipple knobs. It almost looked like Bernadette was about to cum just from that. Rikki removed her hands to Bernadette's growling frustration. Rikki offered one of her own breasts, just out of reach, to her submissive. She pinched the nipple as if asking Bernadette to take it in her mouth. Hard to do with a ball gag, hmm? Ahh, what sweet torture that must be. Rikki's other hand slid down her own torso and found her clit. Just the middle finger was all she needed. It wasn't her girl's sweet tongue, but all good things come to those who wait, right?

Rikki recognized the glimmer of orgasm building in her core and locked her gaze onto Bernadette's. She continued to fuck herself until everything tightened deep inside. She slowed her thrusts to make sure she didn't hurt Bernadette and then exploded. Her moan was long. It was deep and left her breathless. Where her tears came from, she didn't know. She fell gently against Bernadette, hiding her face as she struggled to catch her breath and get a hold of the tears. Once both were mastered, she removed Bernadette's ball gag. Rikki wiped at the drool using the towel she'd draped over the back of the wheelchair.

"Fuck, Rikki," Bernadette growled. "Oh, please kiss me, Mrs. Carmichael."

"It would be my honor, Dr. Carmichael."

# Chapter 21
## Bernadette

The water seemed to run forever in the half bath. What the hell was Rikki doing in there? Taking a full-body sponge bath?

"Rikki?" Bernadette called over her shoulder. Even though Rikki had draped a sheet over her, she was getting kind of cold. And she was tired of being strapped down to the stupid wheelchair. Who knew this instrument of freedom could betray her like this?

Rikki strolled out of the bathroom like she didn't have a care in the world. Bernadette was sad to see that her Domme now wore shorts. And the concert T now hid her lover's breasts.

Bernadette pouted.

"No pouting," Rikki said. There's no pouting in this house. Don't you know that?"

She stopped behind Bernadette and kissed the crown of her head. Why did Bernadette find that so satisfying? Maybe because a hand had also reached down to caress her shoulder.

"Baby, let me see you," Bernadette cried.

Rikki moved in front but didn't speak as she ripped away the sheet. Her intense gaze raked over Bernadette's naked body. Bernadette let out a small noise of longing. Oh, God, she needed Rikki to touch her.

Rikki tested the plastic ties that bound Bernadette to the chair, but she aggravatingly didn't cut a single one. Instead, Rikki leaned down and pressed her lips against Bernadette's, who had no choice but to kiss back. Rikki thrust her tongue inside, gently at first and then with more fervor. Bernadette shivered, and then Rikki pulled away. So mean.

Rikki stepped behind the wheelchair, and Bernadette heard her rustling with something behind her. Blindfold maybe? Ice? No, she hadn't gone to the kitchen. It couldn't be hot wax. Plug? Maybe. Ball gag? Please, not again. Clamps? Let it be clamps.

Bernadette tried to reach up and touch her collar for comfort but only ended up frustrating herself even more.

Rikki moved in front of her. There was no blindfold, no ice, no wax, no plug, no ball gag, no clamps. No, there was only the thigh dildo. This time, it was strapped to Rikki's right thigh.

Rikki reached down and dipped two fingers into Bernadette's center. Without smiling, she pulled them out and held up her glistening fingers to show Bernadette. She caressed Bernadette's mouth with her own desire.

"Taste yourself," Rikki said. Her expression was no-nonsense.

A spiral of desire shot through Bernadette's body at the command. It wasn't the taste of herself on her lips. Oh no, it was the dominant tone of Rikki's command. It was the fact that Bernadette was completely at Rikki's whim and wishes.

"You're ready for me," Rikki said and shimmied herself between Bernadette's still-spread legs. "That's good." She adjusted the thigh dildo so it was at the right height for her desired target. She pressed the phallus down so the shaft rested on Bernadette's mound.

Bernadette tried to open her legs wider. Dang it. She couldn't. Okay, fine. She tilted her pelvis slightly instead. Thank God Rikki took the hint and slid the shaft back and forth across her hooded clit.

Bernadette's head fell against the back of the chair, her eyes closing. "Yes, baby," she encouraged her Domme. "Please, please, please."

"Please, what?"

"Please, Ma'am," Bernadette's eyes fluttered open. "Please fuck me."

Rikki slid four fingers underneath Bernadette's collar and pulled gently but insistently. "Who is the giver of your pleasure?" Rikki's face was now inches from her own. Not close enough to kiss, though.

"You are, Ma'am," Bernadette said. Oh, God, she was so turned on.

"And what would you do if I walked out of the room right now?"

"Probably cry, Ma'am. Cry out of frustration. But I would accept your decision. You are the giver of pleasure."

"All good answers," Rikki said, her tone lightening. She released the collar, bopped Bernadette on the nose with one finger, leaned in closer, and whispered in Bernadette's ear, "You. Will. Use. Your. Safeword. Do you understand?"

"Yes."

"Yes, what?" The T came out sharp and bounced around Bernadette's ear.

"Yes, Ma'am," Bernadette said quickly as arousal spiked through her. "I will use my safewords if I need to."

"Good girl," Rikki whispered. She stood back up. "I want the neighbors to hear you cum. I want Tina and Jaleesa and everyone in their house to hear you. Do you understand?"

"Yes, Ma'am," Bernadette said with enthusiasm.

With no further words, Rikki pushed her leg forward and slowly sank the dildo into Bernadette's body. The method was weird and different, but who cared?

"Oh, so good. We haven't—" Bernadette cut off her own words as sensations overtook her. Her chest and shoulders bloomed with heat. This orgasm was already manifesting.

"That's right, baby," Rikki said, pulling out and thrusting back in. "Cum for me. Let them hear you." Rikki flicked her wrist and smacked the fleshy side of one of Bernadette's breasts. She repeated the motion, alternating breasts. The breast bruise had long healed, and Bernadette didn't need to use her safewords. Quite the opposite. The rhythmic slapping and subsequent pain made her feel alive.

Bernadette ground her pelvis against Rikki's phallus as best she could while tethered to the chair. She hoped Rikki wouldn't be mad that she was cumming so soon, but she felt the beautiful spark ignite inside and couldn't stop it if she tried.

Rikki continued to slap her breasts. Maybe there'd be bruising? Good bruising this time? Yes? Rikki hit a nipple. That did it. Bernadette's body tightened, and the bullet train that was her orgasm slammed into the station.

"Rikki!" Bernadette yelled to the stratosphere. No expletives left her mouth. Just screeches of ecstasy as she came and came. Wave crashed after wave as Rikki continued to thrust in and out. "I love you," Bernadette said, using the only breath she had. Those particular words couldn't wait.

"I love you, too, baby," Rikki said. She slowed her thrusts and then pulled out.

"Kiss, kiss, kiss," Bernadette pleaded, and Rikki obliged. Bernadette had to pull away every now and then to catch her breath but hungrily turned her head back for more.

Rikki stroked her face and then pulled back to look at Bernadette. "I love you so much."

Bernadette willed herself not to cry. Instead, she started laughing.

"Why are you laughing."

"I don't know. It's just the absurdity of this." Bernadette used her chin to point to the wheelchair and her points of bondage.

Rikki chuckled. "Kinda sexy if you ask me."

"For you, I'm sure." Bernadette sighed and then shivered.

"Okay, my love." Rikki reached for the safety scissors. She clipped the four zip ties holding Bernadette to the chair, gently rubbing and easing each limb into a more comfortable position. She went to take off the play collar, but Bernadette protested. "You want to keep that on?"

Bernadette nodded. No other words were needed.

Rikki wheeled Bernadette to the half bath. "Let's get you cleaned up and then back in bed."

"Okay," Bernadette said. "Can I wear one of your T-shirts?"

"You want to wear one of mine?"

Bernadette nodded. "It makes me feel like you're hugging me."

"That can be arranged." Rikki soaped up a washcloth and got to work. "Tell me what to do with the cottage pie, and I'll bring us dinner in bed. How's that sound?"

"Like what a loving partner would do."

"Well, well, I'll let you in on a little secret, little bee," Rikki said and rinsed out the washcloth. "I do love you. And when we get back in that bed to eat dinner, we have to make some definitive wedding plans, like who, what, and where. The *when* will depend on what Dr. Bosco says on Friday."

"Friday can't come soon enough," Bernadette said as Rikki dried her. "Now, take me to bed, woman."

"Bossy, ain't you?"

~~~

The desk chair sat ingloriously in the hallway to make room for Bernadette's wheelchair in her office at the university. Rikki sat in the student chair, smooshed on the other side of the desk. The look on Rikki's face was not a happy one.

"I know," Bernadette said, looking at her small office. "It's a closet."

"It's disrespect," Rikki said.

Bernadette nodded. "But, baby, I'm hoping Wainwright will announce my new courses and new office on the fifth or maybe the third floor today. The new hire is going to be introduced, too."

Rikki looked up at the backward clock. The numbers were in reverse order, and the hands ran counterclockwise. She said, "Do you have everything you need because we'd better get down there. It takes a little longer for us to do things these days."

Bernadette grinned. No one ever took the time to read and understand that backward clock, but Rikki had. Yeah, she'd better marry that woman fast before someone else did. Oh, wait. She already did. Yay. "You're right. Thanks for putting the exams in Shanice's van for me."

"Bianca and Eashon were a big help."

"I have some work to do this evening, don't I?"

"Yes, you do," Rikki said. "Your students and your TAs appreciated you being here in person. That was more than obvious by the way they crowded you when you came in and then again when the exam was over." She pulled on Bernadette's wheelchair from the front and pulled it out the office door even though it was a tight fit. Bernadette wished she could help more, but until she was told she could use her compromised arm, hopefully on Friday, she was pretty useless.

Rikki practically threw the old chair back in and then shut and locked the office door with Bernadette's keys. They headed toward the elevator on the other side of the floor.

"Why do you want to change the courses you teach, little bee?" Rikki asked gently.

Uh, oh. That tone suggested she didn't think it was a good idea or that Bernadette's motivations weren't in line with…something.

"Well, first of all," Bernadette said. "I love the mathematics. And, um, …"

"What?"

"It's just that I think they'll take me more seriously. You've seen my office. Maybe they'll, like, have more respect for me if I teach the upper levels."

"Who?" Rikki pushed the elevator button.

"Wainwright. Professor Yang. I don't know. All of them."

"Your colleagues, you mean," Rikki said.

"Yes, and the students. I worked hard for my doctorate. I want to use it."

"Mm hmm," Rikki said, not sounding convinced. "What did our budding philosopher Madison say to you the other day? That you shouldn't underestimate the effect you have on people, particularly your students. From what I can tell, those Calculus students I just met love you and appreciate the hell out of you. That is quite life-affirming if you ask me. I'm not sure the opinions of your colleagues really matter here."

The elevator door opened, and Bernadette didn't have a chance to reply as a well-dressed woman, maybe in her fifties, came barreling out, almost slamming into the wheelchair.

"Oh, shit, sorry," the older woman said. "You must be Dr. Garneau." She put out her hand.

"It's Dr. Carmichael now." Bernadette shook hands with the woman.

"I was so sorry to hear about your accident." She looked up at Rikki and nodded. "But I'm so glad to have caught you. She backed up into the elevator and said, "Come. I'll walk with you to wherever you're going."

Bernadette exchanged a look with Rikki, who simply shrugged and backed Bernadette into the elevator.

"I'm Mimi Goldmann, professor in the electrical engineering department, but I'm here as a representative of the Society of Women Engineers. I'm the woman whose emails you've been ignoring since January."

Bernadette started to apologize, but the tornado that was Mimi said, "No worries. No worries. I need you, Dr. Carmichael. Students and alums are raving about you. First of all, is this your wife?"

"Yes. Rikki, please meet Mimi Goldmann." Bernadette turned to Mimi and said, "This is Rikki Carmichael, my wife of six weeks."

"Seven on Friday," Rikki corrected.

"Aww, newlyweds. Congratulations," Mimi gushed. "How sweet. It's nice to meet you, Rikki. I hope you can help me convince your wife to take this incredible opportunity."

The elevator doors opened on the first floor, and they headed toward the conference room where the department meeting was to be held. They had a few minutes to spare, so Bernadette asked Rikki to stop at a lounge area where they could sit and talk.

Mimi didn't waste time. "We have a considerably generous grant to promote STEM opportunities for women and girls."

"Stem?" Rikki asked.

"STEM. Science, Technology, Engineering, and Mathematics," Bernadette clarified. "It's an acronym."

"We need a mathematics person," Mimi said. "Dr. Wainwright recommended you so highly, and I hope hope hope you'll help us out. It would entail making twenty-minute videos, maybe longer. We haven't worked that part out yet."

"What kind of videos?" Bernadette asked. She hated teaching onscreen. It made her so self-conscious.

"Teaching lessons that anyone can access, but our targets are women and girls. Any disadvantaged group, actually." Mimi cleared her throat. "We'll start with a few Calculus topics. The market is flooded with those, though, but we want to move up quickly to the higher levels. Linear Algebra, Multivariable Calculus, Group Theory, Differential Equations, Number Theory, Abstract Algebra, Statistics, Combinatorics. Of course, we'll rely on you to fill out the complete roster."

The information was coming too hard and too fast. Rikki put a hand on her arm as if she understood that. She said, "Sounds like my wife needs to find those deleted emails and read them."

"No need. I'll send a description and a contract this afternoon," Mimi said. "I know you have your department meeting now, so I'll let you go."

Bernadette didn't know what to say. "Uh, thank you for thinking of me. I have to give it a look over and discuss it with my wife. Um, I'll need to know the time expectations. I will probably have a lot of physical therapy, which might overtax me."

"Understood," Mimi said. "I completely understand. We have time. My only rush was to get you on board."

They said their goodbyes, and Rikki wheeled her into the conference room whose door was a bit wider than her closet of an office. That was a relief. Bernadette didn't want her colleagues to witness her struggle and think she wasn't capable or strong.

"Ahh, Dr. Carmichael," Dr. Wainwright said as he walked over with someone in tow. Bernadette almost choked. Wainwright never called her by her title. He usually just called her Bernadette. "Please meet Walter Kruk. Dr. Kruk comes to us from the New York City area."

Dr. Kruk was a balding, pudgy, middle-aged man with what looked like a permanent scowl etched into his face.

"Nice to meet you," Bernadette said, reaching her hand up.

Dr. Kruk shook it but not warmly. He nodded to her but didn't say anything and barely looked at Rikki. How can you *not* look at Rikki? Everyone did. She was hot. Bernadette found herself insulted, and she'd just met the man.

"As I'm sure you've suspected," Dr. Wainwright said to Bernadette, "you'll be taking over Dr. Baxter's course load."

*Yes!* It was all she could do not to shout, '*Victory is mine!*' She held in her grin with all her might. This is what she had dreamed of. She shot Rikki a knowing look, and Rikki patted her shoulder as if to say, '*There you go. That's what you wanted.*'

"Dr. Kruk will take over the Calculus course and the Foundations course you developed."

"What brings you to Ohio?" Rikki asked the new professor.

"First grandkid. They live in Denton Heights. My wife insisted we move."

His answers were succinct and to the point. But, wow, there was no warmth, no personality. That's okay. Bernadette figured she'd probably have nothing to do with him anyway.

Rikki leaned down and said she was going to wait in the lobby coffee shop and that Bernadette should text when the meeting was over. Bernadette didn't blame her at all for wanting to skedaddle. "Okay, Rikki," Bernadette said, "I'll text you when it's over." Bernadette took Rikki's see-you-later kiss in stride until she saw the slightly disgusted expression on Kruk's face.

"So," Bernadette said, "do you want me to email you the course outline for the Foundations class? They'll need a bit of review upfront, especially because they come from such varied backgrounds."

"No."

"Okay, I guess there's a copy on file."

"I prefer to dig right into group theory," Kruk said. "None of this babying them. If they're missing something in their academic backgrounds, they'll have to fill in those gaps on their own. Same goes for those Calculus students. I am not here to teach algebra or trigonometry to a bunch of whiny millennials or generation XYZs or whatever they call themselves. Students have a right to fail, don't you think? If they can't handle the course, they shouldn't be in it. Prerequisites are in place for a reason. Put in the work, I say. That's what *we* had to do."

To say she was shocked by his words would be the understatement of the year. An instant headache hit her, and as she sat stunned, trying to form actual words to rebut his assertions, Dr. Wainwright pulled him away to greet another colleague.

Oh. My. God. What had been put in motion? How could Wainwright hire that neanderthal? He was going to undo all the hard work she'd put into making both of those courses worthwhile, meaningful, and accessible. She didn't have time to ponder this nightmare as several colleagues came up to wish her well and ask how she was doing. Many of them had barely spoken to her in the five years she'd been there. There was nothing like tragedy to bring people together.

Miss Olga came up and repositioned the wheelchair to a spot next to a side table so she could take notes. "You okay?" Miss Olga asked quietly. "You don't look okay."

"I'll be fine," Bernadette said. "Just a little tired." She needed to get home and nap. No, they were meeting Lydia and Pammy for lunch at the Indigo Café. Maybe they needed to cancel.

"Olga," Dr. Wainwright called, "are you ready?"

"Gotta go. Duty calls," Miss Olga said and took up her position in the front of the room to take the meeting notes.

"Duty calls," Bernadette echoed. "Duty," she mumbled and wrote the word down. She wrote *duty* several more times and then synonyms for the word. Synonyms like *responsibility, obligation, commitment.*

"Duty," she muttered under her breath.

# Chapter 22
## Rikki

Rikki sat with her decaf coffee, utterly appalled at the lack of discipline she witnessed at the coffee shop in the Mathematics building lobby. "Give me a week, one week with them," she muttered, "and I'll have them all whipped—"

Her phone dinged, saving the day. Bernadette was ready. She left her unfinished drink and used napkin on the table and headed to the conference room. She greeted Olga warmly.

"We'll let you know when the wedding is," Bernadette said to Olga. "It depends on Friday." She gestured to her various injuries.

"Fingers crossed," Olga said. "See you tomorrow, Dr. *Carmichael*. I love saying that," she gushed. "Let me know if you need any help tomorrow."

"Thanks," Bernadette said. Once Olga was out of earshot, Bernadette sighed.

"You look tired, baby," Rikki said. "You okay?"

Bernadette looked up and pursed her lips. Uh oh. Rikki knew what that meant. Bernadette was thinking—thinking about something big. "We should go. Just go."

Rikki paused for a moment and could not for the life of her figure out what had happened to alter Bernadette's mood. The department meeting. What happened? Maybe it was nothing. Her girl was just tired, and this had been a long morning already. And she had all of those exams to grade when they got home.

Rikki grabbed the handles of the wheelchair and pushed Bernadette toward the door. "Do you want to cancel with Lydia and Pammy? Or we could make it a quick lunch. Your call."

"No, let's go. I haven't seen them since before the accident, and I need to."

That was so like her little bee. Tired, but thinking about other people. "Okay, but the instant you start fading, let me know, and we're out of there."

Bernadette reached up and patted her own shoulder. Rikki placed her hand on top and patted her back.

As they passed the coffee shop in the lobby, Rikki was aggravated to see that her unfinished coffee was still on the table. "I'll be right back." She parked Bernadette off to the side near a potted Ficus tree and stormed over to the shop. She grabbed her cup and trash and brought them to the bussing station.

"Ma'am, ma'am," one of the workers said, trying to get her attention, "you can't be back there."

"Well, someone has to do your job, don't they? Look at this place." She gestured to the tables and even the damn counter filled with trash. Rikki turned and headed back to Bernadette, not wanting to witness the young man's reaction. Every step she took helped her feel better. Until she got to Bernadette and saw her stricken expression.

"What's wrong?"

"Take me back." Bernadette pounded the arms of the wheelchair.

"Back where?"

"To the meeting." Bernadette pointed behind her. "Go, go, go."

"Okay, okay." Rikki turned the wheelchair around and headed back to the conference room. Dr. Wainwright and Olga were the only ones left.

Olga looked up with a surprised expression on her face. Rikki shrugged.

"I can't do it," Bernadette said to her department chair. "I thought I wanted it. I did. So badly. But I can't."

"Young lady," Dr. Wainwright said. "Take a breath and tell me what's going on."

"Baxter's courses," Bernadette said. "Don't you see? I can't take them. I can't give that…" She seemed to rethink her words and said a bit more calmly. "I can't abandon my Foundations class. I just developed it. I want to see it become the success I know it can be. I want those students to thrive. And Calculus, they need a helping hand, not indifference."

A knowing and sympathetic expression fell over Dr. Wainwright's face. He exchanged a look with Olga, and it seemed to Rikki that maybe they had hoped Bernadette would change her mind.

Dr. Wainwright nodded and then took a seat to be at the same level as Bernadette. "Do you know what you're asking?"

"Yes." One word. Short. To the point.

"I see." Dr. Wainwright turned to Olga and said, "Can you contact Dr. Yang and Dr. Kruk and have them see me this afternoon? Move things around if you need to."

"Yes, sir," Olga said and made a note on her laptop.

"I was going to surprise you, Dr. Carmichael, but as soon as we can move Dr. Baxter's things out, you're moving in. If that works for you." He looked at Bernadette and then Rikki, who was standing behind her.

"Fifth floor?" Bernadette asked.

"That'll work," Rikki said to Bernadette. "Don't you think?"

"I do think. I'll take it."

"Excellent," Dr. Wainwright said. "And since you're going to be developing the new Foundations course over another semester, I'm going to award you another developmental stipend. And, since we're laying things out on the table, I'm starting your associate professorship evaluation this term. By the end of this semester, I fully expect you to have that promotion."

The look on Bernadette's face was so mixed that Rikki almost started laughing. Instead, she patted Bernadette's shoulder and kept her hand there for comfort.

"Thank you," Bernadette finally muttered. She was clearly in shock.

Dr. Wainwright nodded and then said, "I like what you did with the new Foundations course, but Dr. Allison would like you to add in a lecture or two about the applications of group theory. He specifically wants—"

"Topology," Bernadette finished and laughed when Dr. Wainwright nodded and rolled his eyes.

Rikki grinned at Olga over the tops of the mathematicians' heads as they talked and exchanged ideas in a language so foreign it made her head swim.

"And three graduate students have submitted applications for you to be their doctoral advisor," Dr. Wainwright added. "Their topics look interesting, but you'll need to flesh out their ideas more if you decide to take them on."

He looked over at Olga and said, "Will you forward those applications to Dr. Carmichael?"

"Indeed," Olga said, her grin almost face-splitting.

They finished up a few details, and then Rikki wheeled her girl out and down to Shanice's van.

"Baby, are you sure that's what you want?"

"Yes. More sure than ever," Bernadette said as the lift brought her wheelchair up to van height. "I was focused on the wrong things. I was focused on what other people thought about me." Rikki hopped in the van to wheel Bernadette in place and lock her in. "I wasn't following my heart, Rikki. I need to do what makes me happy. What makes *me* happy. Not…not everyone else. And you know what?"

"What?"

"I love what I do."

"I saw that today," Rikki said, locking her in. "And when you so stubbornly wanted to be with your students, even remotely, at the rehab facility. I mean, c'mon. Who does that?"

Bernadette laughed. "Me, I guess. I don't know why I couldn't see what *I* wanted before."

"Maybe it's like philosopher Madison said, 'You don't know how valuable something is until it's gone.'" Rikki laughed. "Something like that."

Bernadette nodded. "We need to listen to that young woman more often."

"Indeed," Rikki said with a laugh and jumped in the driver's seat. "Indeed," she said again.

~~~

"They're here," Dana announced from her sentry post at the front window of Jaleesa's Beauty Shop and Supplies.

Rikki jumped up from the chair, having just gotten her split ends trimmed by one of Jaleesa's hairdressers. She threw a tip on the woman's station, a generous one because Jaleesa wouldn't let her or Bernadette pay for haircuts, so it was the least Rikki could do.

Jaleesa met Rikki at the window. Jaleesa pulled Dana back against her and kissed the top of her head. Dana looked up with such adoration that Rikki wondered what the customers in her shop thought about Jaleesa's many and varied women. One day, she'd ask.

"What are they doing?" Dana asked.

Rikki broke out laughing. "They're singing. Look." She pointed to Bernadette in the passenger seat, singing into a microphone made by Madison's closed fist. The microphone moved to Madison's mouth.

"Bohemian Rhapsody," Jaleesa said. "It has to be."

"It is," Rikki agreed. "It's on Madison's new playlist. You got one?"

"I did. I need to request a playlist for my shop," Jaleesa said. "You should ask Madison for a coffee-themed one."

"That one could do it," Rikki said.

"Hey, how's Harriet?" Jaleesa asked. "We haven't seen her in a while."

"Tina convinced her to leave the house, finally. She's at your house with the gang right now. Getting everything ready."

"Oh, great. Bernadette will be thrilled. She's been worried. We both have."

"Harriet's doing all right," Jaleesa said and squeezed the woman in her arms until she made a noise of protest. Rikki loved how affectionate Jaleesa was with her subs. All of them. She had such a big heart. "It's not a surprise, is it?"

"The homecoming party?" Rikki said. "No. The other thing taking up half my living room? Yes, that will be a surprise. She doesn't know about that."

"How is Bernadette doing overall?" Jaleesa asked.

"She's doing exceptionally well. We're so lucky."

"Are you suing?"

"She told our lawyer to sue if and only if our insurance combined with his doesn't cover all her medical expenses." Rikki turned to look at Jaleesa.

"Only medical? No pain and suffering? 'Mike Jones got me 1.3 million dollars,'" Jaleesa quoted from the ubiquitous billboards around town.

Rikki shook her head. "Ohio law says we have two years from the date of the accident to bring a suit. I personally want to string that guy up. He was in a hurry to meet his buddies at a bar when he changed lanes too soon and knocked her off the highway."

"Good thing it wasn't *after* the bar." Jaleesa sighed. "We don't know how we affect each other, do we? Individually and globally. All of humanity, I mean."

"Yeah. Things ripple." Rikki pointed out the window and chuckled at the rock stars still in the car. It looked like the song was reaching its conclusion, and the two singers were milking out every last note, especially now that they realized they had an audience. Rikki loved that her girl had gotten over most of her shyness with their friends.

"Wedding in two weeks, Rikki," Jaleesa said. "You ready?"

"Absolutely. Dress picked out. The wedding party's been fitted. I have no idea what Bernadette is wearing, but Shasti says it's perfect. My vows are written, but I keep adding stuff. I hope you're ready for a long exchange of vows."

Jaleesa simply nodded and said, "I'd expect nothing less. Rings?"

"I've noticed that one of two things happen when you're with a disabled person. Either you get over-the-top fast and courteous service, like with our rings. They were sized and ordered instantly. Or you get the treatment she got at the restaurant that we will never go to again. Bernadette was in the wheelchair, and the waiter spoke only to me. He didn't even greet her. He said, 'And what will she be having?' as if she wasn't even there.'"

"It wasn't a D/s thing? Maybe he recognized your awesome dominating presence and knew you'd be ordering for her, which I have seen you do." Jaleesa grinned, letting Rikki know she was teasing.

"I wish. Listen," Rikki said, "I'm just ecstatic to be able to tell the world that this beautiful and amazing woman agreed to marry me and let me take care of her."

Jaleesa nudged shoulders with Rikki and said, "Let her take care of you, too, my friend."

"Something I'm working on."

The driver's side car door opened, and Madison bolted out to retrieve the walker from the backseat.

"You breathing?" Jaleesa asked softly.

Rikki chuckled. "I think so. I've been watching her do this for over a week now. Ever since they declared her leg and arm to be weight-bearing Friday before last."

Madison held the metal walker firm and steady. She was extremely focused on her job and took her seneschal duties seriously. Bernadette swiveled in the seat like they'd taught her at physical therapy, grabbed onto the walker with both hands, and then stood up. A few of Jaleesa's workers and customers gathered around them, but all were silent as they watched the miracle unfold.

Bernadette stood up and then gathered herself. Rikki knew how much effort this had taken – putting weight on limbs that hadn't moved in over six weeks. Rikki didn't go to that morning's physical therapy session because Saturday mornings at her shop during the summer were rather busy. Madison had gladly volunteered to drive Bernadette. And even though Shasti had given her enthusiastic approval and Bernadette was fine with it, Rikki still held her breath when they drove away from the coffee shop that morning. Not because of Madison's driving. No. Because of her own inability to relinquish control.

Bernadette looked up, waved to the onlookers, and then said something to Madison, who let go and backed up.

"Bad leg first, then good," Rikki muttered, urging her girl on. "Move the walker forward. Not too far, not too far." She was relieved when Bernadette adjusted. "Good girl," she murmured.

"Breathe, Rikki," Jaleesa said.

Rikki blew out a sigh in answer.

"This is killing you, isn't it?"

"No," Rikki said. She gestured toward the two making progress toward the ramp Jaleesa had installed in recent weeks. "I'm watching an incredibly strong woman with an amazing spirit overcome an unbelievable setback. It's an honor to be able to help her."

"Methinks you are the one holding onto the trauma of the accident, my friend." Jaleesa patted Rikki on the back. "Isn't that what Shanice's Reiki voodoo witch doctor told you?"

"Yes." Rikki grimaced as Bernadette wobbled going up the ramp. Madison was right there to steady her. "Okay, fine. Both Bernadette *and* I have another appointment with the energy worker next week. And, yes, this is killing me. I'll admit it."

"There you go," Jaleesa said. "The first step is admitting you have a problem."

"Which reminds me." Rikki looked at her friend and said, "We've got sodas and non-alcoholic sparkling champagne as options for the wedding. The alcohol will be at a separate station. That'll do?"

"Absolutely. On behalf of my family and me, I thank you for understanding."

Astute Bernadette had been the one to make the request during their meeting with the wedding planner last week. Bernadette had also insisted on a caterer even though Tina wanted to do it. Bernadette held fast and insisted that Tina be a guest at their celebration. She had wedding party duties to attend to, didn't she?

Dana wiggled out of Jaleesa's hold and opened the front door wide enough for Bernadette to maneuver through.

"I made it," Bernadette declared to a salon now filled with applause and cheering. She stood in the open doorway while Jaleesa's staff and customers offered first their congratulations on her walking achievement and then their condolences on the accident happening in the first place.

Rikki was grateful when Jaleesa politely extricated Bernadette from the crowd and seated her in one of the chairs for a long-overdue trim.

"Thank you," Bernadette mouthed to Jaleesa's reflection in the mirror. Jaleesa stood behind her with a hand resting on each of Bernadette's shoulders.

Rikki sat in the next chair and had an epiphany watching them interact. Having someone close to your head and touching you the way Jaleesa was affectionately touching Bernadette might have sparked their attraction. Or maybe the spark had already been there, and a moment like this had ignited it. And that was okay. The polyamory they shared with Jaleesa was private and something that was welcomed by all three involved.

"What are you thinking about?" Bernadette said to Rikki. She reached over but couldn't quite touch Rikki's hand. "There's, like, smoke coming out of your head."

Rikki helped her out by grasping her hand and squeezing. "I was thinking how amazing you are."

Bernadette gave her a look that said she knew Rikki wasn't quite telling the truth, but she didn't press it. "Umm, baby?" Bernadette said. "Did you see me walk all the way from Madison's car up here?"

"I did."

"You said that RJ and MJ could come to live with us once I could walk."

Rikki looked over to Madison, who was talking Dana's ear off. Dana was very polite, but even Rikki could tell she had just about reached her tolerance level.

"Hey, Madison," Rikki called, and Madison scurried over. "You go on home and get the fur babies for Miss Bernadette, okay?"

"Ooh! Today?"

Rikki nodded. "Bring them and the supplies we discussed back to the house for the party."

Madison bopped up and down and did two slow but well-practiced pirouettes in the middle of Jaleesa's shop. "The kittens are moving in today, Professor," she said to Bernadette.

"Hurry," Bernadette gushed. "But drive carefully. Promise me."

"I promise. Okay, bye." And with that, Madison tore out of the salon.

Once Jaleesa was finished and Bernadette was satisfied, Rikki tipped Jaleesa, who automatically gave it to the young woman who swept the shop and washed the clients' hair.

"Meet you at the house?" Jaleesa said. "I have to shore things up here."

"You got it," Rikki said, helping Bernadette get out of the chair smoothly and grab the handles of her walker.

"Thank you, Miss Jaleesa," Bernadette said. "For everything."

Jaleesa chucked Bernadette under the chin but didn't respond beyond that and a smile.

"Party time," Bernadette said and wiggled like Madison minus the pirouettes. Uh oh. It looked like Madison was rubbing off on certain people. That was okay. It was amazing to watch her girl's transformation.

~~~

Bernadette reprised her exceptional walker skills in front of their friends who had gathered at the house to celebrate her homecoming officially. She had to walk the ramp since she wasn't strong enough to tackle steps yet. Rikki followed right behind her every step of the way. Shanice was the first one to greet Bernadette when she finally made it up to the porch.

"Ready?" Shasti said to the crowd. "One, two, three!"

"Welcome home!" the crowd cheered and then welcomed her inside the house.

Tina stepped forward with Harriet by her side. "We have a wonderful surprise for you."

"Ooh, okay," Bernadette said. Her jaw dropped open when they moved to one side, and she saw it. A baby grand piano sat in one corner of the living room. It was the perfect fit. "Oh, my God." Tears flooded her eyes, and she swiped them away. "Where did you get this?"

"Harriet's old school," Tina said. "They were replacing one of the pianos, and when they heard your story, they donated it to you."

"Donated?"

Harriet nodded. A grin crept up her face, which made Rikki smile. Apparently, smiles and joy had been sparse in Harriet's world lately.

"We asked Miss Rikki if it was okay," Tina continued.

"It was," Rikki said.

"And then Harriet refurbished it." Tina leaned in close and said, "Jaleesa's happy it's out of our garage."

Bernadette laughed and headed around the instrument to the bench. "May I?"

"Of course," Tina said. "It's yours."

Bernadette ran her hand over the cover to the keys. She lifted it and smiled. What she was thinking at that moment was anybody's guess. She played a few scales, testing out the keys. The scales morphed into an upbeat classical piece of music that Bernadette clearly loved, judging by her expression. She stopped playing abruptly and spent a few moments talking quietly with Harriet, who alternately nodded and grinned.

Ahh, Rikki's girl was something else. She knew how to reach people. Tina stayed close by Bernadette's side and finally said to her, "I need you to eat, honey."

"Umm, okay?" Bernadette said, clearly unfamiliar with being bossed around by Tina. Rikki just smirked. She had witnessed Jaleesa getting bossed by that particular submissive many times.

"I want you to sample some things I'm making for the *bye-bye brunch*," Tina said.

"What is that?"

"Sunday after the wedding. The folks who traveled from faraway lands will stop by to eat, give you their best wishes again, and then head out to catch their flights or drive home."

"I love that idea," Bernadette said. She stood, both hands on the walker, while Tina filled a plate at Bernadette's directions.

Rikki's heart was full. Oh, yes, this was what she wanted for her girl— genuine friendship and camaraderie with everyone in their community.

Bernadette looked up the stairs toward the second floor. She said to Tina, "I haven't been up there in almost seven weeks."

"I can't believe it's been over two months since the accident," Tina said and looked back at Bernadette. "I guess those stairs are something to work toward." Tina guided her to the couch, where a controlled crash was the only way to describe Bernadette's sitting.

Aww, Rikki's poor little bee must be so tired. A nap would be the order of the day once everyone left. Shoot, maybe before they left.

Madison loudly announced her arrival, and everyone made way for the box of joy she'd brought in. Jaleesa followed, carrying the rest of the accouterment the kittens would need. Litter box, scratching post, and bags which hopefully contained kitten chow and cans of wet food. Madison placed the kitty carrier on the couch next to Bernadette and opened the metal door. The kittens were shy – probably car sick – and wouldn't come out. Bernadette motioned to Madison to back away and let them come out in their own time.

At this point, Rikki had taken on the important job of holding up the doorframe to the kitchen. Shasti sidled up beside her and said, "The bathroom renovations are gorgeous. That oversized tub upstairs is something else. How did you get the work done so fast?"

"I mentioned Bernadette's accident to the contractor, and he wanted it done before she started walking. Voila! Did you see all the handrails?"

"Perfect for now and for the future."

Jaleesa made her way over to them. They looked on while the kittens slowly made their way out and found Bernadette's lap. When they didn't stop there and began crawling up her t-shirt, giggles overtook her. Tina grabbed the plate of food just in time. The scene was priceless.

"I'm glad you're finally putting a ring on it, Rikki," Jaleesa said.

"Me, too."

"Me, three," Shasti said and patted Rikki's shoulder.

Rikki turned to face her friend. "You know, Shasti. Everyone thinks it was Madison's doing – the whole 'get Miss Rikki and the professor together' thing? But it's dawning on me that your little one sometimes gets her ideas from her Mistress."

"Who me?" Shasti clutched her imaginary pearls. "Whatsoever do you mean?" The grin spreading on her face spoke volumes.

"I should have known," Rikki said and hugged her friend. "I should have known."

# Chapter 23
## Bernadette

The day had finally come. It was the second week in September, almost ten weeks since the accident. It was her wedding day. Bernadette had never been one of those girls who dreamed of getting married, let alone dream of the actual ceremony. And to be honest, it felt pretty surreal. She and Madison were the only ones left in the house. Along with Rikki and Miss Shasti, the wedding party had already gone outside to get in line to process.

"How's my dad doing?" Bernadette asked Madison to distract herself.

"He's good. Your sister-in-law Cathy is fussing over him, but he has a twinkle in his eye." Madison smoothed down her purple tie. "I think you're a Daddy's girl, aren't you?"

"I can neither confirm nor deny that." Bernadette chuckled and then smoothed down her own thin tie and checked the fit of her cream-colored pantsuit. It was more form-fitting than she usually liked, but Rikki enjoyed seeing her in revealing clothing. And today was the day she was giving herself publicly to Rikki. The thin purple and green accents sewn into the pants, sleeveless top, and jacket could have been garish but were surprisingly subtle and didn't overwhelm the outfit. Bernadette had absolutely no sense of fashion, but both Miss Shasti and Madison assured her over and over that her suit was perfect and would match Rikki's dress and the rest of the wedding party. If Madison's suit was any indication, then maybe she could believe it.

"Harriet?"

"She's here," Madison answered the unasked question. "And, before you ask, she seems okay. She's got a camera and is taking candids. Tina said she's a really good photographer. And she won't charge you like your official photographer is."

"I wish she and Dana had said yes to being in the wedding party."

"No, it's better this way," Madison said. "Dana is fussing with the flowers and watching Bailey. Hopefully, he can stay big during the ceremony. And Harriet? She has to have freedom, you know? Mistress explained that Harriet's type of anxiety is called depression and is different from mine."

Bernadette patted Madison on the forearm and nodded. She was still trying to understand Harriet's issues and the whole setup at Miss Jaleesa and Tina's house, but today was not the day to explore that.

A spike of nerves hit her when she realized yet again that she was getting married. Okay, she was already married legally, but this time it would be in front of her family and friends and the softball team and her Monday night darts friends and, oh, shit, a million other people. And had she really agreed to a collaring part of the ceremony? What was her father going to think? Shit. This was real. Really real.

"You'll be okay," Madison said as if reading her body language. "It's only your friends and your family out there. The people who love you, including your very handsome brother named Jordan."

Bless Madison for being able to read the room. "Oh? Does someone have a crush?"

"I can neither confirm nor deny that," Madison said business-like. "Um, the kittens are set in their room." Clearly, this was a conversation changer. "I'll check on them after the ceremony and a few times during the party."

"Thanks, kiddo," Bernadette said. "Got the ring?"

Madison patted her right front pocket, and then her left. "Yep."

"You've been a great help to me." Bernadette reached out and squeezed Madison's forearm.

"You're welcome, Professor. Mistress says I've been awfully grown up these days. You know we only, uh, you know, have private time when I'm big, and so…" Madison turned the most adorable shade of red Bernadette had ever seen.

"Thanks for sharing?" Bernadette said with a laugh and a definite question mark at the end. "Hey, did you see Rikki?" She tried to sound nonchalant but knew Madison wouldn't fall for it.

"Yep," Madison said. "And nope, I'm not telling you a thing other than she's beautiful."

"Does she have flowers in her hair like I do?"

Madison narrowed her eyes as if weighing how much she could reveal. She stood up tall, looked straight ahead, and said, "Madison, *little*, seneschal."

Bernadette burst out laughing. "Not talking, hmm? Fine. At least tell me *my* processional is set up."

"It is. Miss Rachel, who is very nice in spite of her resting-butch face, is ready and knows what to do."

"Resting *butch-face*? Madison," Bernadette reprimanded with a laugh.

"She's scary looking. She's hard, but I like her. Her wife Lisa is really nice, too. We're friends on *Kinks* now. They're from Tennessee."

"I know."

"They have cool accents."

This could go on for days. "How about Jordy? Is he ready?"

Madison sighed at his name. "Yes, he's ready, too." She handed Bernadette a picture. "Umm, I got you this."

The tears that had been threatening to spill all morning finally made their appearance. "Where did you get this?" Bernadette asked, taking a tissue from Madison's outstretched hand.

"From Jordan. I asked him to bring one about this size. You should tuck it into that small pocket there." Madison pointed to the small pocket-watch pocket in Bernadette's pants.

Bernadette nodded, kissed the photo of her mother, and tucked it away lovingly. She dabbed at the tears still brimming in her eyes and knew it would be an entire day of this. But that was okay. During their pillow talk that morning, Rikki told her to be present and feel everything. Feel the nerves, feel the joy, feel the love.

Speaking of nerves, they spiked when the processional music began playing in the yard. Luthor Vandross's "Here and Now" played over the speakers. "Oh, shit," Bernadette murmured. "This is really real." The wedding party must be processing now.

"Yeah, it is," Madison said. "But you'll be okay."

Bernadette barely had her nerves under control when the wedding planner blew into the living room, her energy almost knocking Bernadette over. "It's time. Let's go. Let's go."

208

Bernadette walked out to the front porch, hating the fact that she had to use the cane but grateful that her back wasn't giving her fits today. Miss Shasti made her realize that even though she hadn't broken bones in her back or neck—thank goodness—her entire body had still taken quite a blow in the crash and was still in a bit of shock and bruised up. Bernadette believed it because she still didn't quite feel like herself even though the bones were healed. She was working on flexibility and muscle strength and all of that, but she'd hoped to be much farther along by now.

But today was a good day. Bernadette made sure the brakes were engaged and sat down in the wheelchair. Madison wheeled her down the ramp to the driveway and onto the newly built walkway that meandered around the house to the ample backyard. Rikki said they would keep the walkway and the wedding ceremony deck out back permanently for barbecues and gatherings in the future.

The September early afternoon skies were blue with lovely white puffy clouds in full cooperation with the day's events. They wouldn't have to use the tents for the ceremony, just for the reception and cake cutting. Yay.

Madison handed her the amazing bouquet of flowers that Dana had put together. She clutched them so hard her knuckles were turning white. Relax, she scolded herself and let up.

In front of her, the flower girls were staged to process. Pammy held onto the handles of Shanice's wheelchair, and both looked ready to go. Pammy's blonde pigtails were so cute. Lydia, her Mommy Domme, had obviously done her up. And Marta had put Shanice's hair into two adorable puffballs with purple bows keeping with the color scheme. Shanice's and Pammy's grins were priceless.

"Are you ready, Miss Bernadette?" Pammy whispered from behind the wheelchair.

Bernadette nodded but widened her eyes and took a big breath for their benefit. There were many things to celebrate this week. Next Wednesday, Shanice was going in for what would hopefully be the final fitting of her prosthetic limbs. Everyone had their fingers and toes crossed every which way for her. Bernadette beamed at Shanice, and the *little* waved back, her basket of flower petals in her lap, ready to dispense.

In the yard, Rikki's bride music came on. "Here, There and Everywhere" by the Beatles. Rikki's mother loved the Beatles, so she had chosen that song to feel her mother's presence. Tears sprang to Bernadette's eyes. She wished she could be out there watching Rikki walk up the aisle, holding her bouquet. She'd watch the video later but was sorry she was missing it in real time. Both she and Rikki were walking by themselves—they agreed not to have anyone "give them away." Besides, it would have been incredibly awkward and embarrassing with only Bernadette's dad there and not Rikki's.

Pammy jumped as the wedding planner barked at her to get moving. She dutifully pushed Shanice forward on the boardwalk. Madison pushed Bernadette behind them, still out of view of the crowd. The music changed again. The Piano Guys' instrumental cover of Christina Perri's "A Thousand Years" played over the speakers. This was her music. It had been a suggestion from Kari's piano teacher. Oh, God, this was it. She blew out a sigh.

"Breathe, Professor," Madison said softly. "These people love you."

Madison was such a good seneschal. Very perceptive. Bernadette put her hand on her own shoulder, and Madison patted it. "Let's do it," Bernadette said.

Madison took off slowly and rounded the corner with Bernadette in the wheelchair. Her friends and family got to their feet. Oh, shoot. Bernadette teared up. She had forgotten they do this at weddings. Oh, God. Look at all the people. *Breathe, breathe, breathe.*

She searched for the woman her heart sought. The one who grounded her. She found Rikki on the wedding platform, surrounded by their friends. "Oh. My. God. She's so beautiful," Bernadette murmured, taking in the baby's breath in Rikki's hair piled up on her head with those delicious tendrils falling down her long neck. The flowers somehow brought out the copper highlights in her favorite redhead's hair. And that tight bodice on the floor-length dress showed off Rikki's lovely figure. Oh, yeah, girls, she's mine. Everyone back off!

Bernadette tried not to tear up again as she watched Rikki trying to remain stoic and not get emotional at seeing Bernadette for the first time that day. Bernadette watched Rikki's expression go from one of pure joy to one of concern as she took in Bernadette in the wheelchair. Her eyes and expression asked a thousand questions. Bernadette reached up to touch her collar for comfort but remembered that Rikki had taken it off her that very morning. She felt a little lost without it.

Bernadette answered her telepathically. *Don't worry, my love. Don't worry. All is well.* She felt her own body relax as she calmed Rikki with her thoughts. Odd how that worked.

Madison wheeled Bernadette slowly down the processional walkway between the rows of white foldup chairs. She stopped next to Lisa's Domme, Miss Rachel, who eased the metal walker out to the aisle. Madison scurried around the wheelchair, snapped the walker open, and placed it in front of Bernadette. Once Bernadette was standing, Miss Rachel pulled the wheelchair out of the way. Bernadette chanced a glance at Rikki. A knowing grin took over Rikki's countenance. Good. *She knows, but she doesn't know everything. Now, does she?* Bernadette grinned back.

Bernadette headed down the aisle with the walker until she reached the first row. She smiled at Rikki's sister and brother on her right. She hoped to get to know them better during their stay and maybe get some good dirt on her beloved. Miss Rowena and her submissive Minjung also sat in the front row as Rikki's honored guests. Curiously, there was an empty seat in that row. Was that for Rikki's dad, who couldn't be bothered to attend? Seamus and his boys sat beaming in the second row. His adorable *little* had on the purple and green beanie hat, a gift from Rikki and Bernadette to all the *littles*. She turned to face her own family on the left. All three of them were positively beaming, making Bernadette's heart soar. Her dad had tears in his eyes, though. "Oh, Dad," she said, "don't make me cry." He blew her a kiss. By some miracle, she didn't succumb to the threatening tears and kept her cool.

In the second row, Bianca, Eashon, and Marty, her three now-official doctoral students, sat grinning like cats that had caught canaries. Bernadette turned back to Jordy and handed the walker to him, who in turn popped her favorite cane in her hand.

"Love you guys," Bernadette said to them. She turned, took a deep breath, and walked the rest of the way to the wedding platform—flowers in one hand, cane in the other. She hated that she still had to use the cane, but whatever. She accounted for the slight slope and felt Madison hovering right behind her. Rikki put a hand out, and Bernadette gave her flowers to Madison so she could grab Rikki's hand. She was thankful for the lifelines. She sighed big, and it must have been obvious because the audience laughed and then burst into applause.

Bernadette looked back over her shoulder at the applauders and nodded her thanks while blinking back tears.

"You look amazing, little bee," Rikki murmured.

"As do you, my love," Bernadette said and leaned against Rikki for grounding.

Bernadette took a moment to take in Miss Shasti, Miss Marta, Mark, Miss Lydia, Kari, and Pammy on Rikki's side. They looked so lovely in their matching suits and dresses, with the green more prominent, holding their bouquets of flowers. She turned her head to look at her side. There was Madison, Tina, Lisa, Miss Olga, DeShawn, and Shanice. Purple was the more prominent color on this side. The whole thing had come together so well. She'd made plenty of lists, of course, but it was mainly Rikki, Miss Shasti, Tina, and Madison's doing. She realized that, except for Miss Olga, she hadn't known a single one of these people a year ago, yet in that time, she knew she had made lifelong friends.

Miss Jaleesa cleared her throat gently as if to get Bernadette's attention. Bernadette looked up and melted as she took in their officiant for the first time. The tall and solid Amazonian Black woman that stood at the podium was resplendent in her white minister's robe, the clergy stole draped around her neck. Interestingly, it was piped in alternating greens and purples. An odd coincidence? Bernadette thought not. Her short fro looked relaxed and—what was the right word—elegant. Perfect for the occasion. She was so handsome. So pretty. She was both, actually, and her commanding presence made Bernadette relax.

Bernadette handed her cane to Madison, who had been told to be ready to receive and give it back at a moment's notice. Bernadette took back her flowers and held them with a slightly less death grip.

"Dear friends and family," Miss Jaleesa said, her big voice filling the scene, "we are gathered here to join Rikki Carmichael and Bernadette Garneau in loving matrimony. I have been given the auspicious honor of officiating this ceremony, and I ask you to join me today in acknowledging, honoring, and celebrating their union. By your presence here, you witness and affirm the truth and validity of their love and commitment to each other. Please be seated."

Bernadette heard, rather than saw, the audience take their seats. There was a slight rustle behind them, and both she and Rikki turned their heads to see what was happening. Victoria was making her way to the empty seat next to Rowena. She was led by the chief usher, who also happened to be Miss Olga's submissive husband. Once seated, Victoria looked up and nodded at Rikki, who nodded back. She shifted her gaze to Bernadette, who was still wrestling with this surprise. She lifted her head and decided, yes, it was time to forgive Victoria and move on once and for all. Forgive and, yes, forget. Bernadette smiled and nodded back. Victoria mouthed, "Thank you."

Bless Miss Jaleesa for understanding the exchange unfolding before them and waiting. After another beat, she said, "The seneschals for both brides arranged for photos of the brides' respective mothers and beloved aunt to be placed in honorary witness to their wedding."

Madison held out her hand and pointed toward Bernadette's pocket. When Bernadette realized what was happening, she teared up again. Oh, that little devil. She handed over the picture of her mother, and Rikki handed over the pictures of her mother and Aunt Tilda to Miss Shasti, who clipped them all to a board attached to Miss Jaleesa's podium.

A soft groan of emotion from Miss Marta elicited a slight chuckle from the group on the platform. Mark handed Miss Marta his handkerchief. She wiped away her tears—softy, that one.

Bernadette blinked back her own tears and exchanged a glance with Rikki, who was doing the same. Apparently, she hadn't known about this either.

Bernadette and Rikki held hands as Miss Jaleesa spoke to them and the crowd about the meaning of marriage. She spoke about commitment— emotional, physical, and spiritual. She talked about love, respect, and honor. And then she spoke about the friendship and the mutual respect that she had watched bloom and grow between the two brides. She also cautioned against complacency and assumptions. Her words were well thought out, and Bernadette hoped to watch the video of the ceremony many times over to hear the words again and again. Bernadette couldn't help smiling. She wasn't thinking of Rikki at that moment, though. No, she was thinking how strong, sure, and amazing Miss Jaleesa was. Her Dominance was steady and present. She never faltered, never hemmed, hawed, ummed, or erred.

Miss Jaleesa caught her smile and returned it warmly. It was a smile of friendship and mutual respect, nothing else. Miss Jaleesa finished her oratory with a message about keeping the mind, body, and spirit in balance. She then smoothly segued into the exchange of vows.

"A vow is a solemn promise," Miss Jaleesa said. "It's like an oath from the heart. The brides have written their own vows, and I ask them to please face each other."

They handed their bouquets to their respective seneschals, and then Rikki clasped Bernadette's hands in hers.

"Rikki," Miss Jaleesa said, "if you're ready."

"I *am* ready," Rikki said. "Bernadette, when Madison went to your table at Rocco's Diner and you looked up, my heart fluttered. I was instantly drawn to you. How could a woman that attractive be single? The only thing I knew about you, though, was that you were kiddo's professor. Out of my league."

General laughter went through the crowd, mainly from the lifestylers who knew better.

"My Aunt Tilda introduced me to a way of life that made sense to me, as she knew it would. Oh, my heart soared when I quickly learned that you understood that life but hadn't quite found your place in it yet. That day of the big storm. What did you call it? The best snow day ever? Well, that was the day I fell for you. You jumped in and bused tables while I ushered out the silly customers who didn't seem to care that the blizzard was upon us. You offered to help Marta in the kitchen." Bernadette saw Miss Marta nod out of the corner of her eye.

Rikki looked out to the audience and said, "Loving Bernadette is easy." She looked back at her bride and continued, "I knew you were different, little bee. Your actions spoke louder than your words. You embrace the tenets of consent, honesty, and communication. You are the most beautiful, smart, kind, and generous woman I have ever met. These are the qualities that not only make you an amazing teacher—"

A series of cheers and whistles from Bernadette's three doctoral students made both Rikki and Bernadette smile.

"See?" Rikki continued, "These qualities not only make you an amazing teacher but an amazing partner. Bernadette, you make me understand how good life can be. I get it now. You make me a better person, and I am humbled that you chose me as your partner in life."

Miss Marta wasn't the only one dabbing at tears at Rikki's words, but Bernadette did her best to blink hers back.

"This ceremony affirms my love for you. I promise always to respect you, listen to you, and hear you. I promise to love you for better or worse, in sickness …" she paused as a series of sympathetic noises and "Awws" came from the wedding party and the crowd. Rikki cleared her throat. "In sickness and in health. I want you by my side. Always my partner." She paused for a moment and said with an emotionally shaky voice, "I love you, Bernadette." She reached up and bopped Bernadette's nose with one finger.

Miss Marta's noises of emotion were becoming more and more comical. The wedding party chuckled at her inability to stop crying.

Bernadette rubbed Rikki's forearm and mouthed, "I love you, too."

Rikki clasped both of Bernadette's hands again.

"Bernadette," Miss Jaleesa said, "if you're ready, please begin."

"Yes, Ma'am," Bernadette said, looking straight at Miss Jaleesa. She turned to face Rikki and said, "Rikki, one look into those soulful green eyes of yours, and I was a goner. If I'd realized you were single back then, this might have been a June wedding." Laughter peppered the crowd, relaxing Bernadette a bit. "But then again, I think maybe there were experiences I needed to go through before I was ready for you." She was thinking about the Dommes she'd had in her past. Miss Ciara, Goddess Julie, Mama_Luvs, and Victoria. Each had taught her something. Each had brought her a different and ever-growing understanding of Dominant/submissive relationships and the lifestyle overall.

"I promise to help bear the challenges we face. You don't have to take it all on yourself. You've had to deal with so much with my accident already. The nursing staff told me you were by my side every single minute you were allowed. When did you eat? I mean, c'mon, when did you go to the bathroom?" She had to wait while the crowd laughed.

She almost lost her composure when she saw the tears brimming in Rikki's eyes. "You've shown me how strong and dedicated you are. I hope to be able to do the same for you."

"Ohhhh," Miss Marta moaned as her head fell back. She obviously couldn't handle the emotion.

Bernadette and Rikki burst out laughing when each person in the wedding party whipped out a small pack of tissues and held it toward Miss Marta. Even Lisa, who had just met everyone, was in on the joke. Miss Marta grabbed a few from Mark and Miss Lydia and then waved everyone else away. She motioned for Bernadette to continue.

"And this perfectly brings me to my next point. You brought me amazing friends and a supportive and structured community. They welcomed me into their fold quickly, and that was because of you, Rikki. But let me wrap this up. I'm used to giving one-hour lectures," she said with a laugh. "I promise to be your partner in all things big and small, terrifying and easy. I promise to take care of you the way you have taken care of me. I love you, baby."

Miss Jaleesa held her hand out for one of the tissues, and DeShawn hooked her up. "Oh, wow," Miss Jaleesa said to the crowd. "How do you follow these two? You don't. Time for the rings."

Miss Jaleesa talked about a ring being an unending circle signifying unending love and commitment and then said, "Rikki, do you have the ring?"

Rikki nodded as Miss Shasti stepped forward and produced a small black box. She opened it, and Rikki pulled out the gold band she and Bernadette had picked out together. "Rikki, do you take Bernadette to be your lawfully wedded wife, to have and to hold, in sickness and health, to love, honor, in good times and woe, for richer or poorer, keeping yourself solely unto her for as long as you both shall live?"

Rikki looked Bernadette in the eye and said, "I do." Miss Jaleesa nodded, and Rikki slid the wedding ring on. She then took the engagement ring off Bernadette's right hand and slid it next to the wedding band, locking it in place. Miss Jaleesa explained that this symbolized the love that had brought them together would always protect and sustain their marriage.

"Bernadette," Miss Jaleesa said, "do you have the ring?"

Madison stepped forward and pulled a similar black box from her pants pocket. She opened it, and both Bernadette and Rikki burst out laughing. Inside the velvet box were two Fruity Os. One purple and one green.

Miss Shasti looked fit to be tied, so Madison snapped the box closed and then jammed her hand into the other pocket, producing another black box with the real gold ring.

Miss Jaleesa read the same pledge to Bernadette. However, this time, the word *obey* had been slipped in. Bernadette smiled when she heard it.

"I do," Bernadette said, surprised she wasn't bursting into tears at this point.

She slid the ring on Rikki's finger when Miss Jaleesa nodded for her to do so. Rikki bit her bottom lip and locked eyes with Bernadette.

"Rikki," Miss Jaleesa said, "you had one more symbol of your commitment to your lovely bride."

Miss Shasti stepped forward and handed Rikki a cream-colored, lacy piece of fabric that matched Bernadette's wedding suit. Rikki took it and held it up. She spoke low, making the moment much more intimate.

"Bernadette, will you also honor me by wearing this collar? We're equals, baby. You are never less than or lower. Our power exchange dynamic is one that I think suits your needs and mine. Will you agree that I am the captain of our ship and that you're my very sexy and powerful first mate?"

"One who promises to *obey*?"

"Heh heh," Rikki chuckled. "You heard that, hmm?"

"Mm hmm. Obey, yes. Blindly, no."

"I'd expect nothing less."

"Yes, Rikki," Bernadette said. "I will continue to wear your collar."

Rikki leaned forward and clasped the lacy wedding collar around Bernadette's neck. Bernadette reached up and touched it. She sighed. Yes, that felt like home.

Rikki looked back up at Miss Jaleesa and gave her a nod that said she was finished.

Miss Jaleesa said a few more words to the crowd and then addressed Bernadette and Rikki. "In closing, I want to inform you two that your relationship is an inspiration to all of us. Your mutual respect for one another is clear and present. May you two laugh often and continue to share your light with those around you. And in case you hadn't noticed, you are both loved and cherished by those of us here witnessing your union."

Miss Jaleesa cleared her throat, stood taller, and said, "By the power vested in me by the state of Ohio, I now pronounce you officially and legally married. Rikki, you may kiss your bride."

Rikki pulled Bernadette close. She moved in slowly and pressed her lips against Bernadette's. The kiss increased in fervor until Rikki pulled back with a smile. "I love you, baby."

"I love you, too, Rikki," Bernadette said. No, she would never get tired of saying that.

In her big booming voice, Miss Jaleesa said, "May I now present Mrs. and Dr. Carmichael."

"You changed your name?" Madison gushed behind Bernadette.

Bernadette nodded at Madison, and then she and Rikki turned to face the crowd as their recessional music started. Before moving, they waved while the audience clapped and whooped and hollered. Bernadette burst out laughing when she realized what the recessional song was. "Chains of Love" by Erasure blasted into the yard. The wedding party behind them also laughed when they picked up on the lyrics. It was the perfect song with the perfect tempo and the perfect message. Madison's pick. It had to be.

"Let's do this," Rikki said.

"For a lifetime," Bernadette agreed as they recessed back up the walkway under a shower of soapy bubbles filling the air all around them.

# Chapter 24
## Rikki

Rikki held her wife's friend Lisa loosely in her arms as they danced to a slow song. The reception was winding down, and many of the guests had already said their goodnights and left. Rikki was getting tired, but that was okay. This was a once-in-a-lifetime event, so she would find reserve energy somewhere. The reception dinner had been delicious, although her nerves, not to mention the tight dress, wouldn't let her eat too much. During the cake ceremony afterward, there were no untoward incidents, with the small exception of a bit of white icing dabbed onto a certain submissive's nose.

Lisa's long brown hair cascaded down her back and still looked fresh and styled, even after such a long day. "Thank you for letting me be a part of your celebration," Lisa said as Rikki twirled her toward Rachel, her Domme, who was patiently waiting to take her wife back to the hotel.

"Of course. Of course. You've known her longer than I have," Rikki said with a laugh, which was answered with a similar one. She spun Lisa one more time into the waiting arms of her Domme.

"There you go," Rikki said. "Safe and secure where she belongs."

"Thanks," Rachel said gruffly. "We'll be back for brunch tomorrow morning."

"Yay," Lisa said, nestling into Rachel's arms, one hand holding onto Rachel's shoulder. It seemed like Lisa wanted to say something but didn't. She clearly deferred to her Domme to do all the speaking. This was not, nor would it ever be, one of Rikki's rules, but she had to respect another couple's dynamic. She may not agree with it, but it wasn't *her* life. Just like others might not agree with the way she and Bernadette conducted theirs.

"I'll contact you about your visit in October," Rachel said. "Columbus Day weekend?"

"Yes, Bernadette has a long weekend, and you're only four or five hours away. And listen, while I have you here alone, I want to thank you both for the amazing support you gave my girl as she struggled to find her way in this *lifestyle*."

"Glad to do it," Rachel said. "I'm happy these two found each other." She gestured from Lisa to Bernadette and back again. She took a breath, clearly tired, and stepped back. To Lisa, she said, "Go say goodbye to your new friends. Don't bother Bernadette right now. She's dancing with her father again."

"Yes, Ma'am," Lisa said and skipped away from her Domme. It was almost Madison-esque.

Rikki nodded to Rachel and said, "Thanks again. See you tomorrow."

"Will do."

Ahh, good. It looked like the Daddy/daughter dance was finishing up, so Rikki took that moment to sidle up beside her new bride. Just as she got there, she heard Bernadette's father say, "There's no shame in it, Stinky. We Garneaus are known for being attracted to strong take-charge women." He looked up, saw Rikki, and said, "Speaking of," and gave Bernadette's hand to Rikki. "Take good care of my baby."

"I will, Mr. Garneau," Rikki said.

"She will, Dad," Bernadette said, her cheeks pinking up. Was she embarrassed by her doting dad? That was cute.

"Let me find Cathy and see what we're doing." Bernadette's father hugged his daughter. "I know we'll be back for brunch tomorrow."

"Love you, Dad," Bernadette said as he walked away toward Bernadette's sister-in-law.

"Love you, too," he called back.

Once he was out of earshot, Rikki took her wife in her arms and said, "What was that all about, *Stinky*?"

"I can't believe he called me that right in front of you." Bernadette leaned her head against Rikki's chest as they swayed to the slow music. "Apparently, he had to change one of my particularly stinky diapers when I was a baby." She shrugged.

"And the 'no shame' part?"

"Oh, my God, Rikki," Bernadette picked her head up and looked into Rikki's eyes. "He touched my collar and told me that Cathy told him what it meant."

Rikki's eyes grew wide.

"No, no," Bernadette said quickly. "Cathy's cool. She asked me about it that time I ran away from you to go back home and get my head together. She understands. I mean, I didn't give her every detail, just the gist. But my dad said that my mother was a strong woman, and he learned early on that it was okay to let her lead. I guess I always took it for granted that moms lead the family. He then pointed out Jordy's wife, Cathy, and told me how she takes care of both of them. Did you know that my mother's will didn't leave everything to my father?"

"It didn't?"

"No, she owned the house outright on her own. I don't know why. But she left me, Jordy, and Dad equal child's portions or whatever it's called. When they sold the house, I got my third. That's how I was able to make the down payment on this old farmhouse. My dad always told me to live like you mean it, so I bought the house to do just that."

"And that's what we intend to do, right? Live like we mean it?"

Bernadette nodded. "Oh, and by the way. You're officially on the deed now."

"Well, check that out." Rikki swayed them side to side to the music. "I got a house and the woman of my dreams on the same day. How lucky am I? Thank you for taking care of that."

"Of course," Bernadette said. "My dad said he really likes you and told me he thinks I will be happy with you."

"And that's what's important, my fading little bee." Rikki wanted to spin Bernadette around the way she had many of her partners that evening, including Shanice in her chair, but Bernadette still wasn't strong enough for anything like that. Her back had been hurting her lately, and she couldn't even manage stairs yet.

"Fading? No one's fading here." Bernadette snuggled close to Rikki again. "Oh, and he also said my mom would approve."

"Aww. That's awesome," Rikki said. She squeezed her wife tight and said, "My mom and Aunt Tilda would definitely approve, too."

"I'm sorry your sister and brother had to leave so early. I hardly got a chance to talk to them."

"They had a flight to catch."

Rikki felt Bernadette take a big breath and let it out in a sigh. "Can we maybe talk about your family some time? I mean, not today, but someday?"

"Yes."

"Yes?"

"Don't sound surprised," Rikki said. "I'm ready to open up. I think. Now that I've found someone I trust wholeheartedly."

"Me?" Bernadette looked up at her coyly.

"Yes, you, little bee." Rikki bopped her nose with a fingertip. "Oops, it looks like another wave of guests is leaving. We need to look awake."

"No one here is sleeping," Bernadette said, pulling back. She raised one eyebrow, leaned in close, and whispered, "This is my wedding night. I expect you to be hard all night."

"Oh, ho," Rikki said with a laugh. "I'll see what I can do." She didn't relish spending their wedding night in two side-by-side hospital beds in the *littles'* room. That damn separation down the middle was getting on her last nerve, but as long as she had her little bee, she'd put up with it. "C'mon, let's go see people off. I can see Rachel getting impatient."

After signaling to the DJ that she could wrap things up, Rikki and Bernadette said their goodbyes to their guests, adding to the headcount attending the *bye-bye brunch* the following day. Tina and Jaleesa's crew would be over early to set up and get ready. It was their gift to the newlyweds. Bernadette made Kari promise to play something for them on piano, whatever she wanted, and she reluctantly agreed when Harriet nodded that she should. Those two seemed to be forming some kind of friendship, nothing romantic, but that was nice to see.

The caterers were just about packed up. The DJ was breaking down her station, and a general cleanup and chair stacking had begun by the wedding planner's hired crew. Rikki and Bernadette headed into the house with a few of their friends. Rikki plopped down on the couch, pulling Bernadette beside her. After getting permission from Rikki, Madison deposited not one but two kittens on Bernadette's lap.

"Look," Bernadette said, picking up RJ, "she has on her tuxedo for the wedding."

"So does MJ," Madison added, pointing to the kittens' black and white coloring.

"Aww, c'mere," Rikki said, reaching for her namesake and cuddling her close.

Shasti, who had become one with the oversized chair, patted her lap and opened her arms. Madison flew into them with such a practiced and honed finesse that it made everyone laugh. It was always surprising to see them get lovey-dovey with each other because they weren't overly demonstrative in public, most likely because Madison was often *little* in public due to her anxiety.

"Wedding? Done," Jaleesa said and then pointed to the basement door. "Dungeon? Next on the Carmichael Family to-do list."

"At least the bathroom's done down there," Rikki said. "And the whole thing's painted." She patted Bernadette on the thigh, careful not to smack MJ on Bernadette's lap, playing with Bernadette's fingers.

"You kids have earned a rest for a bit," Jaleesa conceded. She and Tina headed into the kitchen so Tina could get some things set up before the brunch the following day. Jaleesa looked like a puppy following her around, constantly trying to get her attention. She wanted hugs and kisses. It was obvious that Tina enjoyed the attention, but she also found it frustrating that Jaleesa wouldn't let her work.

Bernadette struggled to sit up, "I need to help Tina."

"No," came Tina's quick reply from the kitchen. "It's your wedding day. Stay right where you are, honey. And you," Tina said, poking Jaleesa in the chest, "Go out back and check on the cleanup, would you? Get out of my hair."

"Fine," Jaleesa pouted, but it was a playful pout. She followed the direction of Tina's finger, pointing toward the back door.

Rikki grinned. Those two always found an equilibrium somehow.

Bernadette loosened her tie. "Thank you for the tower of chocolate cupcakes, baby. That was surprising and, umm, special."

"It's called a groom's cake, but neither of us was a groom. Were we?"

"Nope," Bernadette said with a chuckle. "Rikki?"

"Mm hmm?"

"I, uh, I had a bad day that day."

Rikki petted RJ behind the ears, causing an eruption of purring. These little fuzzballs were so cute. "That transgression was punished and long forgotten," Rikki said. Long forgotten in Rikki's mind, so what was bringing this up now? Did Bernadette think the cupcake tower was Rikki's passive-aggressive way of bringing up the incident? It wasn't. Chocolate cupcakes were her girl's favorite, plain and simple.

"I know, but can I explain?" Bernadette had an urgency in her voice that couldn't be denied, and since Shasti and Madison only had eyes for each other and Tina was busy in the kitchen, they had a modicum of privacy. Rikki nodded.

"I'd had a long day and still had the basement painting to do," Bernadette said. "I was cooking dinner, and it was stuff I hate. Broccoli and salmon, I think. *You* like it, and since I was trying to be the dutiful housewife, I cooked it for you."

"I never once asked you to be a housewife. Ever. You took that upon yourself."

"I know, and I'll get to that. But then you called and said you wouldn't be home for dinner. Rikki, I lost my shit. Well, it wasn't just that. I heard you talking to Victoria and thought you were hanging out with her again while I was home slaving away for you. I flung the utensils in the pan, turned off the heat, and blindly went out in search of comfort food. Hungry Hamlet's—"

"Hold on. You went to a fast-food joint that evening? It wasn't just the cupcakes?"

"No, it wasn't. And it was *eight* cupcakes, not two like I told you."

"Bernadette," Rikki said low. "You blatantly lied to me." That was unacceptable.

Bernadette pulled away from Rikki, but Rikki pulled her right back. "Unh uh," Rikki said. "You stay right here. No pulling away. That's what you did that night instead of talking to me like you should have."

"I know. I had this idea that I needed to cook for you and do our laundry—"

"I never—"

"I know. Again, I know. Miss Jaleesa reminded us today about making assumptions. I just assumed a good submissive did these things without being asked like it was part of the role. And, Rikki, I found out that day that I didn't like that role when it wasn't appreciated or even acknowledged."

"I'm sorry I made you feel that way," Rikki said. "I may have gotten complacent in the roles we had taken on as well."

"And I'm sorry I lied back then. I'll take whatever punishment you feel is appropriate, but can that wait until after the brunch tomorrow?"

"No."

Bernadette groaned.

"No, you were honest with me tonight, of all nights, my adorable little bee." Rikki kissed Bernadette's forehead. "I am not super pleased with the fact that you lied to me, and that will certainly not be tolerated again. But I think you've beaten yourself up enough over this. There will be no punishment, but how about this? After the brunch tomorrow, we'll sit down and map out a reasonable schedule for food prep and house cleaning and yard work and laundry for both of us. *Both* of us. Bernadette, it takes two to have a relationship. You have a voice here. I insist on it."

"Okay, but you have the shop and—"

"And what? I'm one-half of this two-person team and should pull my weight. Let's not forget that you also have a full-time job, one that has gotten more intense with doctoral students, as well as a new venture with the math videos you agreed to do for that engineering group."

"Yeah. All of that is true," Bernadette said. Rikki felt her girl relax a little in her arms. And that was good.

"And with both of us so busy, it's going to be difficult for us to find time for our Hawaii trip."

"Baby?" Bernadette sat bolt upright. "Hawaii?"

"Or Alaska. Europe, maybe? Paris, Rome? I have to take you on a honeymoon, don't I?"

Before Bernadette could respond, Tina called from the kitchen, "Take the trip to Paris, honey."

Bernadette chuckled and then said softly to Rikki, "Yes. Yes, you do have to take me on a honeymoon." She snuggled up against Rikki again.

"We'll figure it out. Now, getting back to the other topic. I do want you to try new foods and to eat healthily, but I never want you to suffer through foods you hate."

"Really? I don't have to eat broccoli ever again?"

"No, baby, you don't."

"Yay." Bernadette kissed MJ on the nose and said in a baby voice, "No more broccoli for you, either, little girl."

"Mistress," Madison said in a sleepy voice, "do I have to eat broccoli anymore?"

"Yes, you do, peanut," Shasti answered, but her voice lacked its usual stern tone.

"Darn," Madison said to accompanying laughter from her Mistress and everyone else in the house, including Tina in the kitchen.

"Tell you what," Shasti said. "We'll smother it with cheese. You like it that way."

"Oh, yeah," Madison said and sat up. "I forgot." She stood up when Shasti nudged her off her lap. "Mistress?"

"Hmm?"

"I'm very big right now."

"Is that right?"

"Mm hmm. Very, very big."

"I'll take that into consideration," Shasti said. She looked tired, but Rikki had a feeling her house wasn't going to be the only one rocking that evening.

"Bow chicka wow wow," Bernadette teased, making Madison bury her face in Shasti's dress out of embarrassment.

Jaleesa came barreling back into the house via the front door. "The yard is cleared and cleaned. The chairs and tables are stacked under the tent for the rental place to pick up tomorrow, and we are now free to leave the lovebirds alone."

"Thanks, Jaleesa," Rikki said, standing up.

Bernadette used Rikki's arm to help her stand. "It was a great day. You were incredible. All of you." She put MJ on her shoulder, and by some miracle, the kitten stayed there, content on her human tower.

"I had good people to work with," Jaleesa said and then went into the kitchen to drag Tina out. "She'd be in there all night."

"Would not," Tina protested. "Well, maybe."

Rikki and Bernadette gave hugs and repeated thanks all around and followed their friends out to the front porch after depositing the kittens back in their room. Rikki's eyes grew big when she saw two rocking chairs on the porch, each with a big red ribbon.

"Happy wedding day," Madison called and pointed to the chairs. "Those are from everyone."

"You guys," Bernadette said, sitting down in one. "Thank you!" she called after them as their friends headed toward their respective cars.

Rikki sat in the other chair. What an amazing day this had been. The large full moon lit the yard so romantically as they rocked in their very comfortable chairs. Oddly, she'd thought about rocking chairs that day of the accident before she knew what had happened. That was the day she almost lost her little bee. She reached for Bernadette's hand and held it. Maybe she had said something about the rocking chairs out loud to Shasti. She couldn't remember.

"Our friends are ridiculous," Bernadette said.

Rikki nodded. "You know what else is ridiculous?"

"What?"

"Us. Out here. When I could be showing my wife how much I love her."

"Oh, yeah, that."

"You know," Rikki said suggestively, "we still haven't christened the garage or the yard." She waggled her eyebrows.

"Not on my wedding night, baby. Please." Bernadette struggled to get out of the chair and, with a frustrated sigh, asked for help.

They headed back into the house, and Rikki did a quick check to make sure none of the party lights were still on in the yard and then locked up the house.

"Ready, my dear?" Rikki put out her elbow. Bernadette answered by linking her arm in Rikki's. Rikki started toward the littles' room where the kittens were stashed, but Bernadette wasn't following. Concern shot through Rikki. "Baby? What's wrong?"

"We're going to bed, aren't we?"

"Yes," Rikki said without understanding.

"Let's go then." Bernadette headed for the stairs.

"What are you doing?"

"Surprising you with what I've been working on in physical therapy." Her smile was so big that Rikki matched it with her own. "Stairs are still my nemesis, Rikki, but I'm determined to get up there tonight."

Rikki couldn't speak. Emotion closed her throat as she watched her girl's notably slow ascent up the stairs to the second floor. She hadn't seen it in over two months.

"Rikki," Bernadette cried when she opened the master bedroom door. "I love it! How long has this been up here?"

"Only a week," Rikki said, coming up behind and wrapping her girl in her arms.

"Look at the canopy." Bernadette, using her cane, walked over to the new bed. The old bed, mattress and all, was currently residing in the garage for Bernadette's approval to donate or toss or whatever. She turned her head and said, "It's the one you showed me on that website. Rikki, this is the perfect wedding day present."

"Let's get in there, then. But showers for both of us first," Rikki commanded. "And then round one of—"

"Many."

Bernadette gushed over the master bath renovations as well. She hadn't seen those either. "Bath. You. Me. Tomorrow." Her eyes were wide as she took in the oversized jetted tub.

"You got it." Rikki beamed at the reactions she'd hoped Bernadette would have. Pleasing her wife had quickly become her number one priority, especially since the accident.

Makeup removed, and both showered, Rikki led her bride to their marital bed. It was only fitting that the first time they slept in it was on their wedding night. How special was that? Knowing Bernadette wasn't very mobile, Rikki gently helped her onto her back and crawled on top. She loved skin on skin.

"I love this," Bernadette cooed, gesturing to the closed bed curtains. "I feel like I'm in a cocoon."

"And it will be so warm and cozy in the winter, too." Rikki kissed Bernadette's soft lips.

"Baby, I love when you wear your hair down like this."

"Mmm," Rikki said and kissed her new bride again. Funny how she couldn't stop doing that. "Did you hear Jaleesa's words about being *bound* in matrimony?" She reached behind Bernadette's head and pulled two Velcro wrist cuffs from the headboard.

"Umm, no, I didn't hear that part," Bernadette said coyly, and yet she was holding her wrists steady for Rikki to place the cuffs on her. Both were reattached to the bed frame, the frame that had a million places for securing things like the wrists of a newlywed submissive.

Bernadette arched her body up toward Rikki. Her legs spread apart, whether voluntary or not, Rikki wasn't sure. Rikki brushed her lips across her lover's, making sure she understood who was in charge and that she was loved and adored. The kiss turned deeper, hungrier. Bernadette's kisses were always passionate. Rikki's, on the other hand, were possessive, and she hoped Bernadette felt it.

They broke apart only because they both needed to catch their respective breaths.

"Baby," Bernadette said, "no gags tonight, okay? Please? I want to be able to kiss you and talk to you."

"You got it, little bee." Rikki kissed Bernadette's forehead scar. "First, we kiss the boo-boos and make them better." Her next kiss found the healed bruise on Bernadette's breast from the seatbelt. Several kisses traveled down Bernadette's torso, one for each of the healed or possibly still healing fractured ribs. She would not put her entire body weight on top of her girl that night, even though Bernadette usually loved that. No, she had to be mindful that her girl was still a little bit broken. It was just as well that the basement dungeon/playroom wasn't ready yet.

A quick readjust came next in order to kiss the once-broken forearm that was bound overhead. Kisses then trailed down to one of the chest tube sites and then to the one on the other side. The wounds were now healed but scarred. The long leg scar was next. This spot got several kisses. The kneecap followed, and then several kisses on Bernadette's ankles, where her sprained ligaments were still sore and recovering.

The kisses trailed themselves up her inner thighs.

"There are no boo-boos there, lover," Bernadette said, her eyes glassy with lust.

"There are. Boo boos of neglect and disuse." Rikki looked up from between Bernadette's legs. She kept eye contact as she kissed her way up the inner thighs toward her ultimate goal. "Round one will be soft and tender. Almost vanilla," Rikki said. "Rounds two and on will not. Is that acceptable, little bee? Little bride? Little lover?"

"Yes, Ma'am." Bernadette nodded. "But Rikki, too many words. Too many words."

Rikki chuckled and went to work. Long licks, a thrusting tongue, and fingers sinking into warm flesh had Bernadette crying out in orgasm quickly, her hips bucking.

"Best sound ever," Rikki said. Once Bernadette's breathing was back under control and the hips stopped bucking, Rikki rolled off the bed, almost forgetting to move the curtains out of her way first.

"Come back, baby," Bernadette said. "Let me please you."

"Soon enough," Rikki said. She dove back into the bed and showed Bernadette a brand new set of clips. Each one had a tiny bee etched on top. A wedding present? Sure, why not? There were ten in all. Each one would be placed on her lover's body at some point.

"Oh, yes. Please."

Rikki sucked Bernadette's previously ignored nipples hard. Bernadette, in turn, sucked air through her teeth as the bite of the clips found her tender skin. She shuddered and gasped at first, but those changed to low moans. Ahh, yes, her girl was on her way to subspace. Another clip grabbed the fleshy part of an areola. And then another. And another. Clips trailed down the soft body below her. Rikki grabbed the hood of Bernadette's lovely nub and clipped it wide open. Rikki's lips found the sensitive pearl and kissed it gently. Her tongue got involved and polished the exposed flesh thoroughly. At the first sign of bucking hips, Rikki stopped, and the clips were removed, much to Bernadette's displeasure.

Rikki carefully placed her hands around the calf on Bernadette's good leg. She bent the leg and pushed up so the knee was at Bernadette's chest level. She was testing her girl's flexibility. That one was good. Now the real test.

"Focus now, little bee," Rikki said softly as she repeated the motion much more slowly with the injured leg. "Good?"

"Yes, fine," Bernadette said. "I promise," she added when Rikki hesitated.

"Okay. I choose to trust you." Rikki positioned Bernadette's calves up and resting on Rikki's shoulders. She loved this position because it lifted her girl's center for deeper penetration. She lubed the butt plug, the smallest one, and twisted it inside to many pleasurable moans from her girl. Her baby loved all things penetrative. Next, she attached the strap-on, the medium one. Their largest one—good ole Rocky—and an assortment of ass dildos were nearby for later use.

Rikki ran the phallus over the engorged clit but didn't linger. She sank in, harness deep, making Bernadette squeal in ecstasy.

"Fuck, yes, Rikki," Bernadette said. Her eyes stayed riveted on Rikki's. She arched her pelvis even more.

Rikki obliged and thrust, slowly at first but increasing in fervor. She leaned forward, and the back of Bernadette's thighs now made contact with Rikki's shoulders. This position let her pound her girl deeper, hitting her cervix. Bernadette's wasn't as flexible as before, so Rikki backed off a little and settled on a more comfortable position for both of them.

"Baby," Bernadette cried, "I'm close."

Rikki's thrusts were thwarted by the pre-orgasmic pulses in her girl's body. She had such a tight pussy when she came that it was hard to pull out and push in, but Rikki continued pounding her bride as best she could.

Bernadette's body tensed. She screamed her climax, screeching Rikki's name over and over. Rikki finally slowed down once her girl's body collapsed, obviously sated. Rikki pulled out slowly. Sometimes her girl got sensitive after cumming hard like that.

"I love you, Rikki," Bernadette murmured.

"I love you, too, Bernadette."

"Mmm," Bernadette moaned in lust as an aftershock hit her.

Rikki reached down, twisted the butt plug, and removed it. She replaced it with a medium-sized one. Yes, she wanted her girl stretched for Round Two. Or did they just have round two? Who knew? No one was counting.

Rikki eased Bernadette's legs down gently and then crawled up her body to unclip the cuffs from the bed. She left the cuffs on Bernadette's wrists, though, because they were far from done for the night. Rikki fell to the bed on her side. "We rest now, little bee."

"I need to please you, Rikki," Bernadette said, her voice sleepy.

"And you will. Later I'm going to straddle your head and lower myself to your eager mouth until you make me cum. And then I'll crawl back down your body and oh-so-slowly replace that plug with my still-hard strap-on. I will keep filling you until you give me an assgasm. It's been a while since you had one."

"Yes, Ma'am," Bernadette said, her eyes closing.

"But for now, we sleep." Rikki left the harness on but tossed the dildo off the bed, making the basket by some miracle.

"Sleep," Bernadette echoed. "Okay, Rikki." And then Bernadette did the most amazing thing. She rolled over on her side and pulled Rikki's arm over her body. She wanted her big spoon wrapped around her. It was the first time she'd done that since the accident.

Rikki bit back the tears choking her up. She pulled a sheet over them and then held her girl tight. She held her now like she would do for the rest of her life.

"I love you, Bernadette."

"Lub you, too," came the mumbled, almost incoherent reply.

Rikki gently kissed the woman she'd only known for nine months but knew enough to marry. "This is just the beginning, my little bee," Rikki whispered. "Just the beginning."

~~~ THE END ~~~

# Newsletter Signup

Sign up for Danielle Grainger's newsletter to stay on top of new releases. She also likes to provide recommendations for books to read (other than her own, of course).

## Sign Up Here:

https://mailchi.mp/32c278368547/danielle-grainger-newsletter

# Reviews

Reviews help get my books into the hands of readers who enjoy books like mine. It's often difficult for readers of certain, err, tastes to find books they enjoy. Would you consider writing a review? Let's get the word out. Thank you for at least thinking about it.

# The Wedding Vows

## A Quick Message from Dani:

Miss Jaleesa, the awesome wedding officiant that I have a crush on, said that a vow is a "solemn promise" or an "oath from the heart." I wanted Miss Rikki's and Bernadette's vows in one easy-access place for you, dear reader. They're also here for me to re-read and bask in the love they feel for each other. Theirs is a love story to remember and emulate.

## RIKKI'S VOWS:

Bernadette, when Madison went to your table at Rocco's Diner and you looked up, my heart fluttered. I was instantly drawn to you. How could a woman that attractive be single? The only thing I knew about you, though, was that you were kiddo's professor. Out of my league.

My Aunt Tilda introduced me to a way of life that made sense to me, as she knew it would. Oh, my heart soared when I quickly learned that you understood that life but hadn't quite found your place in it yet. That day of the big storm. What did you call it? The best snow day ever? Well, that was the day I fell for you. You jumped in and bused tables while I ushered out the silly customers who didn't seem to care that the blizzard was upon us. You offered to help Marta in the kitchen.

Loving Bernadette is easy. I knew you were different, little bee. Your actions spoke louder than your words. You embrace the tenets of consent, honesty, and communication. You are the most beautiful, smart, kind, and generous woman I have ever met. These are the qualities that not only make you an amazing teacher but an amazing partner. Bernadette, you make me understand how good life can be. I get it now. You make me a better person, and I am humbled that you chose me as your partner in life.

This ceremony affirms my love for you. I promise always to respect you, listen to you, and hear you. I promise to love you for better or worse, in sickness and in health. I want you by my side. Always my partner. I love you, Bernadette.

## BERNADETTE'S VOWS:

Rikki, one look into those soulful green eyes of yours, and I was a goner. If I'd realized you were single back then, this might have been a June wedding. But then again, I think maybe there were experiences I needed to go through before I was ready for you.

I promise to help bear the challenges we face. You don't have to take it all on yourself. You've had to deal with so much with my accident already. The nursing staff told me you were by my side every single minute you were allowed. When did you eat? I mean, c'mon, when did you go to the bathroom?

You've shown me how strong and dedicated you are. I hope to be able to do the same for you. You brought me amazing friends and a supportive and structured community. They welcomed me into their fold quickly, but that was because of you, Rikki.

I promise to be your partner in all things big and small, terrifying and easy. I promise to take care of you the way you have taken care of me. I love you, baby.

# About the Author
## Danielle Grainger

Dani is an instructor who currently resides in the southeastern USA and has several pampered fur babies. She has always been an avid reader and ventured into writing after reading several novels she felt didn't accurately represent the BDSM lifestyle. With so many rampant misconceptions, she took a chance and crafted admittedly idealized versions of possible experiences. Dani hopes not only to entertain her readers but to enlighten and educate them as well.

Dani's Amazon Author Page:
www.amazon.com/stores/Danielle-Grainger

Dani's Facebook:
facebook.com/danielle.grainger.7777

Dani's Instagram:
DaniGrainger84

Dani's Goodreads Page:
www.goodreads.com/author/show/19699760.Danielle_Grainger

# Books by Danielle Grainger

## THE DENTON HEIGHTS SERIES

The Denton Heights Series is the series that comes BEFORE the Bernadette Series. This group of books tells the stories of the beloved characters who populate the Bernadette Series world and live the BDSM lifestyle. We learn more about the origin stories of Madison and Shasti; Jaleesa, Tina, Harriet, Dana, DeShawn, and Kari; Rowena and Minjung; and Rikki. Victoria (AKA Daddy Vic), Lydia, and Brittany also feature in this series. The Denton Heights Series is basically the "Prequel Series" to the Bernadette Series.

## Under Her Wing (Denton Heights Book 1)
### (The Shasti and Madison Story)

An age-gap lesbian erotic romance with consensual light BDSM aspects featuring *littles*.

\*\*\* 2023 Finalist in the Golden Crown Literary Society Awards \*\*\*

Madison Kim finds herself on a bus headed to Denton Heights, Ohio, a suburb of Cincinnati. Her mother sent her there without notice to care for an elderly Korean woman Madison had never met. Madison is twenty-two-and-three-quarters years old and has a high school diploma, but she isn't smart enough to go to college...so they tell her. Now, she spends her time caring for Mrs. Park, going to the beloved Cincinnati Zoo, and watching movies on her outdated phone. She's not really sure why she's there, but she's taking it day by day. Then, she meets strong, nurturing Miss Shasti at a tea dance.

Shasti Balakrishnan has been looking for someone to call hers for more years than she cares to count. She wants a woman to love and care for in a nurturing Mommy Domme/*little-girl* scenario. She's thirty-two and already a partner in a thriving medical clinic in Denton Heights, but truth be told – she's lonely. She thought she'd found a companion in Amber back in D.C., but that fizzled out once they realized they weren't what each other wanted—or needed. And then she meets adorably precocious Madison at a tea dance.

ISBN: 978-1-953734-10-5 (e-Book)
ISBN: 978-1-953734-13-6 (Paperback)

# In Her Cage (Denton Heights Book 2)
## (The Jaleesa and Tina Story)

A lesbian interracial erotic romance with consensual light BDSM aspects.

Jaleesa Whitmore is a lesbian Domme in and out of fast relationships fueled by sex. She didn't understand addiction. Not yet, anyway. Although she had almost one full year sober, she was done with it. She was moments from heading down the familiar road of drinking that always made her feel good and filled that void. She was about to get her life back on its old track when a fateful encounter with a stranger, who would become a trusted friend, halted her downslide. She didn't know it then, but this encounter would not only lead her to a series of events and people that would change how she looked at life but how she approached it.

Tina Jenkins likes women but is asexual and afraid to try for another relationship. She does understand addiction. Just shy of eleven years clean of her opioid addiction following a dental procedure right out of high school, her parents carefully constructed and monitored everything in her world. It didn't matter that she was thirty-one years old and still living in the pink bedroom in her parents' house. It didn't matter that her mother now had to work from home, and her parents had to track her location and do routine searches of her bag, car, computer, phone, and room. None of it mattered because she was clean.

And then asexual Tina meets promiscuous Jaleesa. And everything changed for both of them.

ISBN: 978-1-953734-28-0 (e-Book)
ISBN: 978-1-953734-29-7 (Paperback)

# Within Her Grasp (Denton Heights Book 3)
## (The Marta and Shanice Story)
A lesbian age gap interracial erotic romance with consensual light BDSM aspects.

"Within Her Grasp" is an age-gap interracial lesbian romance that tells the tale of two women who had settled for unhappy lives. And then they meet.

White, thirty-something Marta Ingersoll was done with people. She just wanted to be left alone at work and at home, thank you. Her inside cat and the outside stray were all she needed. And her sister, Nora, too, of course. But that was it. And then, one fateful afternoon, her instincts to save a woman in obvious distress kicked in, and her life was shoved onto a strange new course.

Black, twenty-something Shanice Ward never got a break. Life had thrown challenge after challenge at the young woman, and this latest thing was too much, but it wouldn't stop. Woken up from a sound sleep by someone trying to remove her clothing, she shrieked for him to leave her alone. He didn't, but then, the most amazing thing happened. She discovered that superheroes were real, and one had just flown into her room to save her, and her life was shoved onto a strange new course.

ISBN: 978-1-953734-30-3 (e-Book)
ISBN: 978-1-953734-31-0 (Paperback)

# By Her Command (Denton Heights Book 4)
## (The Rowena and Minjung Story)
A lesbian interracial erotic romance with consensual BDSM aspects.

"By Her Command" is an erotic interracial lesbian romance containing consensual aspects of BDSM. It finds Rowena Tate in need of a submissive who can also manage her household. It's also the tale of Minjung Lee, who is desperate to find a Domme so she won't find herself homeless again. Trust does not come easily for either of them.

Rowena is a white Domme in her late thirties. Through experience, she has come to believe that most, if not all, submissives are selfish creatures who only want what she can provide without considering the person behind the flogger and the paycheck.

Minjung is an East Asian submissive in her mid-thirties. Through experience, she has come to believe that most, if not all, Dominants are selfish creatures who go well beyond contracted limits because there is no one to tell them not to.

Despite their reservations, both are told by members of the Denton Heights BDSM community that they are a good match and lucky to have found each other. Rowena isn't so sure. Neither is Minjung. Time will tell, won't it?

ISBN: 978-1-953734-32-7 (e-Book)
ISBN: 978-1-953734-33-4 (Paperback)

# THE BERNADETTE SERIES

Dr. Bernadette Garneau holds a Ph.D. in Mathematics and has just gotten out of a four-year relationship. Shortly after the breakup, she began an exploration of her repressed sexual desires. One message from a beautiful and powerful online Mistress and Bernadette leaps into the world of BDSM. The Mistress takes charge, and Bernadette reels in the heady power this stranger has over her. She has gotten a taste of *the life*, and she wants more. She needs more. Several online and in-person experiences with BDSM and Power Exchange have led to cravings she doesn't quite understand. A brief sexual exchange with an online Goddess unleashes an incredible pain-to-pleasure connection that she hadn't understood before. As she sifts through the posers and one-night stands, she homes in on what her submissive nature needs from a Domme. The Bernadette Series follows Bernadette's journey into the world of BDSM and her search for love and sexual satisfaction. As she said, "I want a monogamous partner who wants to not only love and nurture me but who also wants to drape me over her lovely couch and have her way with me."

## Wrecking Bernadette
### (Book One in the Bernadette Series)
A lesbian's exploration of her sexuality with consensual aspects of BDSM.

Dr. Bernadette Garneau holds a Ph.D. in Mathematics and has been out of a four-year relationship for four months. One good thing about breaking up is that Bernadette is free to explore her repressed sexual desires. One message from a beautiful and powerful online Mistress, and Bernadette leaps into the world of BDSM. Mistress Ciara takes charge, and Bernadette reels in the heady power this stranger has over her. She has gotten a taste of the *life*, and she wants more. She *needs* more.

ISBN: 978-1-953734-00-6 (e-Book)
ISBN: 978-1-953734-14-3 (Paperback)

# (S)mothering Bernadette
## (Book Two in the Bernadette Series)
A lesbian's continuing exploration of her sexuality with aspects of BDSM.

Dr. Bernadette Garneau's universe is pushing her toward change. Her initial experiences with BDSM and Power Exchange have led to cravings she doesn't quite understand. A brief sexual exchange with an online Goddess unleashes an incredible pain-to-pleasure connection she hadn't understood until that encounter. But after sleeping on it, she clearly understands that this Goddess would never be the long-term relationship she sought.

Disappointed, she wonders if she should just give up and move back to California to be closer to her family. That is until she meets Mama_Luvs, an online Mommy Domme. The woman is nurturing yet stern from the start and is just … perfect. And then Mama_Luvs wants to meet. Starry-eyed Bernadette packs for a New Year's Eve weekend, hoping that this time she's found *the one* – the one who wants to love and nurture her but who also wants to drape her over a couch and have her way with her.

ISBN: 978-1-953734-01-3 (e-Book)
ISBN: 978-1-953734-15-0 (Paperback)

# Becoming Bernadette
## (Book Three in the Bernadette Series)
A lesbian erotic romance with light consensual BDSM aspects.

University professor Dr. Bernadette Garneau has fallen in love with the world of BDSM. She has a nascent interest in the pain-to-pleasure connection, but she has yet to find partners interested in nurturing the soul within her body that they play with. Admittedly, she's had incredible sexual encounters with experienced Dommes, but all of them left her feeling cold for whatever reason. Most of them simply wanted a sadistic roll in the hay. Bernadette wants a strong Domme who will love and nurture her before flogging her on a St. Andrew's cross and afterward when her body is spent.

One afternoon, she finally musters the courage to venture out and meet some new friends in the local BDSM community. In walks a tall, handsome butch woman with fantastic hair and a confident stride. When this woman asks Bernadette, "Are you collared," Bernadette truthfully answers, "No," and accepts a dinner invitation for that very evening. She is walking on stars when she gets home at 2 a.m. after an ethereal sexual liaison. On the one hand, she wonders who she is becoming – she's never been this promiscuous. And on the other hand, she wonders if this strong butch woman could finally be the Domme of her dreams.

ISBN: 978-1-953734-02-0 (e-Book)
ISBN: 978-1-953734-12-9 (Paperback)

# Desiring Bernadette
(Book Four in the Bernadette Series)
A lesbian erotic romance with light consensual BDSM aspects.

*** 2022 Finalist in the Golden Crown Literary Society Awards ***

Rikki Carmichael finally feels that deep D/s relationship she has been craving since her Aunt Tilda introduced her to *the life*. She embraced her dominant side early on, but finding a suitable submissive woman who wanted more than a quick roll in the dungeon proved elusive. That is until Professor Bernadette Garneau arrived on the scene. Now collared and committed to Rikki, will Bernadette prove to be different, or will she turn out like all the others — fickle and full of lies and deception?

And will this perfect sub stay with her when she realizes Rikki's ship is sinking? She'd almost lost the coffee shop she owns when creditors came knocking down her door en masse, seeking payment for debts that weren't hers. Rikki managed to keep her staff and most of her friends in the dark about it, but she has not been able to get out from under it. With high stakes all around, Rikki looks for the peace she is seeking within her relationship with Bernadette. If this one fails, it may be time to leave the life entirely and go live in a cabin somewhere isolated in the woods. But buying a cabin takes money – money she just doesn't have.

ISBN: 978-1-953734-03-7 (e-Book)
ISBN: 978-1-953734-09-9 (Paperback)

# Loving Bernadette
## (Book Five in the Bernadette Series)
A lesbian erotic romance with light consensual BDSM aspects.

Bernadette Garneau, a beloved professor of mathematics, is a natural submissive. She likes structure and rules and finally found a way of life and a woman who would provide those things for her. The BDSM community she stumbled upon in Denton Heights, Ohio, is where she found Rikki Carmichael, now her dominant partner and fiancée. Rikki is everything she's dreamed of. Yes, Bernadette found the captain of her ship. With Rikki's support and guidance, maybe other parts of her life can finally come together, too — like the respect she deserves but hasn't gotten at the university. Why won't anyone see that she deserves to teach those upper-level courses? And to move out of her closet of an office? What do they know that she does not?

Rikki Carmichael, the respected owner of Rikki's Coffee Shop in town, has finally found the woman of her dreams in super-smart and super-real Bernadette Garneau. Bernadette is a submissive who instinctively knows how to take care of Rikki and accepts Rikki's need to be in charge. Bernadette is the first submissive Rikki's ever had that wasn't solely out for her own gain. Once Rikki can climb out of the deep financial debt she's found herself in, she will finally make their engagement to be married public.

Miscommunication, faulty assumptions, and unmet expectations threaten this union seemingly made in heaven. When life comes at them hard and fast, they must rely on their bond and their loving, self-made family of friends.

ISBN: 978-1-953734-08-2 (e-Book)
ISBN: 978-1-953734-11-2 (Paperback)

www.ingramcontent.com/pod-product-compliance
Lightning Source LLC
Chambersburg PA
CBHW071140260626
47162CB00003B/867